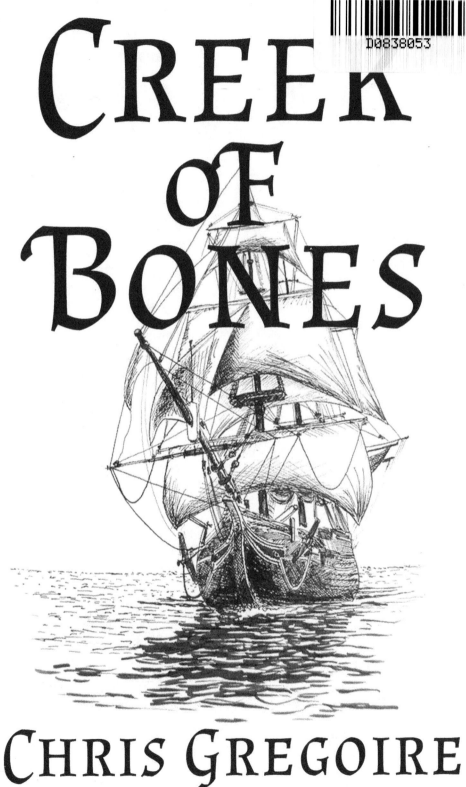

CREEK OF BONES

CHRIS GREGOIRE

Printed in the United States of America

ISBN: 978-1-953910-31-8 (paperback)
ISBN: 978-1-953910-32-5 (ebook)
ISBN: 978-1-956019-05-6 (hardcover)

**Canoe Tree
Press**

4697 Main Street
Manchester Center, VT 05255

Canoe Tree Press is a division of DartFrog Books.

CONTENTS

"Blood alone moves the wheels of history."
—Martin Luther

1589

FOUNTAIN

THE ARMOR-CLAD CONQUISTADOR FOLLOWED A barely clothed native through the rainforest.

While the path was occasionally clear, the small, brown-skinned man often hacked through encroaching vegetation. That's when those trailing the men—five more soldiers and the savage's wife—fidgeted nervously. They had every right to fear the verdant world.

Even when monkeys and birds chattered in the canopy, typically signs of safety, the conquistador scanned the surrounding bush for threats. Harquebus, knife and sword at the ready. During one stop, he raised a curved helmet to wipe sweat from his eyes. The humidity was insidious in the lowlands, but he did not care, for his quest east of the Andes had been wildly successful.

The Spaniards had just found a vast Incan treasure hoard. Quite possibly the gold, silver, statues and gems hidden by Rumiñahui ages ago. Furious that nearby villagers were slow to reveal its location, the conquistador directed his men to exterminate them once the valuables were ready for travel. Blood later ran through the dirt until all were dead—except for the native couple and their two children. Saved by a mother's promise to show the Spaniards a curative fountain.

The conquistador decided to check it out because anything was possible on that Godforsaken continent. After having his best soldiers gather bottles for the new endeavor, the small group had plunged into the jungle. The rest of the men stayed in the village to watch the children and gather supplies for the journey to Cartagena. The fleet would soon gather there, and if the Spaniards hustled, they would reach town in time to offload the hoard into a galleon.

When the group neared the supposed healing waters, a mammoth Tapir gave them a long look—strange behavior for the shy animals. Soon after, an immense black cat mauled a soldier before others stabbed and shot it to death. Then, as the vegetation thinned, an enormous barba amarilla blocked their path—coiled and ready to strike. He lopped the serpent's head off with his blade, then demanded an explanation for the ancient looking creatures.

The native man claimed they drank from the fountain, yet he insisted that no person in recent memory had sampled its waters. When the conquistador pressed him about that, the woman intervened. She announced that her father—a famous healer—had stopped the practice because the hidden fountain hurt people. While drinking from it often showed promise, too many later died—some quite tragically. Like her father before her, she believed the fountain was cursed.

Intrigued by the legend once pursued by Ponce de Leon, the Spaniards soon entered a clearing surrounded by kapok trees. They stretched from elevated roots to the heavens. Sunshine filtered pleasantly through the leaves, and a rocky pool in the middle gurgled turquoise water. As the soldiers quenched their thirst, the woman closed her eyes and chanted. When her husband joined in, the conquistador leaped into action, deftly slitting their throats while avoiding arterial spray and falling bodies.

Once the commotion was over, his men filled the bottles as he drank deeply from the fountain, which he found refreshing, but not unusually so. During a brief rest, he dreamt about delivering riches to King Phillip and seeing his lovely Maria.

DISCOVERY

TWO MEN IN A SMALL boat entered the creek.

With sunrise just minutes away, Kev MacGuire and Rudy Dillon deployed one thousand feet of line between two orange buoys. After tweaking the setup baited with chicken necks, they motored off to the usual spot.

While waiting for blue crabs to ride in on the morning tide, Kev took in the waking creek. Hungry fish rippled its surface, birds sang with joy and the surrounding foliage rustled in the breeze. A stirring preamble to some fine weather near the Chesapeake. Although hungover, he managed a smile. His pending death felt distant, abstract. As if it were coming for someone else.

He eyed Rudy's boyish blonde hair, ruddy skin and hulking frame. Vastly different than Kev's dark, lean look. Both men were now 40, hard to believe. After another glance around the creek, he felt it was time.

"Let's roll, big fella."

Rudy put the outboard in gear, and they glided toward a buoy. Kev snagged the line, placed it over a U-shaped bar on the starboard gunnel and readied a steel net. Necks rose through the murky water, slid over the bar and dropped back down.

Come on, come on . . .

A larger blob signaled a clinging crab, which he caught and swept over to a basket. Kev repeated the smooth motion as the boat chugged toward the far buoy. Once there, he freed the line and Rudy returned them to the waiting spot. After donning heavy rubber gloves, they happily measured the many crabs from tip to tip. The half which did not pass muster went back into the creek. Soon enough, two dozen keepers stared the men down—claws at the ready.

Kev crowed, "Hell yeah! That's the best run we've had in years!" He was a win-at-all-costs guy, now more than ever.

Rudy peered at them. "And they're big as shit, too. You know, I bet those jimmies haven't fed much since the storm. Which means round two might be just as good. Or better!"

Kev shook his head. "You'll never catch me, so take the 'L' with dignity." But that was mostly bravado. Anything was possible, because Hurricane Isabel had produced a storm surge like no other. It deposited all kinds of debris—toilets, bikes, tires, bottles, boats and presumably crab food—along much of the bay's bucolic eastern shore. Hell, he'd even seen a Model T Ford.

Rudy smiled broadly. "Care to bet on that, Mac?" He'd short-ened Kev's last name in first grade, the only person ever to do so.

"Seems unfair. To you, that is."

"Let's see . . . when I win, you get to spread mulch for me." Rudy ran a successful landscaping business.

"How creative."

"White-collar boys should break a sweat now and again. Keeps 'em humble."

"Interesting theory. And if you lose?"

"Won't happen, but . . . how about I wait on you one afternoon? It's no mystery where you'll be."

"Sold," Kev replied, thinking about cool libations on the cottage porch. That vision plus the snappy back and forth made him grin.

The men switched places and resumed crabbing. Rudy caught several of the creatures before a snag sent the boat spinning.

"Put the motor in neutral!" he ordered, then dropped the net and brought the line to his hands. When the boat steadied, he tugged sharply without success, then leaned back hard. The line came free and sent him sprawling.

Kev chuckled. "What was that about staying humble?"

Rudy flicked him off then reeled in the line. Out of the water came a clump of seagrass and mud, caked in and around a skull.

They stared at it in disbelief.

Rudy unloaded, "That's human! And it looks really old. Wonder how long it's been here? . . . Mac?"

Kev snapped into it. "Let's get a better look."

Creek water poured atop the brownish skull revealed a crushed temple and part of the spine. A second dousing exposed a necklace entangled in the jagged bones, its gold shiny and new looking. He whistled softly.

"Score!" Rudy said, reaching in to get it.

"Hold up!"

The man pulled back, surprised. "Finders-keepers! That sucker's payback for hauling in so much crap over the years."

"Maybe. But don't touch it yet."

"If you say so," Rudy grumbled.

A final pour unveiled the edge of a medallion, also gold. Kev jostled the net to see it better, but the piece was stuck. He looked around, perplexed about what to do.

Bright blue sky now capped the pretty morning, with only a few reddish clouds on the horizon. The creek—a highway wide this close to the river—was bordered by a small bluff. It marked the southern tip of Rose Haven, a historic estate owned by Kate Stillwater. Kev lived there in her cottage.

A great blue heron standing in the shallows stirred. After the spooked bird took off with a loud squawk, he noticed that part of the bluff had collapsed. Leaving a path of freshly disturbed clay that ran from a pair of headstones down to the water.

Kev pointed at the mess. "Rudy, look!"

"Uh-oh. Ms. Stillwater's gonna be pissed if we caught a relative. Or maybe she'll be happy . . . I don't know. But you get to tell her since she's your landlord."

"Nice," Kev mocked, then turned serious. "But you're right, she should be the first to know. The bones and gold must have come from her cemetery."

"First?" his friend asked, looking suspicious.

"Yep. The police come next."

"But it's just an old skull, Mac." Cops had been on Rudy's 'do not call' list since a jail term in his roaring twenties.

"You miss that bashed-in temple?"

"They won't care about some broke-ass remains that washed into a creek."

"Not if the fall caused the damage. Anyway, let's wrap up—we should head in and figure this out."

"But I didn't get a fair shake and the line's hopping!"

"You really want to hang out with that thing?"

Rudy looked at the skull again. "Fair point. But I want a rematch!"

As they stored the line, Kev gazed out at the Tred Avon River. His hometown of Oxford was further up on the other side. Framed by farms, forest and manor houses, it had once been a rollicking center of commerce.

He'd returned to the area that spring while on sabbatical from work. After finding a place to live on the water, his next task had been to mend fences with Rudy. There were other insults to remedy, but Kev missing the funeral events for Rudy's father had been next level, friendship wrecking kind of shit.

Kev realized that would disrespect a man who helped raise him. But he did it anyway, because skiing in the Alps with two blondes after a business deal took precedence. Rudy's response to a fictional work excuse had featured a screenshot of a snow-bound social media post. Along with a vow to never see him again.

Yet Kev was determined and Rudy—gregarious and big-hearted—rarely held grudges. When Kev caught him at home after work one day, the man yelled and carried on for what seemed like forever. Even threatened to punch him. But repeated apologies, stories from when they were kids and pleas for forgiveness wore Rudy down. Once Kev gave a heartfelt speech at the gravesite, they hung out again. At first a little, then soon a lot. The tension gradually eased to where it was barely perceptible.

Things were pretty good for a spell until Kev was gob smacked by stomach cancer. While fruitlessly trying to wrap his head around dying young, he'd found that a good buzz or bruising hangover hushed the gnawing in his gut better than prescribed medication. And, since he was so damn competitive, winning at crabbing, cornhole—whatever—muted the voices in his head. They teased that no one would care about his death—which was closer to right than Kev cared to admit.

When asked, he attributed the heavy drinking to a mid-life crisis. One final summer of benders before settling down for good. He'd kept the cancer to himself because hanging with Rudy just felt right, like a perfectly broken-in ball cap, and he was scared of hosing that up. His friend's warning at the gravesite had been clear: No more complications or we're through.

But cancer wouldn't count, right?

Right?

Ah, fuck it. My treatments start in a few days.

I'll tell him then and see what happens.

Although Rudy ditching him in a time of need seemed unlikely, Kev had a plan should that come to pass. Like so many times before, he would take a laden boat out. But on the final trip he'd tie himself down and pull the plug. The crabs would enjoy his remains, which seemed apropos. And his bones might someday make for an interesting discovery—much like their morning catch. The idea was scary, but less so than a lonely, drawn-out death.

He soon fired up the outboard for the ride back to the pier. As he sped them out of the creek onto the river, Rudy's shaggy locks flew back. It made Kev think of simpler times when they were boys. And wish for a mulligan, a do over at life.

REVEAL

KEV AND RUDY HAULED THE basket, net and other gear from the pier to the cottage.

The low-slung building was made of red brick. Its white screened-in porch—Kev's favorite place to chill—faced the water. Once up the modest grade of emerald grass, Rudy dropped his load, breathing heavily. Kev fired up a steamer pot next to an outdoor sink, then gathered items for a crab feast. As he moved about, his friend stared at the covered net.

Rudy finally asked, "How are we playing this?"

"We invite Stillwater over for lunch then tell her."

"Just like that?"

"Not exactly. We should slow-roll it, pick our spot depending on her mood. Maybe after we eat."

"Crabs before bones and gold?"

"Well, we are in Maryland. And I would hate to ruin a five-star meal."

After texting the woman, Kev put unhusked ears of corn into the pot along with the crabs. Once covered, they tried to escape the heat. The ghoulish rattle of claws much beloved by locals served as a warning of sorts. Stillwater was a shoot-the-messenger type, so he'd step lightly when giving her the bad news. He could not afford to piss her off.

Kev shook his head, dismayed. Having Rudy and a freshly minted landlord as his only support structure was pathetic. But he shrugged off the negativity—easy thanks to the morning excitement—as the rattling abruptly stopped. He looked over at Rudy who'd not moved an inch.

"You all right over there?" Kev asked.

"Lunch should straighten me out."

"You seemed pretty animated on the boat."

"I can't explain it, Mac," Rudy said after a glance at the net. "Those bones give me a bad feeling."

Kev broke out his long-dormant eastern shore accent, "That skull ain't gonna hurt you none, big fella. And to think you wanted to keep crabbin' with that grinnin' ghost!"

Rudy smiled at the effort then fished two beers from a cooler. The men sipped the brew while covering a picnic table out front with heavy brown paper. And afterward stocking it with wood hammers, knives, vinegar, butter, paper towels and more beer. They had just enough time to eat outside before the dog days of summer returned with a vengeance.

When the timer rang, Kev stacked the now reddish-orange crabs and corn on a plastic tray. Right on cue, the fresh-faced Kate Stillwater appeared, strolling briskly their way on a path surrounded by pink azalea and purple rhododendron. The pretty, raven-haired woman in her early forties was dwarfed by a stately Georgian Colonial home. Its three-story center was bracketed by chimneys and flanked by smaller wings. Red-bricked and white-trimmed like the cottage.

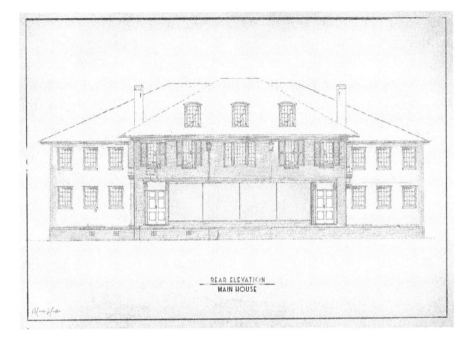

REAR ELEVATION
MAIN HOUSE

She called, "Having me for lunch, Mr. MacGuire?"

The pert lady often shot innuendo his way, but like always he figured it was unintentional. Estate owners rarely went slumming with regular folks, even those who'd made something of themselves.

Her smile was infectious as she came closer and glanced at the tray. "Mmmm . . . they look delicious. But did you have trouble—"

"Acting like I'm not here was pretty slick, Ms. Stillwater," Rudy said coyly. He motioned her toward the table. "We have to keep our budding relationship on the down-low or people might talk."

As she giggled, Kev silently thanked him for the misdirection. He was convinced that the estate owner would take the news better with a full belly. She and Rudy chit-chatted as they sat down. While they got on well, his blue-collar friend lacked the guts to ask her out. The cultural difference was too vast.

But if I was healthy . . .

Kev dumped the food onto the table. The heat and sweet smell made him ravenous, highly unusual since the diagnosis. Conversation came easily as expert fingers removed guts and gills then worked through familiar steps: sip beer, crack open part of the shell, pick out a piece of meat, dip it into vinegar or butter and chow down.

While ripping through his second crab, Kev stared at the distant river. After remembering the mission, he glanced back to his right toward the cemetery hidden by tall trees.

"Your place looks awesome," he declared.

"Thank you," she replied, beaming. "Jake took care of the downed trees and leaves in record speed. That hurricane left quite a mess."

Kev nodded politely. He did not like Jake Tilghman, but at least the brooding estate keeper had a strong work ethic, ever busy on her two hundred acres.

Stillwater next filled them in on the latest news from Oxford, including what could be shared from the town commission meetings. The woman spoke in a relaxed manner, almost like an old friend. But as Kev sipped, cracked, picked, dipped and ate, he wondered if calling her Kate would ever be in the cards. He'd addressed the widow by the customary 'Ms.' or 'Ma'am' for weeks, but felt it was time to break through the formality.

As if to underscore that point, she became engrossed by Rudy's landscaper stories until the carnage at the table ended. Then, seemingly choreographed, the trio rose, rolled the remains in brown paper and bagged it.

After washing up in the sink, Stillwater said, "You guys make crab feasts fun, not to mention rewarding. And to think some folks get skittish about the mess."

Rudy said, "That's my canary in the coal mine right there! People who don't pick crabs aren't worth knowing. I've studied it for years, there's like a perfect correlation."

"I hear you," the woman replied, nodding solemnly. "Now tell me, did things go smoothly this morning?"

Ha! She knows something's up.

Rudy offered plenty of minutia about their outing but skirted the big news. When he ran out of steam, the woman looked over at

Kev expectantly.

He retrieved the net. "Ms. Stillwater, on our second run, the line snagged hard on the bottom. Happens frequently you know. When it came free, we pulled in . . . some human bones and a necklace. Care to see them?"

She nodded stoically, a good sign. "I wondered how two gurus caught less than a full basket."

Kev smiled at her perceptiveness and removed the towel. The bones, having shifted, fully revealed the medallion. It was twice the size of a silver dollar and featured an intricate, sun-like symbol.

What the hell?

"Wow," she said, seemingly dazed before her look sharpened. "Rudy! You left out the important stuff. Where were you on the creek?"

"My bad," he said sheepishly. "We ran our line parallel to the graveyard. We don't know for sure, but the hurricane may have sent the bones and gold into the water." He described the damaged bluff in stark detail.

Kev intervened after she darkened, "What do you make of our catch?"

She studied the items. "Well, the bones look really old. And a fall from the cemetery would explain the broken skull."

"I'm not sure it matters, ma'am, but I think the headstones are still up top." He'd wondered if that meant the remains were from elsewhere.

"It doesn't, unfortunately. The older plots along the river and creek face the water . . . Damn it! I just can't have graves washing away."

"I know," he said gently. "That medallion is something, eh?"

"Sure is. I wonder what the symbol means."

Rudy spoke up, "I bet the curator knows."

Kev glanced at his friend. "That guy's still alive?"

Rudy leaned in and took a picture with his phone. "Yep. He's been a fixture at the museum for as long as I can remember, almost like those artifacts he looks after. I'll swing by on the way home and get his take on the piece. Mac, give the net a shake. I want to see what's on the other side."

Doing so revealed a skeleton's torso.

Rudy said, "How weird!"

Kev found the engraving crude, not unlike a jailhouse tattoo. It rang a distant bell, but he couldn't place it.

"Do you recognize this one, ma'am?"

She sat back. "No. But both are fascinating."

"Could the necklace be a family heirloom?"

"I don't think so, but it may have belonged to someone else who lived here. Checking the cemetery could give us the answer. I'd go now, but I'm booked solid through tonight. In fact, my estate tour starts in fifteen minutes. Perhaps Jake . . ."

"We'll go!" Rudy offered.

"Perfect!"

Kev glared at him. "We covered that ground, big fella. Ms. Stillwater, I think the police should check things out first. That crushed temple looks suspicious to me, and we don't want to trample over evidence. However old."

Her stare made him uncomfortable.

Rudy said, "Mac, you've streamed too many cop shows. Let's go now and call them if the bones came from somewhere else."

Kev shrugged. "It's your place, ma'am. You decide."

"I suppose there's no need to rush. How about I invite Roberts over in the morning, and we can go then . . . say about nine? But don't be surprised if she passes."

"What do you mean?" Kev asked.

"Let's just say that your discovery is unlikely to advance her career."

He nodded. The woman was supposedly a far cry from her father, the original Chief Roberts.

Kev racked his brain after the others left.

Where have I seen that skeleton figure before?

When the heat became unbearable, he gave up and went to the cottage.

DIAGNOSIS

KEV POURED SCOTCH OVER ICE then took his drink to the cottage porch.

He liked everything about it. Thoughtfully grouped wrought iron chairs, chaises and loungers. Colorful cushions, cedar decking. All surrounded by white framing and nearly invisible screens. After kicking back on his favorite lounger, he turned on some tunes. Cooled by a pair of ceiling fans, he watched the river for a bit, which continually changed if one paid attention to the waves, weather and wildlife. Kev then reached for the net. The outer part of the medallion was worn smooth, so he wondered what might have rubbed off. A search online— 'skeleton stick figure medallion'— yielded plenty of hits, but no obvious explanation.

Shrill ringing stopped his examination of the sun symbol. Adding insult to injury, the caller was one of two namesake partners at Gibson & Rogers, a boutique consulting firm in Washington, D.C. Kev had recently been the firm's 'closer.' When big deals got stuck in regulatory mud, he was the guy brought in to convince the feds that the transactions would benefit consumers. His skill—equal parts bullshit, smarts and reputation—had at times seemed magical.

While he'd regularly fooled government employees, hometown friends (apart from Rudy) gave him grief about prices they later paid for stuff. He patiently explained that the transactions created shareholder value which, after an initial round of layoffs, led to job creation and a host of other benefits. After more intense badgering, he stopped speaking to them.

Kev's career had hummed along until two wintertime deals. While the firm made decent money for time spent on the projects, both Gibson and Rogers blamed him for not earning the lucrative success bonuses. He'd objected to being the fall guy. The deals soured for political reasons, and everyone knew it. But the greedy bastards had needed a reason—however thin—to explain why a superstar would not make partner. Anything to avoid sharing profits and keep other minions climbing the ladder.

"Kev, my boy! How are you? Pretty well rested I presume." Rogers' chuckle ended hurriedly when Kev did not play along. "I have to run off to a meeting, so I'll get right to the point. Deal flow is ramping up, so we need to understand your intentions."

"Nothing's changed," he answered coolly. "I'll let Human Resources know when I'm ready to come back."

"We need to put a finer point on that. Are you talking days or weeks? We can't afford to wait much longer . . . it's a reasonable question, don't you think?"

"How about you explain some things first? Like why I didn't make partner? And the real reason you took my team away?"

He got aggressive after hearing a sigh, "Ring any bells, Rogers?"

"Let's put the past behind us. I'm calling because a group of investment bankers have cooked up something super exciting . . . and it kicks off soon."

They must have asked for me . . . toy with this clown.

"Sounds intriguing. I'll make it simple for you guys. Promote me, then my team and I will make the deal happen."

"You'll get your people, but we can't make you partner this cycle. Bring this one home for us though, and we'll do so next year."

"You never were a good listener."

"Perhaps I'm the one not making myself clear. If you won't step up to the plate on this, you have no future here."

After Kev lost his team, he'd been ostracized in the firm. Even by the work buddies he'd thought were upgrades over hometown friends. The situation became a game of chicken: Quit or wait to be fired?

He'd wanted out of the toxic environment but was unwilling to walk away from a fat severance check. The sabbatical idea from a creative attorney took care of the dilemma, freeing him from the office while legally maintaining his employment. The partners had agreed to the unusual move, presumably to assess whether they could land a suitable replacement.

Kev smiled sadly. While today's call confirmed his hunch, the plotting—once so important—had been rendered futile by the cancer diagnosis.

Rogers gently added, "Just take the high road and quit."

Kev laughed. "Seriously, Steve? . . . Call this a termination, pay me the severance and get the non-compete in return. If not, I'll hang a shingle and wreck you guys." He'd emphatically delivered the empty threat.

When his sabbatical began, Kev wanted to avoid colleagues at restaurants and such near his condo. Without a better option, he'd leased the cottage on Rose Haven. After his homecoming was met with deafening silence from those in and around town, it finally occurred to him that he'd been a major league prick. But his grand plans for an Oxford apology tour ended after making peace with Rudy. Kev had not felt well, and it took an alarming number of antacids to settle his stomach.

Crapping blood one night sent him online to evaluate his symptoms. What he read made him contact an oncologist from Johns Hopkins. Kev met with the woman, a former girlfriend, along with her team in Baltimore. On his own nickel to keep things quiet. He knew the way to the famous hospital from his annual physicals, the previous few skipped for one reason or another. The tests, administered over a few days, were invasive, comprehensive and exhausting.

His doctor told him afterward that he had stomach cancer. Even worse, she expected his health to decline rapidly as tumors grew.

The bottom line, delivered in a smooth, clinical manner, was that he had about two years to live. After Kev broke down, she pushed an experimental program to try and better those odds, but it felt like a Hail Mary, particularly since the treatments did not start for several weeks. He left after the doctor claimed that hope was key to survival, but he remembered little from the drive home. Thankfully, Rudy had continued to thaw since that awful day, almost as if sensing something terribly amiss.

"Kev—"

"I can find out who the bankers are. Get me the check and paperwork by Friday, or I'll call them to offer my services. And you know they'll accept."

He clicked off, pleased to finally set things straight. But he should have done it sooner. Truth was, he'd climbed the wrong damn ladder for years, blinded by the high stakes and intellectual challenge of a job which hurt regular folks.

Kev nodded decisively. The medallion would be a great distraction. He had just over a week to figure out what its symbol and skeleton figure meant before the program kicked off at Hopkins. After he freshened his drink and left the porch to get his thoughts flowing, the screen door banged behind him. He hardly noticed.

Could something on the estate explain them?

Records perhaps?

He chuckled inwardly when Stillwater introduced him to her overheated tour followers. A swarthy looking guy named Lucas stood out amongst the seniors. After thinking baldie would be a tough out, Kev headed for the river.

APRIL 2021 - FIVE MONTHS EARLIER

HUNTERS

THE INVESTOR CALL WAS ABOUT to start.

Lucas Chilton paced about his office. It was spartan—desk, chair, credenza, phone—because treasure hunters belong in the field, not some fancy building. But today was different than most. His bosses at Rare Antiquities Salvage Corporation (RASC) were about to unveil the first quarter's financial results and a significant deal. The numbers looked good, but their recent purchase was another story. The execs expected to convince Wall Street that having access rights to *Queen Anne's Revenge (QAR)* was a big plus. But Lucas thought the news would shake things up, and not in a good way.

The quarterly pitch first had to pass muster with a host of razor-sharp analysts. After dissecting any new information, they'd advise investors whether to buy more stock, hold their positions or cash out. If the pitch fell apart, millions in company value could disappear in minutes. And if things got really bad, losing his job would kill any chance he had to gain custody over Theresa, the light of his life.

It was hard to believe that he'd once asked her mother to terminate the pregnancy. He was not much of a people person, and depending on the moment, had found the concept of fatherhood either distant or distasteful. Thankfully, the woman refused. Soon after, he became fascinated by Theresa's development in utero and later worried about her delicate first breaths. One night, when praying for the girl's health and happiness, Lucas realized that he finally gave a shit about someone other than himself. And it felt good.

Her arrival also brought good fortune at work. During his two years with RASC, he'd found a lot of really valuable shit. But there was a downside. An overwhelming desire to provide for his little girl made him impatient with fools who got in the way. His latest outburst, by far the worst, was when he'd objected to leading the *QAR* project. Which was why he was alone and not with his bosses on the top floor of the company's Miami headquarters.

The call kicked off with prepared remarks by Chief Executive Officer John Pederson, Chief Operating Officer Eileen Gomez and the Chief Financial Officer. After Pederson addressed a planted question, the opening salvo of an hour-long barrage, an analyst from Goldman Sachs was next.

"Acquiring the access rights to *Queen Anne's Revenge* is quite a departure from your business model. Can you help me wrap my head around it?"

Lucas tensed up.

Here we go.

"Of course," Gomez replied easily. "Years ago, a competitor discovered a shipwreck in North Carolina. Experts eventually proved that it was *QAR*—Blackbeard's flagship. When financial problems forced that company to put the rights on the block, we took a look, liked what we saw and then pulled the trigger. Now comes the fun part—analyzing artifacts from the dive site. The goal, of course, is to find the pirate's fabled treasure."

"You paid through the nose for access," said a JPMorgan Chase analyst, "which means the company doesn't own a thing. And the way you just put it, the treasure sounds like a fairy tale. Should we expect more transactions like this in the future?"

"Sure—when they make sense. In this case, I'm convinced that Blackbeard buried gold, silver and gems before being killed in 1718. And I'm hardly alone. Countless people have searched for the treasure along the east coast of the U.S. and in the Caribbean, but every one of them failed. We believe that our knowledge and know-how will flip that script."

She added that thousands of artifacts had been retrieved from the dive site over the years. And pursuant to the deal, divers would quickly recover the many still left on the ocean floor. When she announced that Lucas—the company's best treasure hunter—would lead the search, he shook his head.

Bullshit. If I was top dog, I'd have the opus.

Gomez became defensive when asked why RASC would succeed where its competitor failed. And she could not sooth those now worried about the company's pipeline of treasure hunts. Since that drove the stock value, Lucas worriedly gauged how much of it would disappear when the big investors sold out. And if RASC entered a death spiral, that would screw him both personally and professionally.

He'd once thought Pederson might shit-can the deal. But that never happened, perhaps because he was swayed by Gomez's expertise. Regardless, the guy letting her flail on the investor call had brought RASC to the brink of disaster—almost as if grooming her to become CEO mattered more than the company.

Pederson finally intervened, "Look, the deal's simple. We made the investment because we expect to be successful and provide a good return to our investors. Don't forget that this company has *always* delivered on its financial commitments."

He had presence, a gravelly voice and the perfect dose of executive gray on his temples, but on occasion the guy either missed or refused to address important matters. Like Gomez's character flaws and poor judgement.

Pederson continued, "The rights purchase is part of the diversification strategy you heard about last fall. So, I'm confused about the sudden negativity. We've been exceptionally clear that Spanish treasure is unlikely to benefit us at the same level we've historically enjoyed."

RASC had recovered billions from eleven Spanish galleons which were driven into the Florida coast by a 1715 hurricane. While the loss was disastrous for the crown, securing loads of treasure from wrecks widely thought to have been stripped clean was a huge accomplishment for the company. Pederson struck gold for a second time after leading RASC through an oversubscribed public stock offering. Now, its many employees made impressive finds each and every year.

He added, "That's why we've filled our pipeline with viable projects like *QAR*. They won't all be successful—they never are—but I'm confident that Ms. Gomez will bring this one home for us. She is, after all, the world's foremost authority on Blackbeard."

Lucas smiled grimly as he pictured the plain, willowy brunette looking uneasy. Pederson announcing her accountability for the project was unusual, no doubt a heavy burden. And Gomez was off to a poor start. The woman over-reaching on a deal and then clumsily pitching it to Wall Street would normally be something to celebrate. The kind of mistake that cleared the corporate ladder. But since she'd saddled Lucas with *QAR*, it seemed far more likely that he would crash and burn by her side.

Or did Gomez invoking my name create leverage?

The questions on the call soon turned to routine topics, a strong indication that the satisfied-for-now analysts had settled down skittish investors. Lucas checked the stock price to be sure and found it virtually unchanged. Since Pederson had successfully wrapped Gomez's transaction into a strategy unrelated to pirates, Lucas decided that the sleight-of-hand was at least as impressive as the hair and voice.

But QAR is still a dog. And Wall Street will figure that out soon enough.

Ironically, the stock would have shot through the roof had investors learned about a secret project. The company's research team was compiling big data from years when massive amounts of Spanish wealth passed through Caribbean and Florida waters. If Pederson was right about his opus, RASC would someday prove the legend that Spain had concealed the loss of many ships during a 1589 storm. But much like the Spaniards may have done, the company kept the information close to the vest. Alerting ethical competitors about a legitimate search—or even worse, the shady ones operating outside of the law—would be foolish.

Blown away by the science and possibilities of the project, Lucas had lobbied to lead it so he could make some real scratch—but he'd lost out to a plodding peer.

Yeah. Something's gotta give or I'm gone.

APRIL 2021

MOTIVATION

Lucas went to see Gomez.

While waiting for the COO in her conference room, he watched container boats move sluggishly along the glittering Intracoastal Waterway. He then used a mounted telescope to take in the art deco palaces over in South Beach. After imagining himself sunbathing with wealthy neighbors next to the Atlantic, he patted the letter of resignation folded neatly in his jacket pocket. Now that he'd established himself at the largest treasure hunting company in the world, he thought it best to move on before a pirate ship sank his reputation. He felt for the letter again. It was short, sweet and ready to go.

Suddenly angry about cooling his heels, he turned away from the windows to examine pictures clustered on a wall. Each captured Gomez posing with a treasure find, including three of his own. The selfish shots worsened his mood because they insulted those who made the discoveries. And if the company truly believed in the teamwork its execs crowed about, the pictures never would have been tolerated in the first place.

She finally blew in without a word and claimed the chair at the head of a sturdy-looking mocha table. After watching the woman rub her temples as if alone, he almost handed over the letter. But he kept himself in check. It was wiser to first gauge what leverage he'd accrued from being publicly named on *QAR*.

He'd soon had enough. "Did you need me for something?"

She eyed him. "What, are you too busy for your boss?"

"Not at all, but my teams and I are getting after it. We've made excellent progress on the Mayan, Viking and Nazi projects."

"I know," she snapped. "But I want you focused on *QAR*."

"Why? Seems like the others could really move the needle."

She peered at him intently. "Lucas, I called you up for a few reasons. Let's first discuss your recent behavior."

He gave a curt nod. "That's fair. There were better ways to convey my concerns about the project. But then again, you've always told me to be direct."

"You missed the subtleties. When I explained what we needed on *QAR*, you could have saluted after calmly expressing your reservations. Instead, you ranted and raved about not getting the 1589 project. That would have put you on the bench, but my hands are tied. Believe it or not, Pederson has convinced our investors that you're a superstar."

Hmmm . . . better than I thought.

"Was he surprised that I didn't join the call?"

"I told him you had mild symptoms from COVID, so keep a low profile today. But this isn't about him and I'm tired of your delays. Are you ready to start?"

"Not exactly. I read the file like you asked, but it didn't help much."

He'd painstakingly gone through what little was known about Blackbeard. Much of the information had been sourced from contemporaneous news articles. Some came from posthumous books which attempted to piece together the man's mysterious life. Like usual, the research team had done a fine job with what was available. But the accompanying business case was a total reach.

"Seriously?" she asked, her expression hardening.

"Yeah. I'm not worth a damn unless I believe in the mission."

"Lucas, *I* choose what this company goes after. Then you and the other project leads do my bidding. Am I clear?"

"I thought it was okay to explain my reservations." He'd trapped her, and by the look on her face Gomez knew it.

She sighed heavily. "Let's hear them."

"Thanks. Everyone knows that Blackbeard captured dozens of ships during his brief run as a captain. But those vessels carried goods rather than valuables—other than a few personal items. Now, no one's really sure what the man did before that, but he probably crewed for another pirate who achieved similar results."

"I'm familiar with recorded history. What exactly is your point?"

"My point is that Blackbeard's legend is great for movies and video games, but nothing in the file suggests that he accumulated a treasure hoard."

She drummed her fingers on the table. "That file doesn't include my views on the subject. Did you hear what I said on the investor call?"

"Yeah. Having access rights means we can't keep any artifacts from the dive site, so there's nothing to fall back on when we come up empty. And we'll be stepping on the toes of academics and state employees while we do our thing. That's going to require a deft touch, something I'm not exactly known for."

"I didn't realize we had another Blackbeard expert on staff."

"Far from it, but I read every word you gave me. And if that's all we have, our prospects are incredibly weak."

After a staring contest, she handed him a piece of paper. "The Board of Directors just approved some project incentives. You'll earn one hundred thousand stock options if we're successful. Less than me, but still a huge number. This is your moment that matters, Lucas—QAR can make you rich."

He did the math, starting with RASC's stock trading at thirty dollars per share. If that doubled, which could happen if the company found the 1589 ships or made another important discovery, the options would be worth three million dollars. Even after Uncle Sam wet his beak, the paper in front of him teased a financial windfall. But it was as useful as Monopoly money unless he earned it, which would never happen on QAR.

She continued, "We earn them the day RASC owns one of

Blackbeard's 'meaningful' possessions. Look, I need another coffee, so I'll give you a few minutes to chew on that. If you're smart, you'll accept the options and get started." She left through the hallway door.

That's a different ballgame.

Given the intense historical interest in the pirate, any of his stuff found away from the dive site should qualify as 'meaningful.' If Lucas pulled that off, then all he had to do was stay employed and wait for the stock price to rise. But he found the options confusing. RASC prospered when it found treasure—not artifacts. Emotion, however, soon swamped logic.

If I earn those suckers, Theresa's education and wedding are covered.

I could also get custody and move her out of that shitty neighborhood, maybe all the way to the beach.

Making more money in one day than he did over several years at Figuras Ocultas, his previous employer, would be incredible. The 'Hidden Figures' from Central America had taught him the ropes while illegally searching for antiquities, gold and silver all over the world. Lucas enjoyed the work, except when things got rough, and over time developed a knack for converting research and clues into major finds. Only when Theresa's mom became pregnant had he expressed interest in finding another job. One that would make him and (someday) his daughter proud. He was bummed when his bosses laughed him off.

Gomez returned with coffee and frowned at the unsigned paper. "Lucas, I went out on a limb to hire you, then gave you a bunch of great jobs. Stop fucking around." She left the room again, this time through a door which led to her office.

After later getting the green light to leave the organization, he worried about a resume that would be discarded by reputable companies in the sector. As he'd puzzled over his next move, Gomez introduced herself at an industry conference. With his guard down, the man candidly described his methods and discoveries. He could not believe it when she offered him a job.

The COO told others at the company that she once worked with him on classified recovery projects for the U.S. government. Clever, since no one at RASC would expect clear answers about his past. Yet troubling because of her unknown motives. He'd accepted the job anyway because it got him what he wanted. Now, just two years later, he was a top performer.

Yet dirt poor compared to my tenured peers.

He signed the paper.

She gave a curt nod after returning. "It's about time you listened. I've forgotten more about Blackbeard than most will ever know."

What a drama queen.

He smiled. "Apologies, that should have been clear from the start. I appreciate your support and will make every effort to bring *QAR* home."

"That's it then," she said. "You know what to do."

Dismissed, he strolled by the cubicles which housed her minions. Several glanced over furtively, presumably waiting for Gomez's eruption about the investor call prep. She always blamed others for any less-than-stellar performance.

Gomez watched him go.

Unbeknownst to the naïve man, her father had suggested the hiring. Once Lucas came on board, she'd left him alone for months so he could establish his bona fides. He did just that by wowing everyone with a few quick discoveries, then posted the best two-year treasure hunting run in recent memory. Mostly since the guy was a natural, but also because he was edgier than her girl and boy scouts. His only wrong move was pushing back on *QAR*. After stewing over the impertinence, she'd come up with the 'meaningful' stock options idea, which Pederson and the Board supported without scrutiny. Gomez would eventually tell Lucas the reason she brought him on, but the timing was not ripe.

Her father, whom everyone called Padrino, was the brains behind Figuras Ocultas. Fiercely loyal to his people, he'd adopted Gomez at a young age after her biological father was killed on a job. Padrino raised the girl and taught her the business. When ready, she'd received a new identity. Lucas was none the wiser. He'd joined the organization years after her departure.

While Gomez dearly missed living with Padrino, she'd done her part to position Figuras Ocultas for a big heist, advancing in two companies before landing the big job with RASC. As she'd ascended in corporate America, her fiery temper and ego set her apart. Traits that for most signaled an ambitious executive on the rise.

Gomez had been fascinated by the power which grew with every role. After realizing the rank and file were like sheep, the COO demanded daily updates on important projects. The cake was iced when Pederson transitioned most of his duties her way. Now, she was poised to strike when the right opportunity presented itself.

Every once in a while, she considered ditching Figuras Ocultas. But that would never happen while Padrino ran the show. She'd expected that would be the case for another decade, maybe two, before the larger-than-life man was diagnosed with a particularly cruel form of Alzheimer's. He'd accepted his fate with extraordinary grace, but she was tormented by the thought of him forgetting her and dying.

One night, sleepless with worry, she remembered a diary passage. The soldier who wrote it had been privy to the imprisonment, interrogation and execution of the pirates who survived Blackbeard's final fight. Virginia's then governor had organized a raid into North Carolina to kill the man, ostensibly to protect the region from piracy. The attack infuriated the relatively weak leader of the other colony. The soldiers had both illegally crossed the border and violated his pardon of the pirates.

Once transported to Virginia, the surviving cutthroats repeatedly denied the existence of a treasure hoard. One man though, in a bid for clemency, announced that he'd once seen a bottle labeled 'Fuente de la Eterna Juventud' in Blackbeard's quarters. After the prisoner failed to convince his captors, he was hung along with the others. Gomez initially found the Fountain of Youth reference laughable. As silly as the man's claims that the pirate possessed mystical powers and had a body double.

The desperate woman later reconsidered the tale. Hours of research then produced an obscure account from Charleston where Blackbeard was described as surprisingly young looking. Since he'd never been portrayed that way, she convinced herself that the Fountain's waters might be real. That led her to aggressively pursue the *QAR* rights and push the shitty deal through the company.

She shook her head to clear the past. She'd been late to her meeting with Lucas because Padrino had called to learn more about the pirate ship. While Gomez had given the scattered man some details over the phone, she held back her true intentions. It would be unwise to raise his hopes before she found something.

DIVING

LUCAS CONNECTED HIS BREATHING REGULATOR to an air tank.

After making sure the setup worked, he donned a wetsuit. It was hot out, and the ocean swells rolled languidly toward the beach a mile off. Intermittent blue water towers there stood like sentinels. Each one marked a different town along the Crystal Coast, a barrier island in North Carolina.

The other divers aboard the recovery vessel *Shell Point* slowly readied their own gear. The ship had streaks of rust on an otherwise white exterior, and its long, flat deck with a square pilot house resembled a tiny aircraft carrier. The pace of the others soon annoyed him. He was anxious to see the object which had everyone so excited.

To pass the time, he imagined *QAR's* massive sails billowing as the largest pirate ship in the world closed in on a hapless merchant vessel. It chose to run—a dreadful mistake. When in range, the pirates shot small balls linked with chain into the target's rigging and sails. After it was partially disabled, Blackbeard ordered a devastating broadside with his starboard cannon. Then, as the battered merchantman stopped, the pirates raked the sailors on deck with grape shot fired from swivel guns. Dozens of his men soon grappled aboard the bloodied and fiery mess. They finished off those who were still alive and removed the cargo before the ship sank to the depths.

But the vision was replaced by reality—merchantmen nearly always surrendered after Blackbeard hoisted his malevolent flag.

The pirates encouraged that outcome by shooting into the air and shouting threats through amplifying trumpets. But the non-combatants mostly gave up because their skins were far more important to them than the already deep pockets of shipowners.

Lucas glanced at the archaeologists and academics who scurried about the divers. He'd met up with the team that morning at the Fort Macon Coast Guard Station. While the locals on the barrier island and in nearby Beaufort were crazy about Blackbeard and his flagship, Lucas had been surprised to see the 'Coasties' act the same way. After breakfasting with uniformed men and women in a facility that provided a grand view of the Intracoastal, the recovery team had boarded the boat for the short trip out to sea via the Beaufort Inlet.

He snapped back to the present when seagulls screeched near the heavy lift crane at the stern. A young man stood there, life jacket askew, and tossed crackers to the birds. After Lucas shot him a dirty look, the man flushed and put the snack away. The others stopped their preparations only when Ben, their leader, explained the dive plan. The sunny man came over afterward.

"Lucas, you geared up quickly!"

"It's been way too long, Ben." After appraising the activity aboard, he added, "This is quite an operation."

"Thanks. I've got a great team other than that straggler who'll soon walk the plank. Any questions about what we're doing?"

"Nope."

"Good deal. I'm freakin' pumped about this concretion!"

Lucas smiled. The energetic comment reminded him of his first visit to the *QAR* research facility over in Greenville, two hours inland. During an introductory meeting, he'd learned that Ben helped discover the wreck years ago and later proved it belonged to Blackbeard. The low-key man, famous in his world, had been gracious and welcoming from the start. Perhaps because RASC had secured the funding which enabled him and his team to dive again after a long hiatus.

Lucas remembered interrupting Ben that spring day, "Sorry to be slow, but what do you mean by concretion?" He'd never searched for anything but gold, silver and antiquities.

"My bad. Concretion is a hard, concrete-like substance—hence the name—which contains one or more artifacts. It's created when iron corrodes in saltwater. As that happens, molecules from the metal bind to other stuff nearby, like man-made objects or natural things on the ocean floor. Add barnacles and vegetative growth, and it's hard to distinguish concretions from the seabed. Except for artifacts like cannon and the anchor. Those are so big they retain their original shape."

He'd pointed out example pictures around the room. "They're spread out over a wide debris field. We've been untangling them for years, and it will take a few more to finish the job. But I would have retired halfway through without gradiometers. Oh, and of course the money you got us."

The devices he'd mentioned located metal objects by highlighting changes in the earth's magnetic field. While iffy on the science, Lucas sure as hell liked the result: a searchable map divided into dozens of grids.

"We also use a dredge hose which brings silt up to *Shell Point*. My folks sift through it carefully, kind of like miners panning for gold. They've found buttons, iron shot and canvas, even trace amounts of gold dust. While that effort is underway, a handful of us pry away concretions—which usually contain the most significant artifacts. It's slow going down under, but that reminds us to be careful with our cutting tools. Damaging an important artifact, particularly right out of the gate, would really suck."

After months of hard work, the RASC team had sorted through many of the artifacts ashore. Impressive progress fueled by a library of digital photographs and mostly on-site storage. Lucas had driven his folks hard, secretly caring only about his stock options. But he eased off after it became clear that a clue, should one exist, would most likely come from a new discovery. He finally asked to dive with

Ben and the others when the removal of a cannon exposed the potentially exciting object.

The man spun him around, inspecting his gear. "You're all set, buddy boy. The last treasure hunters never went into the water, so I just assumed that y'all were wimps. Had I known you were different I would have invited you out weeks ago."

"You may regret this," Lucas said, grinning. "I'd much rather be here than in Greenville."

"Spoken like a true archaeologist. You're gonna love it, and tomorrow we'll have another go if need be. That'll be our last chance for a while if Hurricane Isabel blows like they're expecting. Big storms move things around down there, so I suspect we'll have to re-map the site before resuming operations."

Lucas and the five other divers soon took long steps off a platform. After hitting the water, they formed a loose circle. When Ben gave a down signal, Lucas let air out of his vest. The wind, waves and voices shut off and he equalized his ear pressure on the way down. He scanned the swirling silt for something menacing but saw nothing other than translucent fish. Once the group reached the shallow floor, Ben located a stake, and then headed across the sand. Lucas followed with the others. They held the dredge hose and a basket linked to the crane.

Ben spoke on the crackly radio as he swam, "Lucas, as you can see, the sandbar Blackbeard crashed into is long gone. They come and go in big weather. Who knows, maybe this storm will create a new one."

After reaching a large patch of rocky bottom covered with shells and waving sea grass, the other divers positioned the basket nearby. Vacuuming the area more than tripled its size.

"See the imprint from the cannon?" Ben asked. "That sucker was over two thousand pounds, a cast iron beast . . . Okay fellas, have at it."

Two divers carved into the bottom with small tools. They occasionally called for the hose as more silt settled in. After Ben finally gave a slow-motion fist pump, Lucas swam in for a closer look. The concretion had broken free into three pieces, including one over a foot long.

The divers placed them into the basket and then gripped its edges like pall bearers. Ben instructed the crew to winch it up. On a safety stop designed to remove excess nitrogen from their bodies, Lucas felt giddy, like he was a step closer to his dreams.

SEPTEMBER 2021

GRAVES

KEV TOSSED A TENNIS BALL to Sandy near the cottage.

Playing with the Chesapeake Bay Retriever was always fun. Little seemed to bother Stillwater's chestnut brown dog, but he was sweating profusely, unaided by a breeze that pushed the boiled air around. Soon, an errant throw just missed Jake as he came around the corner. Kev unsurprisingly fielded a death stare.

But for a park ranger-like uniform, the tall, broad shouldered man with thinning red hair would have been the perfect extra in a medieval film. He did not say a word on the way over—never did, unless his boss was nearby. As Kev resumed throwing, he briefly wondered about the duffel bag slung across the man's shoulder. The retriever sprinted back and forth without pause, a testament to her breed.

Stillwater soon arrived. Like usual, she wore a baggy T-shirt and loose-fitting shorts.

"Happy Monday, guys. Where's Rudy?"

"Off doing damage control on a job," Kev said, summarizing an earlier text message.

"Sounds serious. Can you let him know that Roberts will be here at one? If he could join us then, she won't have to come back."

"Will do. Are we still going now?"

"Of course. I'm anxious to know what happened."

Yes! Fingers crossed for a lost grave.

After Sandy ran down a final toss, Stillwater added, "The chief told me to look but don't touch—like I was in grade school. You believe that crap?"

She marched off without waiting for a reply. Jake fell into formation while Kev labored to catch up. Sandy ran ahead and barked periodically. Apparently oblivious to the shimmering heat, the woman led them through the fields toward an enormous oak tree. She finally stopped there, her shape tiny in the green and brown giant's welcoming shade. While catching his breath and mopping face sweat, he guessed that the tree was as wide as it was tall. Its gnarled limbs would be perfect for a movie set in the deep south. Or a bevy of tree houses.

Stillwater admired the oak until he asked its age.

"Four hundred years, give or take. The town arborist—yes, we have one, stop looking at me like that—says it's the oldest white oak in the country. Can you imagine what it's witnessed over the years?"

Kev counted on his fingers while replying, "Generations of white-tailed deer, squirrels and hedgehogs, not to mention legions of assaulting woodpeckers—"

"I'm serious," she said playfully. "You must admit it's impressive."

"Sure, for a tree."

"Stop qualifying! Say Jake, can you go up ahead? I forgot to speak with Kev about his rental agreement. We won't be long." Both men looked surprised before Jake shuffled off.

When the man was out of earshot she said, "Let's keep the medallion between us for now. He only knows about the bones."

Weird but okay.

"Gotcha. It's Incan by the way."

"Pardon me?"

"The sun symbol appears to be of Incan origin. You know, from South America."

"The curator told Rudy that?"

"Yep."

"Interesting. But how did it get here?"

"He has no idea. Maybe the cemetery will provide answers."

She nodded. "Did he recognize the skeleton figure?"

"Nope. And I struck out online."

They marched onward. After passing through rustling grass and yellow flowers, a loud yell spurred them forward. They followed similar noises into the largest patch of woods on the estate, where dogwoods and red maples mixed in with towering tulip poplars and white pines.

Jake hollered again as he swung a machete. The blow finished off a thick vine, one of several which spiraled to the tops of trees. Clear water gushed from the severed one onto the ground.

Stillwater asked, "Everything okay?"

"Yeah. These bastards take a lot of effort. I'll come back tomorrow for the rest."

Kev observed, "This is new."

Stillwater replied, "We're removing all non-indigenous plants as part of the 'Pure Maryland' campaign. But there are more than we bargained for, so it's turned into quite the operation."

Stillwater led them out of the woods and stopped by two white Adirondack chairs which faced the river. Several boats were out racing, their sails vibrant and full. After watching them jockey for position, the trio moved south along the steadily rising shore.

Cresting a slope revealed about fifty headstones set around the tip of the peninsula. Those closest to the river and creek were gray and weather worn. Next came marble grave markers—some quite ornate—which swept toward three facing stone benches. Lush grass ran from there to more woods.

The estate owner lingered near a marker which read Stillwater.

Feeling uncomfortable about her dead husband, he offered, "It's a nice resting place."

After she nodded absently, he followed Jake over to the creek side bluff. As the men approached the precarious headstones and disturbed clay, Stillwater announced, "Those graves belong to either the Devons or Armisteads." He glanced back, impressed.

She added, "I played on every inch of the estate as a kid . . . And I've spent a lot of time here paying my respects."

"Were the Devons the original owners?" he asked, keenly focused on his footing. As he crept forward, Jake hung back. Little remained of the turf near the two headstones.

"Yes. Lord Baltimore granted them the land in the 1600s."

Kev evaluated the damage. "One grave is completely gone, no surprise given the trail of clay down to the water. But I'll need a better vantage point to see who it was."

"Careful!" she warned. He gingerly stepped onto a plug of dirt which jutted out to the right of the headstones. It felt shaky, so once in position he became very still.

"Man, these are in rough shape . . . but I think the intact one says 'Edward.' "

"That's Edward Armistead then. Which means the grave that washed away must belong to his wife, Elizabeth. Can you make out any letters on that one to be sure?"

"Just a T and an H," he finally replied, then worked his way back. When the ground felt solid, he jumped toward the unhappy looking Stillwater.

"I guess that settles it," she said.

"Looks that way," he replied, masking a growing excitement. "And Edward's not far behind her."

Jake unpacked his bag and positioned stakes around the landslide. After hammering them into the ground and attaching yellow string, he surveyed his work.

"How awful," she said while scratching Sandy's ears. "But I'm glad you and Rudy saw this before it got worse."

He nodded. "At least it wasn't one of your relatives."

"There is that. But I'm supposed to look after everyone at rest here. If only the cemetery was somewhere else . . . oh well. Jake, when we return to the house, let's discuss who should fix the bluff once and for all. Funds are tight, but this is unacceptable."

Money is an issue here?

She was so grim afterward that he let her be.

I'll ask about records later.

MONDAY AFTERNOON

COPS

KEV, RUDY AND STILLWATER WAITED on the front porch of the big house.

White columns gave it a regal look. Her long driveway, lined by orderly red maples, swept to a wide circle before them. An expansive storage building—Jake's home base—was on their left, while a four-car garage stood to the right. Kev, worn out from the earlier walk, greatly enjoyed the shade. The lack of energy made him mournfully imagine sand falling from an hourglass.

Stillwater looked at her watch. "Roberts is late."

Rudy added, "I hope she hurries up. Harry Homeowner was some kind of pissed off when I ran out of there."

Kev smiled. "Would you like to hear about the Incans while we wait?"

"Yes," they replied, then laughed about their enthusiasm.

"Well, I think the curator is right. Incan symbols like the one on the medallion are all over the internet. The South American natives loved intricate designs and worshipped the sun. And if it isn't a fake, the piece might have been stolen by conquistadors. They removed boatloads of treasure from the continent when Spain was a world power."

Rudy said, "The curator thinks it's real."

"Then take it to the bank," Stillwater replied. "Kev, did the Spaniards steal everything of value from those poor people?"

"As much as possible. But at least one hoard—the Treasure of the Llanganatis—was hidden from them in Ecuador. It's been lost to history after being moved a few times."

Rudy asked, "What makes that one so famous?"

"It was part of a big double cross. The Spaniards were promised a room full of gold, silver and gems if they freed the Incan king. But they killed the guy before the exchange took place, which allowed the general who'd gathered the valuables to escape. He was later caught and tortured but never revealed their location."

"When did this happen?" Stillwater asked.

"In the 1530s. It took decades, but the Spaniards eventually conquered an empire that stretched from Colombia all the way to Argentina. They captured modern cities and roads first. Mountain hideaways and jungle villages fell later."

Rudy said, "Sounds like the Incans put up a good fight."

"I guess. Most warriors were wiped out by disease, just like the Indians in North America. Superior armor and weaponry took care of the rest. Anyway, that's all I've got. Bottom line—we know where the medallion came from and possibly who took it. But how it got here is a mystery."

A police cruiser turned in and came down the driveway. When it stopped, a lithe, blonde woman in uniform hopped out. As she catwalked over, a male officer who'd been driving—the stout Deputy Daniel—hurried to catch up.

"Ms. Roberts," Stillwater said coolly.

The chief replied, "Good afternoon."

She frowned when the estate owner hugged Daniel. Roberts had managed to alienate half the town since her promotion. Among other insults, she'd demanded new SUVs, assault weapons and body armor to better protect one of the safest zip codes in America. Stillwater had squashed the formal budget request when it came across her desk. Then advised Roberts to smarten up and slow down when gunning for change. Instead of taking that cue, she complained about funding deficiencies all over town. Which created an impassible chasm between the two women.

Daniel and Rudy shared a laugh off to the side. Kev was surprised since the deputy was the one who put the big fella behind bars.

The chief asked, "Care to share that with the rest of the class?" The question hung in the air like a bad curveball. Kev, who'd moved away before she came through the ranks, introduced himself while taking her measure. She was flat out gorgeous, yet he sensed something ugly about her.

"You found the bones," Roberts said, suddenly all business.

"Me and Rudy, yeah. Ms. Stillwater and I figure they belong to a former estate owner."

"I heard. Was the cemetery any help?"

"Yep." She crossed her arms as Kev explained the damage.

Roberts shook her head once he finished. "You're putting the cart before the horse. Those bones could have come from anywhere."

Okay, Columbo.

Daniel objected, "I don't know, Chief, that would make for one hell of a coincidence. Rudy just told me they ran their trotline next to the cemetery."

She stared the deputy down until Stillwater intervened, "Roberts, I thought you were coming alone to keep things quiet."

"Daniel will be circumspect with the interviews and such."

"I'm sure. But what if there's a violent crime in town?"

The deputy shielded a grin.

"Officer Johnson's on duty and ready for anything, however unlikely."

Stillwater winked at Daniel while opening the front door. "I'll be sure to remember how unlikely such events are during the next budget cycle."

Before a now angry looking Roberts could respond, Stillwater entered the house. She passed by the stairs which led to the upper floors and entered the rectangular great room. When Kev caught up, he was drawn to a bank of windows. Floor to ceiling, covering much of the room. With nary a smudge on their plate glass, the view of the river was marred only by the cottage.

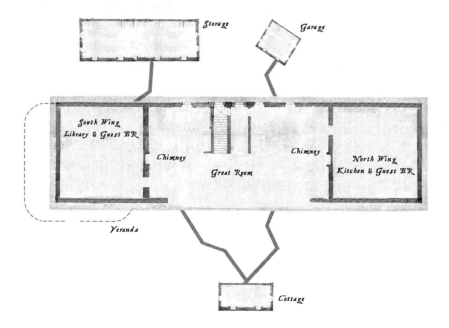

Daniel looked around. "What an amazing room!"

Stillwater beamed. "Thank you! This is where I entertain when the weather is not cooperating. Before you go, remind me to show you the library. It's my favorite room in the house."

The deputy nodded. "How old are the fireplaces?" he asked, eyeing two brick behemoths, each six feet wide.

"They're part of the original house, so just shy of three hundred years."

Roberts flared, "Can't we just see the bones?"

Stillwater frowned as she led them into the kitchen. Immaculate with a bereft pantry, the place suggested its owner preferred take-out. A country table and chairs filled one corner, but visitors tended to gather near an outsized granite island. The covered crab net rested there on brown paper. The chief strode over and plucked off the towel.

"The skull's broken like you said, Ms. Stillwater, same as the neck bone. And what a necklace! Daniel?" She stepped aside as the deputy took pictures. Then, after donning gloves and untangling the jewelry, he photographed each item individually.

The deputy announced, "The necklace kept the skull and vertebrae together. The soft tissue which once linked them is long gone."

Roberts dispatched him to interview Kev and Rudy. After Daniel led them to the table and produced a notepad, she put gloves on and examined the skull. Kev listened to her as Rudy briefed the deputy.

"Thankfully I used our meager training budget to get us smarter in forensics. That's how we learned that uneven, dark shades like these mean the bones are pretty old. But I can't tell—"

Daniel interrupted, "Fresh bones are ivory colored. If we didn't know about the cemetery, I'd say it's even money whether they were in dirt or the creek. Buried remains are often tan and brown, but they can also look that way after a long stay in water. It really depends on what they absorb from surrounding minerals and organic matter."

The glaring chief snapped at him to finish the interview.

"What he said makes sense," Stillwater offered. "Elizabeth Armistead was in the ground for a few centuries before Hurricane Isabel came through."

Roberts replied, "*If* it was her, the skull could have broken when it fell. Or maybe old bones collapse inward, I don't know."

The estate owner rolled her eyes.

The chief continued, "On to the jewelry . . . the necklace is beautiful and likely real gold. But the medallion is different. One side is elegant, the other so coarse. Ms. Stillwater, do you recognize the symbols?"

"I don't. But that's not surprising since the piece belonged to Armistead."

Kev wondered why she did not mention its Incan origin.

The chief looked disappointed as she put the necklace down.

"We're supposed to have forensic experts analyze bones that display trauma. If there was evidence of ownership, I might be able to bend the rules, but without it . . ."

Stillwater snorted, "It'll be obvious who it was when you see the lost grave."

Roberts motioned to Daniel who said, "If things aren't clear, I'll drive the bones over to Annapolis. It could take a while for the anthropologists to start, but once they do, the process moves pretty quickly. In the meantime, I'll get the curator's take on the medallion."

"None of that is circumspect," Stillwater said, shooting daggers at the chief.

"Standard protocol," Roberts declared.

"Does that involve common sense?"

"We're done here," the chief said angrily. "Let's go to the cemetery."

After Rudy left for his troubled job site, the others repeated the earlier trip. Once the deputy examined the headstones, Stillwater declared that the investigation should be over. The chief shrugged that off and said little on the way back to the house. Once there, Daniel bagged the bones and gold.

Roberts prompted him, "Tell her, deputy."

"What now?" asked Stillwater.

He was clearly uncomfortable. "The anthropologists create a paper trail."

"Internal?" Stillwater asked, looking suspicious.

"For now. I initiate the process with a police report, which eventually gets released to the public."

"This gets better and better," she said, shaking her head. "Who reads those?"

"The Easton paper and a few hacks. You've seen the occasional write-ups of petty crimes and DUIs in the area? Those come from our reports."

"Unbelievable."

"Sorry," the chief said, looking anything but. "I thought the chair of the town commission would understand the process."

"Keep your phone on—I'm calling you every few hours until things are resolved. Daniel, that undoubtedly means the heat will flow to you. So, I suggest you press the anthropologists to work quickly. I want to re-bury Elizabeth before I field a bunch of stupid questions."

Kev and Stillwater soon watched the cops drive off.

She said, "Think I'll tell the police in Annapolis and Baltimore about our talented chief. Maybe they'll relieve us of our burden."

"Roberts doesn't listen," he complained. "And she ran rough-shod over the deputy who I thought was pretty insightful. You know, now that I think about it, the chief may have missed her calling. She'd make one helluva cop on TV." He feigned examining something while muttering, "My brilliance suggests that this old skull was damaged when it fell."

Stillwater laughed. "She's no Perry Mason, but maybe I'll rec-ommend her to a gal I know who writes screen plays. It's a shame really, her old man was an absolute pro. But at least Daniel and the others absorbed his lessons before he retired."

Kev nodded. "Are you aware that the deputy once arrested Rudy?"

"Yes. I'd just become a commissioner when that happened. His turnaround after prison is pretty remarkable. The whole town's proud of him."

"I'm surprised Daniel got past it. He was a real pain in the ass during the case."

"Well, he's no longer a hothead. We all change, Kev, and the deputy is now a trusted ally."

"Then why didn't you mention the Incan connection?"

"Because Roberts was here. If she knew, she'd blab it all over town. And believe me, I've had my fill of publicity."

"The horse racing stuff?"

"Exactly."

Kev said, "Ma'am, that piece will make a big splash. Even without the Incan headline."

"Will?"

"Yep. Two cops are in the know. Which means the rest of the department, including the admins, will hear about it shortly. Then we have our museum curator. Mix in the anthropologists, their support staff and some pillow talk, and that's quite a list."

She looked prim. "The curator won't tell a soul, not even the police. Roberts screwed him over a few months ago. As for the others . . . you really think someone will talk?"

"Small town like this? Hell yeah. And once the news gets out, folks will speculate like crazy about the bones and gold. Unless we tamp things down first."

"How do we do that?"

"Prove that the medallion belonged to Elizabeth. Then when the story leaks, it's boring—just old remains that fell from your cemetery."

"Makes sense, but again—how?"

"You got any old records around?"

She brightened. "Let's go to the library."

LEGACY

KEV'S SENSES TINGLED AS HE followed the estate owner through the house.

The renewed sense of purpose was not unlike working a big-time deal. But this was much better, pure in a sense. After they passed through an arched doorway into a sea of books, he admired the quirky bust of Einstein, Stillwater's stately desk and a smartly grouped set of club chairs. A spiral staircase led to the wrap-around upper level. Sliders across the room opened to a veranda.

"This way," she said, moving left toward a dark credenza. It featured flower inlays made from different woods. "The older records are in here."

"Any from Armistead's time?"

"I'm not sure, I've never gone back that far. And it's been years since I opened this beast."

"Yeah? What were you after?"

She hesitated. "Information for my family tree."

He smirked. "You estate owners sure have it rough."

"I needed something to do during a blizzard! And stop throwing shade my way—I'm just a regular gal."

"Yes, your highness."

She stuck out her tongue before unsuccessfully trying the top drawer. "Care to give it a shot? You look pretty strong."

It screeched open to reveal a chaotic mess of documents, folders and newspaper articles. A brief examination revealed that they addressed family or estate matters in the late-1800s. The second and third drawers yielded similar caches but from different eras: the early-1800s and late-1700s.

"Gettin' warmer," he said. Since the last one would not budge, he sat and braced his feet wide against the sides of the credenza. After grinding the drawer open, he gasped, "Jake should soap these things."

She smiled. "Make sure I'm around when you tell him that."

They rifled through the contents.

"Everything's in good shape," he observed.

"Paper lasts forever. Leonardo da Vinci's drawings are still intact, and they're twice as old as what's here."

"See, you are different. Only an estate owner would say something like that."

She adopted an imperious air while opening a thin folder, then got excited. "These are the purchase documents for Rose Haven!"

"Your relatives bought it from the Armisteads, right?"

"No, the White Marsh Church."

"Really?"

"Yes. The Armisteads donated it to the local parish because they had no heirs."

He nodded. "What did a few hundred acres of prime real estate go for back in the day?"

"Strange . . . I don't see that. You can figure it out." After placing the folder into a cardboard box, he uncovered a series of small hardcover notebooks. The first, dated 1723, began with an artistic drop cap F. It was followed by smaller lines of neat, masculine script.

For the sake of posterity, I will chronicle our lives on this beautiful plantation. We just inherited it from Elizabeth's father . . .

Kev said, "Edward wrote this! It's some kind of journal." He handed it over, then inspected a few other volumes. "These are also his . . . the last one's from 1750. Ms. Stillwater—we hit the jackpot!"

"How fun! You may be the first person to read them."

Once finished with the drawer, Kev added the journals and some articles to the box.

"This may take a while." He'd feigned being aloof, but his heart raced with excitement.

"I bet. Call if he mentions the medallion. No pressure or anything, but like you said, I need to get ahead of the rumor mill."

On his way out, Kev flinched when he saw Jake. The man had taken apart a toilet in the adjacent powder room.

So much for keeping secrets.

Kate Stillwater smiled.

She'd rented Kev the cottage to make some extra cash. At first lukewarm to the idea, she embraced it after a background check and their lively phone calls. But when they met in person, Kate found him so good looking that she stumbled over her words and acted like a fool. Completely embarrassed, the estate owner later scolded herself for having urges inappropriate for a widow.

After cooling down, she frequently sought out his company. And he was receptive—perhaps because his hometown friends would not speak to him. Kev's appearance eventually blended in with the landscape. Yet by that time she'd been hooked by his easy intelligence, playful personality and seemingly broken spirit. Kate then peppered double entendre into their conversations. But he either missed or ignored those not-so-subtle signals, even when together for a nightcap. It made her wonder if other estate owners had trouble getting laid.

When Rudy came around, she almost asked him if Kev liked her. But the 'Ms. Stillwater' side of her squashed the sophomoric idea. Kate did not have multiple personalities or anything, but the moment her father died, she became a 'Ms.' and everyone treated her like royalty. Almost as if the happy-go-lucky 'Miss Kate' they'd known for years had ceased to exist. After it became second nature, only Joe—her beloved husband—could break down the unnecessary gravitas. But when he died, she reverted back to the old ways.

Stillwater grew anxious when her desk phone rang. Kev's presence had lifted her spirits, but the sunniest person on earth could not alleviate her fears about a recent property tax assessment. She'd fought it tooth and nail for much of the last year. While deadpan bureaucrats had listened to her pleas, they were hung up on comparable estates selling for top dollar. The final outcome was so alarming that she hired a new advisor. Who'd called just now to provide a realistic view of her financial situation.

After exchanging pleasantries over speaker, the man walked her through the expected cash inflows in the plan he'd sent over. They were meager. The only decent chunk of money on the way was from the pending liquidation of a once impressive endowment. Its low balance was the key reason she'd severed ties with her previous advisor. That loser had recommended a wide spectrum of poor investments, far different than most who hit the ball hard after the last market crash.

"Ms. Stillwater, you spend a lot of time on the town commission and other boards. Any way to get compensated for those efforts?"

"No, they're volunteer positions."

"Okay. How about charging for tours?"

"Oh, I couldn't do that. That's another way I give back to the community." He next turned to a long list of expenditures, headlined by the new tax burden and her hefty loan payments. She inwardly cursed the crippling debt. Then remembered a rant to Joe.

"Dad dug us in deep. Starting a thoroughbred operation from scratch using Rose Haven as collateral was silly *and* debilitating. Remind me to burn that empty trophy case which touted a Preakness Stakes victory he never sniffed. It's embarrassing to have around, and the hubris which brought it here still ticks me off. The man used to spout 'build it and the wins will come' while downing mint juleps and smoking cigars with Pop-Pop. Kentucky cocktails in Maryland for Christ's sake! Neither of them knew a damn thing about horses—other than how to bet on races—and they weren't even particularly good at that."

"Well," Joe had said, "selling the land across the road will give us a decent cushion. Near as I can tell, we won't get much for the stables and such, but the parcel itself is quite valuable. That should put us in a decent place, so long as the financial markets cooperate. And you control that spending gene of yours."

"I hope so. And I shouldn't completely bash the dead. At least the son of a bitch never made me wear a fancy hat. Anyway, I feel guilty for dragging you into this. This is my problem, not yours."

"I'd do anything for you, sweetie."

Stillwater snapped back to the present.

"Ma'am, you'll be insolvent by spring, even with the influx of cash from the endowment. And the bank will foreclose after you miss payments. We need to avoid that at all costs because it would result in a distressed sale. Which could mean very little money left for you after the bank gets paid."

"My last advisor had me tighten the belt when things got rough."

"Well, that guidance was . . . incomplete. I took a look at your spending patterns. You've reduced your day-to-day costs, which is great. But unplanned projects with steep price tags have really set you back. Even if you avoid big expenditures and cut back further, it won't matter much. The higher tax bill just isn't sustainable."

He was being subtle. Kate was addicted to improving Rose Haven at the expense of common sense. It eased the pain from losing Joe.

She asked, "Can't I just borrow more money?"

"I wish that was possible. The credit line is tapped out because of new, more restrictive regulations."

She'd once thought that her financial flexibility would keep pace with the rising value of Rose Haven. But without another significant increase that assumption had proven faulty, perhaps fatally so. Kate almost mentioned the pending cemetery project but held back. It was none of his damn business.

"Ma'am, I doubt it makes you feel better, but a lot of people around here have valuable property without the means to sustain it."

Yay. I'm a member of the land-rich-and-cash-poor club.

"It doesn't. How can I avoid foreclosure?"

"Page twenty has you selling Rose Haven. The realtor I trust believes the estate should fetch one hundred million dollars, right in line with the final tax value. You'd pay off the eighty plus million in debt, invest the difference conservatively and never worry about money again."

Kate replied, "I don't want to move." But what he'd said was logical. A widow living alone on a large estate did not make much sense. And a sale would allow her to travel again, donate to her favorite causes and prop Jake up after the new owners let the unusual man go. But the prospect of a sea change terrified her, and the weight of the family legacy demanded a better solution.

"Perhaps the next option will be more palatable. Here, you'd keep Rose Haven, but clear the land and lease it to farmers. The income would help cover your expenditures, but only if you become frugal. Which means no big projects, employees or contractors."

"I'm sorry, but I could never cut down that many beautiful trees."

"Understood. The last option has you sub-dividing the estate, then selling the individual parcels except for the buildings and driveway. That allows you to stay and keeps much of the land intact, presuming the new owners enjoy pastoral landscapes. The money left over after satisfying the debt should keep you comfortable enough."

"I have a plot next to Joe," she said flatly.

"The land near the water would have to go since it provides the highest payoff. But the buyer of that parcel might permit visitation and internment rights. The same holds true if you sell the entire estate. We'll make those rights a priority as we move forward."

With no apparent silver bullet, Kate felt her chest tighten and had difficulty breathing. The analysis confirmed what she'd suspected after the taxes shot up and the banks closed the spigot: Rose Haven was at a tipping point.

"Ms. Stillwater, I know these seem like terrible choices. But you asked me to show you what's realistic . . . Are you still there?"

"I am," she said in a small voice. "Are there other options?"

"I'm afraid not." His voice was gentle and soothing, the words anything but.

She imagined a host of relatives staring at her. Even Joe.

"I need time to think these over."

"I'll check in early next week. Not to be pushy, but we need to get moving."

Stillwater looked over at Einstein after she hung up, but her plea for inspiration fell on deaf ears.

Jake rolled his eyes after MacGuire complained about the drawers.

But he perked up when Stillwater mentioned a medallion, which he envisioned as big, golden and mysterious. Since she'd kept that from him, he decided to snoop around and catch a glimpse of the piece, maybe even figure out why she and the prick now skulked around.

After MacGuire left the library, Jake's heart sank during Stillwater's phone call. Not being a numbers person, he could only imagine the financial papers she reviewed. His fate, however, seemed clear regardless of the path she chose. He snuck away a few minutes later, immensely frustrated.

1589

CARTAGENA

THE CONQUISTADOR FINISHED CLIMBING, LIT a cigarro and gazed upon the port town.

Native men carried treasure along the wharf to 'his' flagship. Armor-clad soldiers lined the way, lances and swords at the ready. He felt for his own trusty blade. He'd pack it away for good once the king rewarded his efforts, then return to Maria in the white town. Its people would worship him, for he'd finally bested his father and grandfather, both famous explorers in their own right.

Beyond the wharf were dozens of ships from the Tierra Firme fleet. Over the past few days, he'd watched them deliver goods from Spain, then stand-off in the harbor. When it was time to load, non-descript vessels docked first to receive exotic spices and other goods. Well-protected galleons were then filled with valuables. When it had been the flagship's turn, the conquistador climbed the hill to watch and reflect.

He and his men had passed through miles of rainforest to reach what amounted to civilization in these parts. When threatened by savages on the way, the Spaniards had brandished their arms or, when necessary, fired into the air. That scared the little but danger-ous men away each time. Fortunate because protecting burdened pack animals while in battle was difficult.

The Spaniards made good time. But they could have done bet-ter if several men had not been stricken by the invisible diseases which plague that Godforsaken continent, including three who required stretchers. Fevers, chills and worse had taken thirty of his soldiers over the past two years, with twenty more killed by the enemy, accidents or their own hand. Losing half of the men and leaving remains behind troubled him. But at least they'd cleansed numerous savages from the mountains and jungle.

This time, however, he'd done more than wait for sick men to recover or die. Sips of fountain water soon cured them, just as it had nourished the creatures in the rainforest and made him feel incredibly robust. Since the effects were obviously potent, he'd decided to keep the bottles in his personal belongings. And later hide them from the crown. High treason, but well worth the risk.

Horns blaring in the distance signaled a nautical event. The spectacular number of ships would more than double in Havana when combined with the New Spain fleet. The largest convoy in history would then sail to the Canary Islands before provisioning there and heading for home.

Home! Where his beautiful Maria waited for him in the hills of southern Spain. He missed the woman's adventurous spirit, and memories of her sultry body often consumed him. So much so that he'd raped pretty natives at each and every opportunity. Earlier that day, the conquistador joined the many soldiers readying to confess similar transgressions. He'd successfully angled for a priest known to be gentle with penance and now enjoyed an unencumbered soul.

He looked toward the horizon. The view from up high was impressive, but this sea was no match for the azure Mediterranean. Leaders from towns near its coast would no doubt enlist his help with their affairs while Maria raised the children. He fervently hoped most would be boys. That way, they too could conquer vast amounts of territory. A girl or two would also be nice, for he might require care after the boys sailed off for high adventure.

Or perhaps not, if the bottled water retained its power.

When the activity below slowed, he crunched what was left of the cigarro under his boot and made his way to the harbor. They would sail at dawn.

MONDAY EVENING

SAFEHOUSE

KEV GOT COMFY ON THE cottage porch and plucked a few items from the box.

He lost himself while tripping through the past. When the final pages of a journal piqued his curiosity, he paused to print the notes he'd taken on his laptop. After he collected them and made copies, his landlord marched by.

Kev called, "Got a minute, neighbor?"

Stillwater climbed a short run of steps, opened the screen door and then collapsed into a chair. He'd never seen her look so stressed.

She asked, "Find anything?"

"I've struck out so far on the medallion. But I want your take on some other stuff."

"Okay."

"Is something wrong with our resident royal?"

"Wrong doesn't begin—"

"Hey guys!" Rudy boomed. He'd just rounded the far corner of the cottage.

"Big fella!" Kev replied. "You get your job sorted out?"

"Yeah. All is well again in the landscaping world." Rudy eyed the papers and books after joining them. "What's up?"

Kev said, "We found Edward's journals and some other documents in the library. We're hoping one of them mentions the medallion."

Rudy grimaced. "Sounds fun. Any luck?"

"Not yet, but there are some things worth sharing. Since you're here and all."

Rudy asked, "Did Elizabeth write any of this stuff?"

"Nope."

"Bummer. I bet she'd explain that weird figure."

"Good news! Edward writes like you talk. So, he'll probably address it at some point."

Rudy feigned being hurt as he removed a bottle of beer from the outside fridge.

After taking a pull he said, "All right, college boy. A few of these can get me through anything. Where do we start?"

"From the beginning."

"You didn't jump to her funeral? Elizabeth took that medallion to her grave."

"Nope. Edward may have given it to her early on, and I'd hate to backtrack. They were married for over thirty years."

While organizing the copies into packets Kev added, "I'll give you guys a visual to kick things off. Both husband and wife were pale with dark hair. One article suggested they could pass for siblings. Interesting since he was twenty years older, eh?"

Rudy said, "Get to the good stuff. Was she easy on the eyes?"

"Very. Edward raved about her beauty, as did others in the community. If I did the conversion right, he was the size of an NBA wing. She was also tall, but nowhere near his height."

"It'll take more than a hoops reference to hook me," Rudy said, stifling a yawn. "Do you guys really care about this stuff?"

Stillwater smiled. "Don't you appreciate a good love story?"

"Ma'am," Rudy said, "no matter how you couch it, this feels like a history lesson." He pointed at his own chest. "And this guy hated those classes like no other."

"These will win you over," Kev said, handing out the packets. "The first set addresses some family matters and the second focuses on Rose Haven. That'll be like gold to you, Ms. Stillwater. The third . . .

well, I'm not sure how to describe it. You'll just have to wait and see."

Kev read the first passage aloud:

Elizabeth is smiling again after a long period of mourning. Now that her father is at peace, she frequents his grave in our new cemetery at the confluence of the river and creek. We chose the spot because Devon enjoyed it more than any other.

They were quiet so Kev added, "We just can't get away from that graveyard."

"It *is* the nicest part of the estate," Stillwater said wistfully. "But what happened to Devon? It sounds tragic."

"I use the word *confluence* all the time," Rudy said chuckling. After fielding Kev's stare, he added, "Okay, okay. How did the guy die?"

"From tumors," she said while reading ahead, "which Edward attributed to *lymph*. In the early 1700s, folks believed that poisonous body fluids caused cancer."

Kev was morbidly curious, "How'd you know that?"

"I read up on the disease when my husband had melanoma. Anyway, Devon soon had company. His wife's remains were moved over from White Marsh a few weeks after his funeral."

"That old church creeps me out," Rudy said, shivering. "There's just a wall of it left now, and the grounds are haunted."

Kev inwardly thanked him for changing a subject close to home.

Stillwater moved on, "The couple was religious, particularly Elizabeth. Oh! . . . there's another difficult matter here. The Armisteads were unable to conceive. How awful!"

Her reaction suggested a close familiarity with the issue.

Kev said gently, "Building a new house might have been a welcome distraction for them, if that makes sense . . . which is a good segue to the next set of papers. There's a lot here about construction plans, materials and the like, but I'll just hit the wavetops. Rudy, someday we'll discuss Flemish brick patterns over a beer."

"As long as there's a game on."

Our new home will be fifty feet long and half of that wide. Its numerous windows will provide lovely views of the Tred Avon. Twin fireplaces and chimneys are to anchor each end.

We will stay in the Devon house until ours is ready this spring. Work will begin after that on the kitchen, stables, new slave quarters and guest cottage.

Elizabeth was difficult today. While we agree that the plantation's name must match its magnificence, she has rejected my every suggestion without making one of her own.

Rudy said, "They argued like regular folks! Ms. Stillwater, I assume your family re-purposed some of the buildings?"

"Yes, the garage used to be the stables and the storage building was the slave quarters. I'm not sure where the outdoor kitchen was, but it would have been near the house. You know, that last passage is a real tease. It's always been a mystery how the estate got its name."

"Not anymore," said a grinning Kev.

"Really?" she asked, then anxiously flipped forward. "Bingo!"

While strolling on the peninsula at twilight, I was struck by the rose-colored water reflecting the last bit of sun. Thus inspired, I suggested the name Rose Haven for our plantation. And Elizabeth agreed!

"The folks in town will go nuts over this! And it wouldn't surprise me if Estate Magazine ran an article!"

He hid a grin while Rudy was diplomatic, "Ma'am, we obviously lead very different lives. But I hear you—it's fitting that both the name and story match the beauty of this place."

Kev moved them along, "Okay—last packet. Edward often wrote that he and Elizabeth danced a 'Goat's Jig.' And he frequently referred to something called a 'Flash Ken.'"

"Goat jigging, eh?" Rudy said, eyebrow raised. "I've never heard it called that before. Even when I was a frat boy at Frostburg State before . . . how shall we say . . . the administration invited me to leave."

"You went right to the gutter, big fella, but that's exactly right. Now, take a look at the Flash Ken passages."

Where to put the Flash Ken? My FK has a home! Work on the Flash Ken has begun!

"He sure flashed Ken a lot," Rudy said, making himself snort. "Why didn't you start with this packet? It's way more entertaining than the others."

"How about a little focus?" Stillwater asked with a smile. "Kev, did you look up 'Flash Ken' as well?"

"Yep. It's either a safehouse for thieves or a brothel."

She looked perplexed. "Those don't make sense."

"Not so fast!" Rudy interrupted. "Eddie was a randy dude, at least with Elizabeth. Maybe he was a scoundrel who ran a love shack!"

"You're so weird," Kev teased. "But if she wore the medallion, I suppose anything's possible."

"You think Elizabeth was in on it? Maybe the Madam? You'd better get cracking on the rest of the journals. Inquiring minds want to know!"

Stillwater objected, "I hate to burst your boys-club bubble, but it's crazy to think that there was a brothel here. There would have been talk from customers or the 'help,' if I may be so crass."

Kev said. "Okay, so he had a safehouse for thieves. Whatever that means."

Stillwater replied matter-of-factly, "Which also is ludicrous."

Kev asked, "Why?"

"The Armisteads had no reason to consort with criminals—they were the richest folks around. But Rudy's right in his own special way. Kev—please keep at it. If nothing else, it's nice to learn more about my place."

Rudy seemed intrigued. "They were loaded, eh? Maybe they socked money away in the Flash Ken. Mac, you should look for it.

You have nothing else to do."

After they left, Kev read until his eyes tired. He then gazed out at the river, where the pinkish-red water mirrored the last gasp of sunset. The view inspired him, but differently than it had Armistead long ago. Kev poured himself some scotch, selected a dark cigar from the humidor and soon had it burning smoothly.

He drew in and blew out a cloud of smoke, pleased that the mystery had grown. While there could be simple explanations for the medallion and Flash Ken, his instincts suggested otherwise.

REGRETS

JAKE STOMPED THROUGH THE HEART of Oxford.

Impeccable homes lined the two-lane avenue. Most had markers advertising historic significance. Antique, knick-knack and packaged-goods stores mixed in here and there, along with a few stone churches. Broad trees towered over the street. Their roots unseated the occasional sidewalk brick, an accepted outcome of a battle between ancient rivals.

He'd come from his sad little cottage on the outskirts of town. He grew up in that home, and for years trekked into Oxford for school, groceries and such. But he avoided the place these days, except when drawn to the tavern at the Robert Morris Inn. It was his favorite watering hole, and he needed alcohol after Stillwater's financial call. Perhaps even some company.

He smirked when two well-dressed women said hello. Like many in town, they were sweet sounding rich folks who'd carve people up for less-than-ideal behavior. Working for Stillwater had largely protected him from such attacks over the last decade. But with that about to end, he wistfully remembered another job that would have had staying power *and* brought him respect. One that Pops, in his heavy country drawl, had killed off years ago.

"Boy, who's taking you on as a mate? No one, eh? See, all you do is talk, talk, talk about becoming a fishing boat captain. But you haven't lifted a finger to learn that trade or any other. Getting started in something takes a good reputation, which you don't have. I mean, you've been in trouble since Christ was a corporal and you barely graduated from high school. Let's face it, you need the family tradition, not a pipe dream. It'll take time, but you can become a good estate keeper, maybe better than me. So, get your head on straight—we leave tomorrow at six."

Pops had trained him relentlessly for the role. After a bad ticker forced the man to retire, he handed over the reins. At the time the transition felt natural, appropriate. But when Stillwater later let on that she'd been unsure about it, he realized the apprenticeship was a test. Pops dying before hearing a proper thank you used to make Jake feel guilty. But now he wanted to curse the man. Estate-keeper skills would not translate well in the real world.

After arriving at the squat, two-story building the color of fancy mustard, he muscled through its crowded outdoor patio, practically begging for trouble. The warm inside of the tavern—brick walls, small bar, scattered tables and fireplace—took the edge off. Jake, perhaps more than most, intuitively understood why the place had attracted folks for centuries.

The bar was full, so he took a proffered Bud on the way by to a table. He was good for at least a half-dozen long necks on work nights with no such weekend prohibitions. When not at work, asleep or in a bar, Jake watched TV, hunted or fished. Usually by himself, sometimes with other gruff men. Those outings provided plenty of guy time, but he rightly feared that his persistent eye for the ladies was misconstrued. He tried to overcome that by scouring sources—friends, extended family, online services—for dates, but second chances were few and far between, third nonexistent. Sheer determination, his one positive trait, never fixed the problem. While deep down Jake was lonely, he rarely thought in such terms. Mainly because his job at Rose Haven gave him immense pride.

His somber mood evaporated when a red-haired woman slipped into a neighboring chair.

She said, "Well, if it isn't my fellow heat-miser!"

Lucy looked fabulous. Jake tried to disguise a long-simmering hunger as he absorbed her skimpy yellow dress and sun-kissed neckline. She'd entranced him since third grade. Mean classmates that year had blamed the two redheads, or so-called 'heat misers,' for an unusually cold winter, strangely claiming their hair absorbed the little available warmth.

While she overcame the verbal abuse and became popular by springtime, he was left behind to plot his revenge. Once he grew big, he beat the holy hell out of each offending boy. That success, such as it was, had encouraged him to make lists of transgressions—both real and imagined—ever since.

He went right for his comfort zone, "Hey, Lucy. Buy you a drink?"

"Yes, thank you." After he signaled the bartender, the man brought over another beer and took her order.

Her green eyes sparkled. "It's great to see you again! You still at Rose Haven?"

"Yeah—same ol', same ol.' And you're more famous than ever!"

"Far from it," she giggled. "I love that little paper, though. Circulation's still strong, but I wonder what'll happen when the retirees around . . . you know." The Easton Daily covered the happenings in that nearby town, a thriving metropolis compared to Oxford. But the paper extended its reach through its lead reporter when there were stories worth chasing. Jake nodded but kept quiet, uncomfortable with taking the lead.

She asked, "What about you, handsome? Does Stillwater still work you like a dog?"

"Yeah, I mean, it's a lot of effort. Has been ever since her husband dumped the rest of the staff a few years ago. But I couldn't ask for a better boss, and she encourages me to get outside help."

He'd added the last bit because Lucy was connected. If Stillwater heard that he'd in any way disparaged his job, her recommendation to potential employers would be tepid. Or even worse sink him in rich person code.

"Thank goodness for that!"

"Yeah, she's solid . . . What brings you back to Oxford?"

"Dinner with friends on the restaurant side. They went home early, so I dropped in to see if any cool cats were around."

"Gotcha," he said, surprised to make that cut. As he considered what to say next, he looked through a photograph on the wall. It was a shot of James Michener who'd written part of *Chesapeake* while at the inn. A thought struck Jake. Lucy grew up on the same street, but she was accepted, welcomed even. Before it stuck, the familiar awkwardness from conversing with women took over. Otherwise, he might have realized that friendly people did just fine in and around town regardless of economics. He adjusted himself to camouflage the angst which was his mom's fault. She'd run off before giving him sisters.

Lucy appraised him. "So, what's new?"

"Nothing really."

"I've heard differently."

"What do you mean?"

"A little bird told me that some strange things were caught in Devon creek."

"Oh, that." For a moment, he'd wondered if she knew about Stillwater's financial problems.

"Wait, is there something else?"

Shit.

"Nope." He'd said it firmly to move her along.

"Thought you . . . well . . . Anyway, I don't know what they are yet, but I expect to find out soon." She flashed her winning smile. "And having a source who knows the place would be icing on the cake."

She's gonna find out anyway.

And telling her what I know could open the door for a real date, maybe more.

"It'll be off the record."

As he gathered his thoughts, Lucy added, "Come on, I'll be your best friend!" She'd successfully used that line for years.

"Tell you what," he said under his breath. "Spring for these beers and dinner Friday—"

"You got it, handsome. Wherever you want to go. Now spill it!"

Which he did.

AUGUST 2021

CLUE

SHELL POINT RETURNED TO HER slip.

Once the boat stopped, two baby-faced Coasties fielded the bow and stern lines. As the helpers tied them off, a rusty gangplank crashed down. Ben was the first ashore, toting a cooler which held the chunks of concretion. After securing it into the bed of his pickup truck, he drove away.

Lucas, caught in a throng of academics leaving the ship, eventually made it to his rental car. He exited the Coast Guard station and made his way down the barrier island. Once across a small bridge, he turned on the news. Ben had it right—Hurricane Isabel would soon smack the North Carolina coast. The governor instructed those in low-lying areas to run for the hills.

Most of the travel across state was on country highways, where the extreme heat made the distant pavement appear wet. The illusion repeated as he progressed, but the homogenous towns that cropped up periodically were real enough. Each had a dollar store, gas station mart, fried chicken restaurant and a church, sometimes two.

Reality set in on the way. While the earlier discoveries seemed exciting, the chunks of concretion most likely held artifacts with nary a clue. After a two-hour trip, he was welcomed to Greenville by the pirate mascot from the local university.

Fitting.

He drove through town then along quiet roads which led to the *QAR* research facility. Lucas parked in a spot under Blackbeard's proudly waving black flag. Ben pulled in afterward and went around the main building. Made of beige brick, it resembled an upper-crust middle school. Once inside, Lucas followed the noise to a cavernous two-story lab. The place was jammed with people, possibly the entire staff. But not his folks. They were in a separate wing analyzing artifacts.

Everyone seemed excited except for the bushy-haired lab head. The dour man stood by while two women ran the show. One super tall, the other quite short—an odd pair clad in white coats. After Ben backed the truck in through a tall garage door on the far side, he brought the cooler over to a worktable. He then stuck around to watch, something that rarely happened after a dive.

The women donned gloves and examined the chunks. Most packed in close while Lucas climbed a set of steps to see better.

The short one took charge, "No surprises here. We'll need X-rays to see what, if anything, is in them." A waiting tech brought the objects to an adjacent room. When he announced that at least two contained artifacts, the crowd's excitement was palpable.

The tall specialist received the X-rays and held up the first sheet. She clearly enjoyed the spotlight.

"And the artifact that has everyone so excited . . . is cylindrical . . . and much different than anything previously found at the dive site. Here's the best part—the metal shows up vividly, so it must be silver." The room exploded with whoops and high fives. Discovering valuables usually fired Lucas up, but he was in a wait and see mode.

"It has embedded . . . parts I guess, for lack of a better description. I'm not sure what this sucker is, but we can work on it right away. Air won't harm the precious metal."

She continued the play by play with the next X-ray, "This artifact is an iron tube. One end has a sharp protrusion, kind of like a nail. And there's something circular on the other side. Could be a weapon . . . maybe a tool. We'll find out more once the salt and negative ions are gone." After placing the chunk into a nearby tank and examining the last X-ray, she set aside the third object, likely an encrusted piece of rock from the ocean floor.

Ben cleared his throat. "Folks, if I can have your attention . . . I'm probably getting ahead of myself, but these artifacts look real special. I just wanted to say how proud I am of what y'all do." He then walked around and shook hands. The well-received sentiments made Lucas wish he was a better leader.

When Ben finished, the women pulled up protective masks and lowered eye shields. As they carved around the silver artifact, their air scribes looked and sounded like miniature jack hammers. Guided by the X-ray, they carefully stripped away excess material, layer by layer. Once it was down to a thin covering, they placed the artifact into a second tank.

"Folks, that's the end of tonight's show. The current will loosen up what's left of the concretion and make our job easier in the morning. See you bright and early!" Lucas returned to his hotel in town, where he grabbed a bite then crashed, exhausted yet hopeful for a clue.

Parts of the blackish cylinder were visible the next day. After watching the same specialists work on it for a while, this time at a slower pace with gentler tools, Lucas stepped out to check on his other projects. Once done with the calls, he told his on-site team about the new finds. That led to an impromptu briefing in a bland conference room, where they walked him through the remains of weapons, navigational instruments and cooking items, including some that were fairly intact. But their enthusiasm seemed forced, presumably because they had not found a clue. Lucas feigned interest but often drifted, thinking about the work in the lab.

After his people wrapped up, he said, "You've made great progress. Keep pushing—we're due for a break!" The lie seemed to give them a lift.

Much of the concretion was gone when he returned. The tall specialist soon fidgeted with the artifact, and when it more than doubled in length everyone cheered—they'd found a telescope. Most babbled that the spyglass once belonged to a pirate, perhaps even Blackbeard himself. The lab head thought it might be captured loot, a theory which Lucas found more likely. When things simmered down, the short woman carefully polished the intact lenses before raising the telescope to her eye.

Amazingly it still worked. He was ensnared by the hoopla until he remembered that the interesting artifact would not earn him the stock options.

She spoke up, "Hang on folks, there's script on one of the segments!" The crowd hushed as the woman cleared material from the letters. Artifacts from *QAR* were often engraved in different languages since Blackbeard was an equal opportunity offender, but a translator was not needed this time. The message was in English.

Guide my love to Oxford.

AUGUST 2021

PLOTTING

LUCAS LISTENED TO HIS TEAM debate next steps.

The storm had finally blown through. Since the QAR facility was closed for repairs, he'd rented the banquet room at his hotel. A big, mostly empty space with threadbare carpet, peeling wallpaper and an outdated chandelier the size of a small car. He huddled with his folks around a handful of circular tables that were covered with laptops and power cords. The researchers participated by phone from Miami. When the large doors were shut, the group could safely hash out differences of opinion.

Lucas stayed out of the fray for a while. His teams were all different, and this one was most creative when he was on the sidelines. After seeing 'Isabel' pop up on a corner TV, he cranked up the volume. Everyone stopped talking once the anchor loudly proclaimed the hurricane to be the storm of the century. He smirked at the overused line until pictures of the destruction—mangled boats, piers and houses—ran across the screen. Jurisdictions were still counting, but so far dozens were dead from the fierce winds and storm surge. The hurricane had slowed over land, but forecasters expected the storm to gain strength as it swung northeast toward the Chesapeake Bay.

His people reanimated when the channel went to commercial. After several months of frustration, they were fired up about the inscription. Most of the academics had also been stoked before Lucas and the lab head convinced them that the telescope was pirate loot, its message intended for someone else. After accepting the logic, they pivoted away from dreams of silver and gold to the anniversary events marking Blackbeard's death. The telescope would be the star of the show, thankfully a few months away.

But Lucas let his team, many of whom were convinced that the inscription would lead to pirate treasure, go mostly unchecked. Their passion could score him an artifact or two away from the dive site. A more realistic possibility, and for him the most rewarding.

He spoke up when some aggressive folks got out of hand, "Simmer down. You guys have come up with some interesting ideas but now you're off course. If the telescope belonged to Blackbeard or an officer—"

One of his vets objected, "Lucas, I don't get the 'if.' This is a big deal!"

"The spyglass certainly has potential. But we need to determine whether it belonged to one of the pirates. So, forget about visiting Oxford, England. There's no way they could have completed the journey in the known timeline. And I seriously doubt that 'Oxford' was a name used in the third person."

"I'm confused," a newbie chipped in. "Do you believe what you told the folks in Greenville or not?"

"I got them out of the way so we can do our thing. For those returning to the facility—"

Good-natured groans erupted.

"Come on, people. We've got to finish our work there in case the inscription doesn't pan out. When you're back on-site, preach the same message I did. Think about it . . . if we show excitement or pull out of town, folks will get chatty, well before they unveil the telescope to the public. Now, a leak might happen regardless of our precautions. So, Yvonne, your research team needs to put us way out in front. Try to link the pirates with towns named Oxford on the east coast of the U.S. or in the Caribbean. I also want to find the craftsmen who made the spy glass. That's probably a reach. But if we pull that off, their records might have clues."

Someone called out, "You're as pumped as we are!"

He grinned. "I just hide it better. But again, the key is to stay cool, work the problem and stop chasing wild theories. Speaking of which, Gomez wants a brief tomorrow in Miami. So, let's re-convene first thing. You can tell me everything you've learned before I fly out."

After the prospects of an all-nighter elicited more groans, he added, "If we look sharp for the boss, you'll get a three-day weekend. If not, she'll be all over us. Trust me—that's the last thing we want."

Lucas was in Gomez's conference room the next day by 11 AM. She breezed in afterward with a big smile.

"Does my ace have anything new?" He'd updated her by phone the day before, which made him question being summoned to Miami. Calls were much more efficient.

"We've decided that the inscription could point to where Blackbeard or one of his officers spent time with a lover. Those are the only paths I see to something meaningful. But to be honest, there's a better chance the telescope was captured loot."

"I'm betting on black! That search grid where you found the telescope includes what's left of the captain's quarters."

"I hope you're right. But we both know that pirate officers shared cabins, including that one."

She looked dreamy. "Are your folks looking for the right Oxford?"

"Yeah, they've really gotten after it. Turns out there are twenty towns with that name in the U.S. Of those, seven are in east coast states. One each in Florida, Georgia, North Carolina, Maryland, New York, Massachusetts and Maine. Our preliminary look suggests starting in Maryland or North Carolina."

"What about the Caribbean?"

"The islands are a dead end."

"Got it. Well, Carolina's not surprising since Blackbeard lived near its coast for several months. But I've never heard of an Oxford there."

"It's up near the Virginia boarder, just off I85."

She frowned. "But that's several hours from the ocean."

"Yep. Four by car, which would have made it quite a hike in those days. Even by horseback."

"Hmmm. Tell me more about Maryland."

"That Oxford is on the eastern shore. With easy access to the Chesapeake Bay."

She looked thoughtful.

"Shall we start there?" he asked hopefully. It seemed like the most logical place to search.

"I was leaning that way, but the pirate never visited the colony . . ." She drummed her fingers. "Tackle North Carolina first. It's close to your current base of operations, and my gut tells me the treasure is somewhere in that state."

He wanted to roll his eyes. "You sure?"

"Yes. Pirates travelling to the interior goes against conventional wisdom. But maybe that's for the best. No one's ever found a damn thing near the water."

"Fair enough. While I'm there, the research team will evaluate the other towns. Online to keep a low profile. And, in case the inscription doesn't pan out, we'll examine the remaining artifacts."

Gomez appeared satisfied. "Lucas, by 'lover,' did you mean a woman who lived in one of these places?"

"Yeah. It's well known that Blackbeard was a ladies' man."

She nodded. "How will you narrow them down?"

"We'll focus on wealthy ones who were single at some point between 1713 and 1718."

"Wealthy because of the telescope?"

"Exactly. That's one expensive gift."

"Blackbeard was killed in 1718 . . . so the end of your range makes sense. Did you pick 1713 because he was once a privateer?"

"Yeah. Those types rarely strayed from the Caribbean and Gulf of Mexico."

She was quiet so he stroked her ego, "Does our approach make sense? You know more about Blackbeard than anyone."

"Yes! I've waited a long time for that lovely inscription! Press the team to move quickly though. That telescope's too juicy for it not to shake loose at some point."

"Roger that. But please be patient. It could be weeks before we make a connection, if one exists."

Her snarl disappeared as quickly as it had formed. "Happy hunting and send me daily updates."

Hope stirred in her belly.

Gomez had done everything possible to prioritize *QAR*, first by doubling the usual number of staff. She'd added more people over the summer as they freed up from other assignments. After the COO saturated the team with resources, there was nothing left to do other than wait. And pray.

The summer had felt even longer during visits with Padrino, once the highlights of her year. The man's frail physique and poor memory provided constant reminders that his time was running out.

She'd almost given up before Lucas called with the news. While the recent events were both clear and extraordinarily promising, Gomez summoned him to Miami so she could evaluate his sense of urgency. Everything sounded good until Lucas preached patience. That's when the COO had decided to bird-dog his progress. He seemed prepared for a long road, which of course would not do.

I should have put a deadline on the stock options.

But sweating him will yield the same result.

She smiled while reaching for her cell phone. The truth might give Padrino the strength to hang on.

SEPTEMBER 2021

CONNECTIONS

Lucas called Yvonne after visiting a dusty museum.

"North Carolina is a bust. The town name comes from the first house built here, which the owner named Oxford to honor his hometown in jolly old England. He was here for several years with his old lady and kids before others settled nearby. The town was established later, but by then Blackbeard had been dead for years."

"Damn. We should have caught that before you schlepped out there."

"I found the information in an old book which I doubt is online. Plus, I only get a feel for a place by putting boots on the ground."

"Read anything about a tall guy with a beard? Unexplainable happenings? Someone fascinated by pirates?" He smiled at her persistence. She was an invaluable resource who challenged hunters in the field to turn over each and every stone.

"Negative, it's similar to most American towns that are near interstate highways."

"Bummer."

"Don't be too disappointed, there's value in eliminating one of our candidates. So, let's talk about Maryland. How's the Oxford there shaping up?"

"It's a mixed bag. Blackbeard never visited the colony according to the experts. But there are rumors to the contrary."

"Are the rumored spots close to our town?"

"Well, they're on the same side of the Chesapeake."

"Yvonne, that's almost half the state!"

"Hear me out. The buccaneers who frequented the bay cleaned their vessels over there on remote patches of water. Blackbeard could have done the same thing and gone to town for supplies and such."

"Okay, let's roll with that theory for minute. What was Oxford like back then?"

"A lot busier than today. For years it was one of two places where goods could enter or leave the colony, which of course made it a trading mecca. From our research, I get the sense that no one asked questions as long as business was good. Tobacco was the featured crop and made lots of people rich. Many of whom lived on big plantations."

"Did they get destroyed in the Civil War?"

"Maryland was part of the Union, silly . . . well sort of. But no, most are still there—some even owned by the original families. I guess the cash that rolls in from agriculture and what not has sustained the plantations—now called estates—for generations. They have the cutest little names."

"Like what?"

"Somebody's 'Pride' or something 'View'—you know, shit that rich and idle people make up."

"Any pirate-related?"

"You think I'd keep that from you?"

Lucas chuckled. "So, if we want to find a woman who waited for a seafaring lover, kind of like Brandy in that seventies song—"

"Old timer, the only Brandy I know of is from Cali, and she doesn't sing about sailors. But if our mysterious lady existed, it's reasonable to believe that she came from a tobacco family."

"That must narrow down the possibilities."

"One would think. But we can't figure out who lived on the plantations during the years you set forth. Except for the men who owned them."

"You've put a lot of thought into this."

"We have a list of places ready to go. You'll just have to figure out who the eligible ladies were the old-fashioned way."

"You mean go door-to-door? I'm sure that will be well received."

"Actually, we're in luck. September is a big tour month for old estates. So, all you have to do is visit and ask a bunch of questions."

"Most estates offer tours?"

"All but two . . . which I guess are owned by assholes. As for the rest, inviting strangers to your home must a thing when all you do is count money. The tours run three days a week, and here's the best part. When I sensed that North Carolina was a dud, I went ahead and booked you for this Sunday, then every tour day thereafter until we're tapped out."

After a brief trip home to visit his daughter, Lucas flew into Baltimore-Washington International Airport. Once on the road and over the Chesapeake Bay Bridge, he followed signs to Oxford. Everything felt slow when in town, so he matched the pace while taking in the immaculate main drag. Shorter than he expected, it ended at the Robert Morris Inn, right on the river. The town was pretty, tranquil. It was hard to envision a once hectic port.

Once checked in, Lucas oriented himself downhill at a spartan ferry terminal. He then headed right along a moneyed avenue which led past a small beach. When a marina marked the end of the craggy peninsula, he worked his way back, this time along grid-like streets. A number of friendly folks strolled about, many with compliant dogs. After Lucas had a feel for the place, he found the right bench and waited for the tour bus.

The first stop failed to produce eligible females who fit the criteria. As they pulled into the second, he admired the lovely home with its Tara-esque columns.

A pretty woman greeted them outside, "Good afternoon and welcome to Rose Haven. My name is Ms. Stillwater, and this is my estate. You're visiting several places today, but you'll be here long enough to get a feel for the place. Tours always start in the Great Room, and today is no exception. So, please—follow me."

As folks chatted about the trappings and view through the plate glass, she distributed a sketch while describing the buildings. After she mentioned that her family purchased the plantation in 1752, Lucas raised his hand.

"Excuse me, who lived here before that?"

"The Devon family was first, followed by the Armisteads."

"Devons, Armisteads, Stillwaters—got it. Ma'am, it was before your family's time, but were any single ladies around in the early 1700s? I want to make sure the novel I'm writing is realistic."

She smiled. "Oh, an author! My maiden name is Nelson, not Stillwater. And yes, the Devon's had a daughter who lived here from cradle to grave. I'm not one to tell people how to approach their work, but the information you're after is probably online or at the library."

"Yes, ma'am," he said, feigning embarrassment. "But since I'm here, I assume from what you said that the girl married an Armistead?"

"Very perceptive—yes, Elizabeth was born in 1700 and she and Edward tied the knot in 1718."

Hmmm . . .

"Was Armistead from the area?"

"No, he was a trader, originally from England."

Better . . .

"Did they have a long courtship? I understand those were once fairly common."

The estate owner looked at her watch before answering, "He called on her for a few years. I'm sorry, but I have to keep moving or the tour folks will kill me . . . Anyway, where was I? Oh yes, the families here grew wealthy from tobacco, but those markets were not that lucrative after the American Revolution. Like most others, we eventually switched to wheat—the next big cash crop—but my family's interest in agriculture waned after the abolishment of slavery. You see, the economics . . ."

Lucas thought about it. Elizabeth had been single at the right time, but the length of the courtship would have put her at fifteen or sixteen before the trader first came around—likely too young for a dalliance with the pirate. Disappointed, Lucas refocused on Stillwater.

"In the twentieth century, my family got into the oyster business. They hired men who dredged the shellfish from beds once so large they were navigational hazards. Take a good look at the river. It looks blue from here, but up close you'll see that its murky. It used to be crystal clear when the oysters filtered every drop of water. Isn't that amazing?

"Once most of them were harvested or dead from disease, we bred thoroughbred horses. I was around for that venture, which ended unfettered by success. Now I spend the bulk of my time serving the community in a variety of ways."

This place seems like a dud.

But he had to be certain. "Were pirates ever a threat here?"

"Yes. Space was the first line of defense, which is why large homes like this one were set back from the water. That gave folks time to escape with their valuables and slaves. They'd return later, hoping to find their houses and other buildings intact."

"Was Rose Haven ever sacked?"

"No . . . perhaps because the early owners kept an armed sentry by the water. But piracy was only a concern in the early years. It had largely been eradicated by the time my relatives bought the place."

"Did the sentries use telescopes to look for trouble?"

"I assume so. Why do you ask?"

"Oh, just curious."

She soon led them through the rest of the first floor. "The two wings were added in the 1800s. The library was a luxury, but as my family grew, they needed the kitchen and extra bedrooms. The third story came later, but as you can see, the width of the home today is still the original twenty-five feet."

When they went outside it felt like an oven. He mopped his brow as she described Georgian Colonial homes like hers, once popular both in England and the colonies. On the way back from the river, she introduced the group to two men. The first one was a large redhead who looked after the estate. And the other guy—lanky and either ethnic or deeply tanned—lived in her cottage while on sabbatical.

Must be nice.

TUESDAY MORNING

BATON

RUDY'S HEADLIGHTS REVEALED MAC IN front of the big house.

After climbing into the black truck, he muttered, "You didn't answer my text."

Rudy laughed. "Good morning to you as well, sunshine!" He'd always tormented his friend when grumpy, but things seemed different now, more serious. He examined Mac closely. The deeply curved ballcap was pulled low, but not far enough to mask anguish.

Yep, he's hungover again.

If this keeps up, I'll lead an intervention.

Small group, though. Me, him . . . maybe Stillwater.

The others all hate his guts.

"You don't look so good."

"I asked you to cancel."

"At the last minute? You're nuts!" Rudy left the real reason unsaid. He'd scheduled the trip—camouflaged by a biggest fish bet—to break up his friend's destructive routine.

Mac finally looked around. "You got enough lights on this thing?"

Rudy grinned. "I think she could use a few more."

"Thank God Stillwater sleeps on the other side of the house."

Rudy couldn't help himself, "Wait. Have you been in her bedroom?"

"Don't be a douche."

"Come on! Don't you see the way she looks at you? And those comments—"

"Stop."

"Sure, she's a few years older, but I bet that bod is as tight as a drum. If I were you, I'd play indentured servant boy."

Mac sighed. "If we're really doing this, get me some java."

"Too much booze again?"

"No, I was up late with the journals."

Sure buddy.

"Learn anything good?"

"Tell you later."

Rudy put the truck in gear and drove to the general store for coffee, then perfectly timed the Oxford-Bellevue Ferry. A sign claimed it was the longest-running private service in the country. Once the vehicle was chocked, the men left the cab for the mile-wide river crossing. As Rudy watched the dark water slip by, he fondly remembered simpler times with Mac.

As boys, they'd both enjoyed video games, girls, beer and weed—pretty much in that order—while excelling at hoops and lacrosse. Yet there were differences. Mac, the son of teachers, helped Rudy get through tougher subjects at school. And he taught the always smaller boy how to fish and crab. For those reasons, they eventually agreed that Mac would someday have an office job. While Rudy worked in the great outdoors.

After the ferry docked near the Robert Morris Inn, Rudy drove off. He followed the shore road for a stretch, desolate at the early hour. The marina lot was largely empty, so he parked near four brightly lit boats. He led the way toward them as diesel engines thumped his chest, like heavy bass at a concert. Mac stopped him halfway down the pier.

"It's over for me at G&R," he said, then proudly explained what had transpired.

That fired Rudy up, "You're finally free of those asshats! When did this happen?"

"Sunday after crabs."

"You sat on a bombshell like that?"

"Sorry. Yesterday got away from me."

"Say, can you damsels hurry up?" They looked toward *Reel Good*, where a grizzled woman leaned against the port gunnel. Smoker's voice, large belly. "We're gonna miss the morning bite."

"Sorry, Cap'n," Rudy called as the men approached the forty-six foot long craft. She had a ruby red hull, white deck and was chock full of gear. The clean lines made him miss his boat, the *Kasey Marie*. Named after a high school sweetheart who got away.

The captain said, "Well, it *is* the one and only Rudy Dillon! I was surprised to see your name on the manifest. Your business is going off!"

"Well, someone had to babysit this punk." He'd pointed at Mac.

"Ah," she replied, waiving them aboard. "It's Mr. High and Mighty."

His friend ignored the poke. After they stepped down into the wide vessel, the first mate handed them cans of beer. He then introduced two female tourists, a blonde and brunette—both over-dressed and girl-next-door pretty. Rudy watched Mac get smiley and hold court. Coffee in one hand, suds in the other.

He's always been a dog.

After welcoming everyone, the captain said, "Folks, we're trolling for rockfish today. You New Yorkers may know them as stripers."

"Why are they called rockfish here?" asked the brunette.

"Because we Marylanders like to confuse outsiders with quirky names for stuff." Her brusque tone was offset by a lopsided grin. "Seriously though, the fish cluster near jetties, bridge supports and rocks on the bay floor during the hot months. Since they're on the move again, better weather must be on the way."

When the last line came free, the captain eased the vessel into the channel. The other boats swung in behind her. The small flotilla churned down the Tred Avon toward the larger Choptank River. Rudy watched ghostly sea nettles glide by on the surface, too many now for river swimming. He again thought about his friend.

Mac's life had been fairly vanilla until the summer before high school. That's when his parents were killed by a runaway tractor trailer on the Chesapeake Bay Bridge. The loss cut Oxford deep. Parents and kids alike had revered the public-school teachers.

When Rudy and his dad heard the awful news, they raced over to Mac's house. With their help, he stoically navigated the funeral events and parades of well-wishers. He finally broke after the burial. When they found the boy sobbing on the hood of his mother's car, Rudy's dad put him to bed then asked about adoption. But he was to live with a nearby uncle, an enigmatic yet solid sort.

Rudy watched over him after the move. While Mac in many ways seemed untouched by the tragedy, he would not discuss his parents and made sure others followed suit. Rudy felt that strange yet gradually took his eye off the ball as his friend ran in the right social circles, posted terrific grades and eventually landed a full ride at the University of Maryland.

The mate interrupted the memories, "Another beer?"

Rudy accepted the fresh can while watching Mac. Little now separated him from the blonde, so maybe she'd be his next squeeze. While the guy's stressful job had long kept serious relationships at bay, Rudy wondered if that would change with him now free of G&R. If so, he hoped that Mac would improve upon his own brief attempt at matrimony.

A little bored, he stood watch over the fish finder in the covered wheelhouse. The Choptank soon opened to the broad expanse of the bay—calm and twinkling in the early morning sunshine. Several boats had lines in the water.

The captain sniffed the air theatrically as she waved everyone over.

"Can't you just smell them rockfish? Gather 'round so you can see where the baits will go." As she explained her plan, Rudy pointed out fish marks on the digital screen.

"We'll work the edge of the shipping channel. It was originally part of the Susquehanna River which now feeds the bay from up north. The rest of what's around you was created when sea levels rose eons ago. That gave us one of the largest estuaries in the *entire* world and a state with an amazing shape."

When the show was over, Rudy lost himself in the steady hum of the engines. While instinctively compensating for the small waves rocking the boat, he recalled drinking with Mac on the man's final spring break from college. They'd laughed a lot one night in a bar before things grew tense.

"Hey Mac, remember when your mom caught us with a bowl? We thought no one would ever see us hiding in that big Forsythia bush. But when smoke came out of it like a teepee, she raced out of the house and broke a wooden spoon on your ass! Damn, I thought my sides were gonna split!"

A grim look had killed Rudy's laughter.

"Sorry about that." He recalled feeling like a dumbass for letting a good buzz drive him into taboo territory.

His friend had wiped away welling tears, something not seen since the death of his parents. "It ain't your fault, big fella. I have a hard time remembering them, almost like they're in a fog or something. But what never fades is how they were always on my ass to be perfect. Higher test scores, more points in a ball game. You know, shit like that."

"Parents push kids. What's the big deal?"

The reply had been barely audible, "I think they'd be disappointed in me."

While Mac occasionally complained about his parents when they were alive, Rudy had ignored him since good teachers were supposed to be tough. That night, with little trauma experience to leverage, all he could figure was that his friend's memories of good people had gone horribly awry. Which led to frustration.

"What the hell are you talking about? You landed a solid gig with the feds, your top choice. Being a civil servant will make for a fine career. And your parents would have thought so, too. I mean, they spent most of their adult lives helping folks."

Mac's transcript and demeanor had impressed several large

firms on the interview circuit, but he opted to begin his career with the Federal Trade Commission. While Rudy expected him to work for a more prestigious organization, he stayed out of it. All he'd ever done by that age was sell weed and work construction.

"You don't know the full story. They expected me to make the big bucks. That won't happen with the government."

"Then accept a different position."

"Almost did, but something held me back. Like they were too good for me. Guess I just want Mom and Dad to be proud of me wherever they are. That would never happen if I washed out somewhere. But at the same time, I know the FTC wouldn't impress them a bit. I don't know, man . . . I'm just all fucked up."

"Catch-22," Rudy had observed, unsure what else to say. Friends arriving killed the conversation, never revisited by men who rarely expressed feelings.

Lowered outriggers on the boat spurred the mate into action. He attached green and white lures to several rigs. Once finished, he put them on large rods, then played out their lines. Soon, several stood ready in holders around the boat.

The captain puffed up when the tourists gawked at the setup. "Impressive, eh? Baits out wide, shallow and deep should get us some rock. And if one of 'em hits on an outrigger, the noise will stay with you for a long time."

They trolled for a while without any action. After the mate passed out more beer, the captain rubbed her belly and chanted, "Rub-a-dub-dub, rockfish jump in the tub!" Everyone laughed. Charter boat captains are often eccentric, and she was no exception. It helps distract customers during slow periods.

Mac finally came over. Rudy thought his clothes were too loose, but he blew it off because the guy had always been skinny.

"Okay, booze hound, do you remember what you found in the journals?"

Mac objected, "I had two drinks last night. But if you really want to know, Armistead wrote about the Flash Ken a lot. He liked where it was and visited all the time."

"Any details?"

"Nothing substantive so far," he said, looking frustrated. "It's driving me crazy."

"What about the medallion?"

"Zippy."

"Well, you must have learned something!"

"Sure. Armistead wrote extensively about the house and other buildings. And since the tobacco markets were booming, he eventually lengthened the fields out to some oaks. There's also a lot about the slaves, almost like they were family. Oh, and he's the one who added benches to the cemetery."

Thrilling.

He did not understand why Mac was so intense about the mysteries. But at least his focus had limited the drinking for a night.

Rudy tried to be diplomatic, "Sounds like you've covered a lot of ground."

"I guess." With the subject exhausted, they stared at the water. He soon wandered back to the past.

It seemed crazy now, but Mac had warped just as he straightened out. Almost like he'd passed an accursed baton to the guy. His reformation began with a jail term for dealing drugs, followed by a landscaping job in nearby St. Michaels. When he showed interest and aptitude for the work, Mac encouraged him to start his own business. Even lent him the seed capital for earth-moving equipment and such. Rudy's work ethic, natural charm and life lessons took care of the rest, and he soon repaid the funds along with an unasked-for return.

Mac, meanwhile, had become a seasoned regulator. But his career really took off when he left the government to work for Gibson & Rogers. He then led deals all over the world. As the pace grew more frenetic, he and Rudy hung out less and less. And when they did his friend would only discuss business. Eventually, it became clear that the deal maker had grown too big for his britches.

Rudy finally got fed up when the guy bragged about fooling consumers. The running jokes about the feds were one thing, but an apparent disdain for regular folks had touched a nerve. After the lengthy pissing contest, they saw each other only on major holidays, but those interactions felt forced, artificial. Rudy finally ended the friendship, or so he'd thought, after his dad died of a heart attack. Mac had missed the funeral, ostensibly because of an overseas work commitment, completely dissing the memory of a man integral to his upbringing.

He left Rudy alone for a few months. But spring brought a series of apologetic calls, texts and emails. Rudy ignored him until Mac showed up to grovel for forgiveness. The big man was still unsure why he let his suddenly needy friend off the hook, particularly since the guy had frolicked in the snow while the old man was put to rest. Powerful shared experiences undoubtedly played a role. Surely the length of their friendship. But mostly Rudy just liked the guy. Always had.

He called, "Cap'n!" and pointed off to where birds fed in the water. She turned that way—gradually to avoid fouling the lines. Those on other boats had also taken notice. A slow-motion race ensued to reach bait fish being attacked from above. And hopefully from below. He tensed when *Reel Good* passed through the area.

When two lines ripped out of clips on the port outrigger (ZZZZZZ!), the mate snatched the rods from their holders and gave them to the tourists. Rockfish are not big fighters since they swim with their tails—not entire bodies like tuna. But to make reeling easier, he had the women place the rods against their stomachs, then periodically pull up to create slack. Soon, the mate netted the silvery striped beauties from the stern.

After unhooking and measuring them he called, "Both thirty inches." Smaller than spring trophy rock but better eating.

After that, the fish practically jumped into the boat, almost as if cajoled by the captain's earlier song. Once each passenger reached their limit, she motored away to shallow water. There, they caught other types of fish using smaller rods.

Everyone was all smiles on the way back to Oxford—even Mac who'd lost the fishing contest by a wide margin. Rudy inwardly toasted the guy for being so relaxed. But his friend's obvious need to prove himself to long dead parents remained a worry bead.

First it was the insane job, now he's after the medallion and Flash Ken.

Investigating mysteries should be fun, not manic.

Something to keep an eye on.

Rudy flashed back to the funeral. He and Mac had been through a lot together. But if the guy's win-at-all-costs attitude returned, Rudy would drop him like a bad habit.

TUESDAY AFTERNOON

FLAG

KEV FILETED THEIR CATCH ON a dockside table.

When done, he tossed the carcasses into the river for the crabs. Rudy then stuffed rockfish into resealable plastic bags and hosed off the table.

Once everything looked pristine, he said, "Mac, would you like a chance to redeem yourself? Those poor guys you caught were barely legal!"

Kev replied, "If you're clamoring for another shot at the title, Stillwater can decide the winner. She has the chops to recognize culinary talent."

"You're on—a fish fry at Rose Haven! We can do it tomorrow."

After storing the bags in the truck bed cooler, Kev led the way across the gravel lot to the Cracked Claw. There, they bellied up to its rustic dock bar and were greeted by an exotic looking woman. Her tied-off black T-shirt revealed a gold belly ring. Daisy Dukes completed an ensemble which left little to the imagination.

Once Kev had a cold beer, he soaked in the place. The wooden bar, stools, railings, tables and chairs were heavily lacquered to protect against the elements. A guitar player in the corner crooned a Jimmy Buffett tune.

"I like those flags," Rudy said, pointing to the back of the bar. Set between neon beer signs, one said, 'Only pirates get away with saying Yo Ho!' Another ordered prey to 'Surrender the Booty.'

He then spoke in a pirate voice, "Meghan the barkeep will surrender *her* booty one of these days. Aaarrrggghhh, I'm sure of it."

As if in response, the woman worked a church key from her back pocket and opened a beer for another customer. Before she noticed him staring, Kev looked down the bar and spotted another flag.

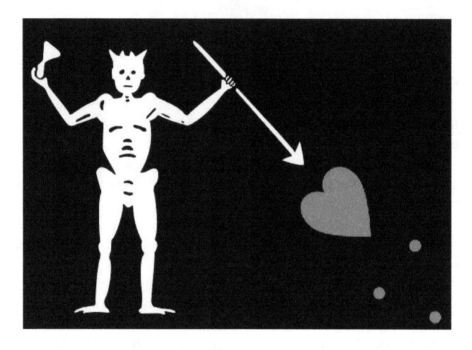

Holy shit! Am I imagining things?

"Rudy, check that one out!"

"The funny ones are better."

"Does it remind you of anything?"

"Let's see . . . a skeleton, arrow and heart . . . How about Jason playing cupid in a new Halloween movie?"

"Focus on the torso, big fella."

Rudy nodded then broke out his phone. After examining a picture, he declared, "That part is similar; the rest not so much."

"No shit—the outside of the medallion rubbed off. Hey Meghan! Can we get another round?"

After she delivered the beers, he asked, "I'm digging the pirate flags, but what's that one all about?"

Meghan looked where he'd pointed. "I have no idea, but the owner flies it on his boat. He'll be here for the dinner shift if you want to ask him."

Kev thanked her, and then typed 'pirate flag skeleton arrow heart' into his phone's search engine. When several pictures popped up, he clicked and read.

"That's a replica of Blackbeard's flag!"

Rudy seemed disinterested. "Yeah?"

"Get this, the symbols on it are pretty morbid. The hourglass in the right hand meant that targets better surrender fast. And that's a spear in the other hand, not an arrow. It piercing the heart signaled a sure death for uncooperative sailors. The circles are drops of blood . . . which suggested the process would be agonizing."

"Surrender fast or die in pain. Sounds like one helluva guy."

"No kidding. This is interesting—his given name was Edward, but no one's sure about his last name. And the man got around. He may have had fourteen wives."

"Wonder if any of them were as cute as Meghan. I'm scared of having number two, but if she were game, I'd seriously consider—"

"Wait, there's more. Blackbeard was well over six feet tall—"

"Hold up! We've learned about two towering dudes in as many days. Weren't people shorter back then?"

"They were," Kev said, frowning in thought. "Except for pirates and plantation owners, I guess."

Rudy nodded toward a nearby bottle of rum. "Was the guy swashbuckling? Like Captain Morgan?"

"Let's find out." Kev found a passage from Charles Johnson's *Pirates* and read aloud:

So our Heroe . . . assumed the (nickname) of Black-beard, from that large Quantity of Hair, which covered his whole Face, and frightn'd America, more than any Comet that has appear'd there a long time. This Beard was Black, which he had suffered to grow of an extravagant Length; as to Breadth, it came up to his Eyes; he was accustomed to twist it with Ribbons, in small Tails ... and turn them about his Ears.

In time of action, he wore a sling over his shoulders, with three brace of Pistols, hanging in Holsters like Bandoliers; and stuck lighted matches under his Hat, which appearing on each Side of his face, his Eyes naturally looking fierce and wild, made him altogether such a Figure, that Imagination cannot form an Idea of a Fury, from Hell, to look more frightful.

"Jesus," Rudy spluttered.

Kev nodded. "That helps explain how he captured dozens of ships in 1717 and 1718."

"Just two years?"

"Yep, but the pirate and his band of cutthroats made the most of it. They wreaked havoc along the eastern seaboard and in the Gulf of Mexico before soldiers killed him and most of his men. That happened in November of 1718 near Ocracoke, North Carolina."

"Been there," Rudy said, snapping his fingers. "Now that you mention it, there *was* pirate gear all over the place . . . Wait, our boy Eddie began his journals around then, right?"

"Five years later."

"So, if the flag is a match, maybe Blackbeard's exploits inspired Armistead to carve the figure on the medallion."

"Would his wife really wear something like that? I get an Incan medallion, but . . ."

"Maybe she felt obligated. Even though hubby botched the engraving."

Kev tapped fingers against his beer bottle, lost in thought about skeletons and giants.

BLUDGEON

KEV JOLTED AWAKE IN HIS bedroom.

Insistent knocking came from the porch. Realizing that he'd locked the door out of habit, he removed a pirate book from his chest and entered the living space. The carpet felt good on his toes as he passed by coastal themed furniture, an ancient fireplace and a flat screen TV. The kitchen was off to the right, separated by a long countertop which held his laptop, printer and other gadgets. Wood beams throughout crisscrossed an otherwise white ceiling.

Opening the door revealed a frantic looking Stillwater.

"Kev, I need you! A reporter from Easton called about the police report!"

"It's out?" he asked groggily, running a hand through his short hair.

"Yes! Daniel gave me a head's up earlier, but I didn't want to bug you. Plus, I expected to have a day or two before someone at the paper noticed. Too bad Lucy was on the news desk today."

"Who?"

"The reporter I mentioned!"

Wait, does this hose up my search?

"Sorry," she added. "I'm all over the place."

"Nah, it's me—I just woke up from a nap. Did the police ID the bones?"

"No."

"The cops issued a report without knowing that?"

"It's hard to believe," she said, clearly exasperated. "I guess we didn't understand their process. Anyway, Lucy wants pictures of the medallion and an interview. She's writing an article for tomorrow's paper!"

"I'm not sure I understand. Are the ones in the report blurry or something?"

"There aren't any," she said, handing him her copy. "Take a look for yourself."

He grew perplexed while reading at the counter. "No conclusions, no pictures . . . the damn thing raises more questions than it answers. Did Daniel say why they released something so half-assed?"

"No, he hung up quickly. Presumably to avoid the wrath of Roberts."

"She's making your life difficult. The deputy said the report would stay internal for a while."

Stillwater smoldered. "I'll get her back, believe you me. Anyway, if we knew for sure that you found Elizabeth, I could show Lucy the lost grave. That would settle things down. But now . . ."

"When will the anthropologists be done?"

"This week apparently, but they wouldn't commit to a particular day."

Better tell her the other news. Gently.

"Hey, not to pile on, but Rudy and I figured out where that skeleton figure came from."

"Where?"

"Take a look," he said, handing over his phone. "When we got off the boat, we went over to the Cracked Claw for beer. That flag was at the outside bar."

"It's quite strange."

"Blackbeard flew one just like it three hundred years ago. You know, the famous pirate."

She studied the picture before declaring, "The torsos definitely match! What do you think that means?"

"I'm not sure, but I have a weird question for you: Is there any chance the Armisteads knew Blackbeard?"

She looked thoughtful. "I don't see how, Kev. If someone like that came to town, there'd at least be rumors."

"Then how do we explain the match?"

"Edward probably copied his flag. People still fly it today, so imagine how popular it was back then."

"That's what Rudy thought. Could it be that simple?"

"Sound logic usually is. Anyway, how would you suggest handling Lucy?"

"I'm not sure. What's she like?"

"Sweet, smart and vivacious as hell. If it was just her, I could trade information to delay the article by a day or two. But the boss man over there is a son of a bitch who worships the almighty dollar. There's no way he pumps the brakes on a story about Rose Haven."

"Not a friend, eh?"

"Far from it. Years ago, he pimped my father's horse racing operation. Then, when I had to shut it down and let the workers go, he became my harshest critic. This has all the makings of a similar time-suck. Which I really can't afford right now."

"Because of what you referenced yesterday?"

"Yes, but I don't want to talk about that right now."

He nodded. "Well, since you don't trust the paper writ large, have you considered making a statement instead of giving an interview? That way you can shape the story. If you're concise, I bet Lucy includes the whole thing."

Stillwater liked the idea and they worked up a draft:

The bones and necklace found in Devon Creek are believed to belong to Elizabeth Armistead (1700 - 1750), a prior owner of Rose Haven. If confirmed, her remains will be returned to the estate cemetery and the jewelry stored in a secure location.

"That's pretty solid," he said. "Now, how do you want to handle her picture request? If she includes one in the article, someone might link the medallion to the flag—just like we did. Or at least uncover the Incan angle."

"She's not getting one from me."

"Smart. Make her go to the cops. That might buy you enough time to get a read out on the bones."

Her phone rang—it was the chief.

Kev tried to follow along as Stillwater attacked, "Roberts, the Easton paper is all over me. Why on earth would you issue an incomplete report? . . . You bet I'm pissed! . . . No, *you* created this situation!" After listening for a few seconds, the estate owner found a pen and took notes.

"Say that again . . . You must be joking . . . What does that mean?"

She soon hung up and straightened her blouse. "Well, so much for a statement."

He raised an eyebrow.

"The bones are from the same era, but they don't belong to Elizabeth. They're from a large African male."

"That's quite the curveball," Kev said, digesting the new information. "What else?"

"There's a lot of algae inside the skull. Enough for the anthropologists to conclude that the bones were submerged for years."

"Interesting. So, a black dude who wore—

"Wait, there's more. I thought you were being paranoid about the broken skull the other day, but that's exactly what killed him."

She glanced at her notes. "He died when a large implement struck his right temple . . . that's a scientific way of saying the man was bludgeoned to death."

Lucas arrived back at the inn.

He passed by a plaque honoring a visit from George Washington then went upstairs. After digging out an old-fashioned key, he entered his room. Its light green walls were trimmed in white. An antique table and chair were on the near side, both too small to be useful. Sunshine poured in through a small window. A bit tired from the latest tours, he plopped down on the four-poster bed and pulled out a notebook. While evaluating a now lengthy list of female candidates, he re-prioritized a few names before Yvonne called.

"Hi, Lucas. Have you thought about giving me a raise?"

"I was actually about to admonish you. For not delivering."

"Well, put that on hold and get my paperwork ready! Our cop buddy in Maryland just bootlegged us an interesting police report. Get this—two guys found bones while crabbing near a former plantation. Remember Elizabeth Armistead from Sunday? The cops think they're hers!"

"The young woman from Rose Haven?"

"Yep. The guys found the bones the same day you toured the place."

He looked at his notebook. Elizabeth was at the bottom of the list because she'd married an English trader in 1718, the year Blackbeard died.

She was single before that but . . .

"The timing's no good with her, remember?"

Yvonne said, "They also caught a gold medallion," then described what happened.

Hmmm. Could be nothing. Could be everything.

"Is there anything unusual about the jewelry?"

"I don't know. I sent you the report, but it doesn't have pictures. Not even a description beyond what I've told you."

"Seriously?"

"Yes. Maybe the cops don't care about remains which came from a cemetery."

"Can your source get us a pic?"

"No, he only sees what's sent to the central repository."

"Got it. What happens next?"

"They've asked anthropologists to confirm the age and sex of the bones. And, if possible, a cause of death."

He drummed his fingers. "Yvonne, we need a picture. Should I ask Stillwater for one?"

"That might blow your cover. A freedom of information request would be better."

"How long would that take?"

"A few days. The police are generally forthcoming with information unless it's pertinent to a current investigation. And this one's older than dirt."

"I like it. Just make sure the paperwork comes from one of our shell companies. Anything else before I drop to read the report?"

"Not nearly as good."

"Yvonne!"

"Okay, okay—Stillwater's relatives bought the plantation from a church. I doubt it means much, but that makes Rose Haven unique in a way." She provided the details.

That's one hell of a gift.

Why didn't the estate owner mention that during the tour?

"Understood," he said, thinking the information was likely irrelevant. "We'll check it out later. And thanks for calling—the medallion is welcome news."

After reading the report, he was pretty sure that he'd met the MacGuire guy at Rose Haven, but not Dillon. His bones tingled. Dying to see the piece, he considered how to finagle his way into the tiny Oxford police station.

It could work. I've been silky smooth lately, like when I convinced the archeologists in Greenville that—

Shit!

Like a dumbass, he'd run off without explaining his departure to Ben and the others. Which might make them second guess why the treasure hunter had downplayed the Oxford inscription.

He called to assess any damage. Thankfully, Ben had been so busy remapping the artifact field after the storm that Lucas being on 'vacation' took him by surprise. He hung up after shaking loose from the archeologist, mission accomplished. The chatty man would surely spread the word about their phone call.

WEDNESDAY MORNING

NEWS

THE HEADLINE WAS DRAMATIC.

MURDER, BONES AND GOLD!

A few pictures jumped out as Kev advanced the article on his phone. The first two were clear shots of the medallion's sun symbol and skeleton figure. The other—murky water lapping against the bluff—was captioned 'CREEK OF BONES'.

That reporter got what she wanted. But from whom?

And she sure knows how to stir the pot.

He soon put his phone down. Lucy had cogently described the bones, jewelry and cemetery damage as well as the African angle. Quotes from the police added little to the story though, as did her suggestion that the victim was possibly a slave from a nearby tobacco plantation. She promised to follow up if her investigation revealed more information.

Lucy could become a real pain in the ass.

Stay ahead of her. She'll soon realize that a slave wouldn't have owned a valuable necklace.

And if the story hasn't already gone viral by then with its catchy headline and picture caption, it sure as hell will if she learns about the Incan symbol or pirate flag.

There's something intriguing here, I can feel it. Blackbeard had Africans on his crew, so the bones and medallion could mean they were in the area.

But where? Close by? The remains might have been dumped far away and flowed into the creek from the Tred Avon. Maybe even the Choptank.

Yet a Flash Ken, the 'Safehouse for Thieves,' just feels significant, connected somehow. Could the pirates have operated out of Rose Haven for a spell?

The river is deep enough.

Lucas steered a small boat into the creek and puttered around.

Yvonne soon called. "We've got pics! They're in an article I just sent."

"Hang on!"

The opened link stunned him. To be absolutely sure, he compared the skeleton figure to the flag which flew in front of the *QAR* facility. The torsos were a clear match. The other side of the medallion surprised him as well.

So, the pirates were likely here. Crazy.

But how did they get an Incan medallion?

He imagined a few of them rowing by in a skiff. Dirty, dangerous and drunk.

She continued, "I knew you'd recognize it. Our dead African either really admired Blackbeard or—"

"Crewed for him."

"Right! The plot thickens."

"Rose Haven suddenly looks promising, doesn't it? Maybe Elizabeth got around . . . Yvonne, I'm floored."

"That's a first. Cue the hunt!"

"Yeah, we now have a real shot at an artifact or two. Perhaps mixed in with old bottles of rum and rotted cargo."

"Lucas, you're the master of understatement. There could be something special on or around Rose Haven! And who cares about artifacts? If you want, buy some from North Carolina. They have boatloads."

"We'll see," he said, sounding doubtful.

"Can't I dream?"

"While you do that, I'll need to canvass the estate—quietly. Find out when MacGuire's lease is up. Living in that cottage would be perfect. And it's exactly what a novelist would do. But since that's probably too good to be true, get the team cranked up. We need ideas."

He next spoke with Gomez. After absorbing the news, she said, "I knew my ace would score!"

Lucas took it slow, "We may have a long road in front of us. And that article could complicate our search."

"Good grief!"

"Don't get me wrong, the medallion is very exciting. But I'm worried that other treasure hunters or the folks in Carolina will see it and make the same connection we did. If so, we're going to have company."

"Why so negative? This is huge!"

"You really believe in the treasure, don't you?"

He kept at it after her frustrated sigh, "Regardless, we need to search the estate without raising suspicion, so stay tuned for our plan. You should know, however, that one of our ideas is toast. It's impossible to find the craftsmen who made the telescope."

"Lucas—"

"I also caught up with Ben yesterday, the head honcho in Greenville. His folks identified the iron artifact we brought up with the telescope. It's a urethral syringe that was used to treat a painful stage of syphilis. Pretty gruesome really."

Her voice was icy, "I don't care about venereal diseases or who made the goddamn telescope. It's hard to believe, but I prefer the ornery you over Mr. Methodical."

"Slow and steady gets results."

"Catch the next flight to Miami. I want you and Yvonne to work up charts for a Friday meeting with Pederson and the rest of the leadership team. During which you'll clearly convey how close we are to finding Blackbeard's treasure."

CONJECTURE

ANGRY LOOKING CLOUDS WERE ON the way.

Kev moved the porch table to a spot that would remain dry. As the thunderstorm approached, temperatures would cool drastically, perhaps by as much as twenty degrees. And if they were really lucky, it would break up the area of high pressure which had gripped the eastern shore since Sunday.

He rejoined Rudy in the kitchen. Their banter became loud as they prepared side dishes for lunch. When they turned to the rockfish, Rudy tried a new sauce—capers, garlic, tomato, red pepper and olive oil, while Kev stuck with old reliable—butter, spice, wine, lemon and Worcestershire. Bowls, cups and measuring spoons piled up in the sink. Cooking together for the first time in years felt good, perhaps another step toward normalcy—such as it was in his terminal world.

He said, "Smells terrific in here."

"It should," Rudy replied. "What I'm making is the bomb!"

"We'll see. And big fella, after this little contest is over, I'll broach our new theory with Stillwater."

"Tread carefully or she'll get rattled. Those reporters must be all over her."

"She can handle it."

"I don't know, Mac. Your landlord gets awfully cranky when things don't go her way."

Stillwater soon arrived looking distraught. Rudy, who'd donned a tiny Baltimore Ravens apron, came out to greet her.

"Welcome to the main event! Too bad the competition is ill-prepared."

Kev said, "Don't mind him, ma'am. He's like the annoying brother I never had, always coming at me and getting destroyed."

She nodded half-heartedly. "I'm glad you guys are having fun today."

To lighten her mood, he explained the culinary debate as if standing before a cooking show judge. Not to be outdone, Rudy formally led Stillwater to the porch and presented her with a linen napkin. When small talk did not break her reserve, the men served the fish, spinach and seasoned rice. As he ate, Kev worried over Rudy's outstanding effort. Lunch was uncomfortably silent until rain pounded the roof like an anticipatory drum roll and sheets of water swept across the lawn.

The estate owner said, "This could send Edward's remains into the creek. The ground is still soaked from the hurricane."

"It'll be over before you know it," Rudy replied. "Just sit back, enjoy the cool air and let Kev down easily."

She continued, "Losing another grave would be a disaster."

Kev moved her along, "Three news vans around here must be a record."

Stillwater exploded, "It's been absolutely insane! I knew the reporters and phone calls would drive me crazy, but Roberts has been the worst. She wants me to hold a press conference! To talk about *your* catch!"

"I take it you told her no?" Rudy asked.

"Absolutely! She acts like you guys caught the bones and medallion on my estate. I . . . er . . . forcibly reminded her that event happened on a neighboring creek."

"Forcibly?" Kev asked.

She cracked a smile. "I told her to fuck off!"

Both men laughed.

Kev said, "Sorry we've caused so much trouble. Mr. Popular over here is getting hit up as well. I've never heard so many ringtones!"

The big fella chucked. "I have Queen's 'Another One Bites the Dust' queued up for your demise."

"Better stick with 'Loser' by 3 Doors Down. For you, that is."

She again turned dour. "I'm going after the chief's job when things settle down."

There's the volatility Rudy mentioned.

"For cause?" Kev asked doubtfully. "What's her take on all this?"

"That the police took the appropriate steps. But she was awfully defensive about it, so I think I'm on to something."

"Like what?"

"Since Lucy got the pictures she wanted—and also knew about the African—I went through every word of her article. And guess what? It has details that were not in either report! Someone's leaked additional information, and I bet it was Roberts."

Kev nodded. "Wouldn't surprise me a bit."

Rudy took a bite of fish then said, "This is so freakin' good. Take some weight off your shoulders, Ms. Stillwater. Tell Kev I won."

"Patience," she said. A warning.

"Come on, just—"

"I'm not ready!"

Kev raised an eyebrow. He wondered why Rudy had poked the stressed woman, particularly after his own advice to take things slow. But then again, the guy often missed social cues.

She turned sheepish. "Sorry, that was too harsh. And Kev, I've been thinking—I really liked that statement we came up with yesterday. Something similar will remind folks that the media circus has nothing to do with my place. I'll add that, as a concerned citizen, I expect the police to drag the creek and solve the murder."

"Clever—that'll push them to find Elizabeth."

She nodded. "I'll work up something after lunch, which by the way is wonderful."

The decision seemed to relax her, so Kev dove in, "If you're up for it, Rudy and I have some thoughts to share about the medallion and flag."

She acted horrified, but her narrowed eyes suggested real concern. "What now?"

"Well, after kicking it around some, we think your estate might tie them together."

"How so?"

"It struck us that a safehouse for thieves could have been a pirate hideaway."

"You're serious? You think a famous buccaneer spent time at Rose Haven?"

"It would explain a lot," Kev replied combatively. He did not have much time for kid gloves.

She smiled her disagreement. "It was probably a man-cave."

"Call it what you want, but the point remains."

"Kev, we've chewed this gum. Like I said before, the Armisteads had no reason to consort with thieves."

"Then why did Edward call the damn thing a Flash Ken? Here, maybe these will sway you." He handed her the safehouse references he'd shared with Rudy on the boat.

The big fella said, "Uh, Mac, another time might be better—"

She interrupted, "Nothing here links pirates to my estate!"

The rain let up, seemingly emphasizing her point.

Kev replied, "It's inferred, not explicit. I also meant to tell you that 'Flash Ken' and 'Goat's Jig' were slang terms favored by the working class in the eighteenth century. Which included pirates."

She took a deep breath. "Before Edward married Elizabeth, he built a fortune trading goods on the eastern seaboard and in the Caribbean. So, he probably picked up the lingo in a port. They've never been delicate places."

Kev chewed on the new information.

"You see?" she said, smiling triumphantly. "It all makes sense when you have the proper perspective."

That annoyed him. "Why didn't Armistead mention trading in the journals? There's not a single word about that part of his life."

"Good grief, you're like Sandy with a bone! He was probably

laser-focused on Elizabeth and Rose Haven. I'm sorry Kev, but I don't buy your theory. The Flash Ken, however, is—"

"Rudy has an even stranger one."

His reluctant friend said, "Ma'am, Armistead and the pirate were practically twins, except for the beard. They also shared a first name and were the same age."

"What do you mean?"

"Speaking plainly? I bet the pirate shaved his beard then used an alias. All to start a new life."

"Et tu, Rudy?" she said, shaking her head in disbelief. "There must have been a million people in the colonies by the 1700s, some no doubt tall with dark hair. And Edward's been a popular name for centuries."

Rudy turned beet red. Like most folks did when ridiculed by an estate owner.

She added, "Kev, what do the history books tell us?"

"Very little, but Blackbeard's final hours are well documented. The soldiers who killed him cut off his head and hung it like a trophy from the bowsprit of a ship. Armistead of course lived another thirty years after that, give or take."

"Did the pirate ever visit the Chesapeake?"

"He came close. But there's no mention of him or his men ever being in Maryland waters."

"Rudy, I assume that changes your mind?"

Kev intervened, "I disagree with the big fella, but the evidence suggests that Blackbeard was on or near the creek at some point. And perhaps stayed a while."

"I'm not convinced. Someone, presumably the African, carved a popular skeleton figure on the medallion. He wasn't necessarily on Blackbeard's crew, which is what you're insinuating. Even if the poor guy was in cahoots with a murderous pirate, there's no proof that Blackbeard had anything to do with the Armisteads. Or my place."

"You just raised one possibility. If Edward was a trader, he might have supplied the pirates with goods and such. And not to defend

Blackbeard, but he wasn't much of a killer. His actions were mostly theatre, intended to avoid damaging fights by terrifying merchant ships into submission. The flag symbols were part of the act."

"Perhaps not, but he was a thief and . . ."

She's re-thinking the safehouse for thieves!

Stillwater shook her head seconds later. "If you two believe that the African sailed with Blackbeard, why haven't you gone to the police?"

Uh oh.

Kev said, "Well, we wanted your take on things first, much like we did after crabbing. But to be honest, I haven't considered calling the cops."

"You pressed for their involvement a few days ago."

He nodded at the fair point.

Stillwater kept at it, "I think your focus is misplaced. Solving a murder is what's important."

Kev sat back. She was right in a way. He'd blown past the crime to chase what intrigued him. But his mind was made up.

"Ma'am, if Roberts finds out about the flag, she'll have that press conference—with or without you. And the national networks will be here shortly thereafter."

"You'd suppress potential evidence? About a murder?"

"No one cares about the African or who killed him. Too many years have passed. The better play is to keep quiet while we do our thing."

"I'm inclined to divorce myself from the entire affair. Since you and Rudy spotted the flag—just like you caught the bones and medallion—the decision is yours. Tell the police, don't tell them, I don't care. Just leave me and my estate out of it!"

"But how can you ignore—"

"When we thought the medallion belonged to Elizabeth, I encouraged you to find out more. But now I don't care!"

"What about—"

"You're not listening!" she said, slapping the table. "I don't have time for pirates! Remember those news vans?"

Rudy grew wide-eyed as Stillwater pushed her chair back from the table. When she teared up, Kev figured he'd better cool things down. Losing out on the mysteries would be a bummer, but he needed a comfortable place to stay while undergoing treatment.

"I'm really sorry, Ms. Stillwater. I completely botched this discussion."

"Yeah," Rudy added. "We just dropped a ton of bricks on your head. Completely unfair given the circumstances."

After a long pause, she replied, "I don't know what's come over me." The estate owner wiped her eyes before adding, "It's embarrassing to act like my father."

"No worries," Kev said. "I deserved the vitriol for being so stubborn. But I'm convinced there's more to this story."

"Well, it's hard for me to believe the couple knew Blackbeard. Or that Edward was once a famous pirate."

After Rudy looked at his shoes, she added, "But I can be biased on matters involving Rose Haven."

Kev waited to see if she was coming around.

"Look, if you guys still want to investigate—fine, it's your time and I respect that. But please, leave me out of it unless you connect Blackbeard to my place. If that happens, I'll eat crow and re-engage. But if not, I expect you to call it quits after a week or so."

"That's fair," Kev said. "We'll let you focus on more important things."

She nodded. "Yes, like dealing with the press and finding the Flash Ken."

Kev stared at her.

"Did that confuse you?"

"Yep. I thought you were out."

"You've missed the key distinction. Whatever it may be, the Flash Ken is, or was, somewhere on my estate. And, as Rudy has suggested, it could be full of money. So, is there anything new to consider on that topic other than those journal passages?"

Kev found separating things irrational but rolled with it, "No, but I have more to read."

"Do you need help getting through them?"

"Your plate is already full. But there is one thing."

"What?"

"There could be church records which address the estate donation. A list of assets, or something like it, could provide a clue."

"Great idea," she said enthusiastically. "St. Paul's replaced the old one that burnt down. The pastor there is a friend, so I'll make an appointment for you to poke around."

She sighed after checking the time. "Well, I'd better go. Thank you for lunch . . . and for putting up with me."

Kev asked, "Is there anything we can do to ease your workload?"

She looked thoughtful. "Jake's worked at light speed to get bids in for the cemetery project, however, he won't discuss them with me until his process is complete. Whatever that means. Rudy, could you try to move him along since you're familiar with that type of work?"

"I'm on it." After getting up he asked, "What about the rockfish?"

"I wish there was a clear winner."

"Come on! It's not even close."

Kev laughed. "Now that's something we can agree on, big fella."

"I'll just say it, gents. Both recipes are really good, but next time I'll show you a thing or two."

Rudy cackled while leaving. Once he was gone, she said, "I'm too tired to deal with it now, but I need your advice on a financial matter. I hear that you're the master of deal negotiations."

"Say the word."

After she departed and the dishes were done, Kev read on the porch. While he could not connect Blackbeard to Maryland, the man's whereabouts for much of his life was a mystery.

WEDNESDAY AFTERNOON

BIDS

JAKE WAS AT HIS DESK when the phone rang.

He sent the unknown caller to voicemail, then glanced around his 'office.' Parts, gadgets and hardware covered much of the concrete floor and strained the surrounding shelves. A footpath snaked from where he sat to another room which housed heavy equipment. Others might not appreciate the place, but he'd miss it badly once Stillwater sold out.

Suddenly anxious, he answered the next call.

"Yeah?"

Lucy snapped, "Where have you been? I've tried to reach you for hours."

Jake had tossed and turned the night before, worried that her article might expose his disloyalty. But fears were put to rest when the story kept him clean. Relieved, he'd downed some coffee and doughnuts then driven over to Rose Haven. While thumping away to classic country.

The news vans parked near the gate had surprised him. Gawking at the reporters and camera men made them rush over, so he'd hit the gas and shot by onto the estate. Once they followed, Jake blocked the driveway then leaped out, ready for battle. But he'd called the cops instead when freedom of the press shouts threw him for a loop.

Deputy Daniel's lecture about personal property rights had been a hoot, but the fun ended when Jake stopped two seedy-looking dudes from scaling the black fence along the road. He retreated to his office afterward to fire up long-dormant security cameras.

He'd kept an eye on them while returning calls, mostly from buddies wanting to discuss the bones and gold. While Jake did not play ball, he'd hinted that free beer could later loosen his tongue.

"Lucy, this ain't your number!"

"It's my office line. Don't you check messages?"

"I haven't got to yours yet."

She giggled. "Okay, bigshot. I'm calling to make sure the article looked okay. You're my last check-in before I get on with my day."

Wonder who the others were?

"I think you told the story real clean. It's crazy that those bones turned out to be from a n—slave. I bet that shocked the hell out of most people."

"Jeez, Jake! You're such a redneck!"

"My bad," he backpedaled.

"I can't stomach people who talk like that."

"Sorry. It was a stupid thing to almost say."

He thought she'd find that funny, but the deafening silence told him otherwise.

"Lucy, are we still on for Friday night?"

"That was our deal. How does seven grab you?"

He grinned after hanging up. Without hesitating, she'd agreed to the Italian place near her condo. And he couldn't wait.

A good fuck would really take the edge off.

"Now that's a shit-eating grin."

He flinched before turning around. Rudy stood in the doorway.

No! What did he hear?

"You scared the hell out of me!" Jake grimaced at his squeaky sounding voice.

"Sorry about that," Rudy said, looking anything but.

"Good, because you almost gave me a friggin' heart attack." Jake searched the man's face, but it was inscrutable.

Feel him out.

"Well, what can I do you for?"

"I don't want to be a bother," Rudy said, surveying the messy room. "You look busy."

"I've got a lot of irons in the fire," he replied, gesturing around.

Rudy was enigmatic, "I've never seen anything like it."

"Believe it or not, Stillwater wants me to better organize the place. I don't know why she cares. It works for me, and the estate looks sharp." He described a recent project to build distance from the call.

Rudy finally interrupted, "Tell her this is where shit gets done. Speaking of which, did you see her text?"

"No, I'm way behind on calls and stuff. I've turned into a god-damn celebrity!"

"Yeah? Who thinks that?"

"Mostly buddies wanting scoop on the bones."

Rudy pointed at a folded newspaper on the desk. "That reporter a friend of yours?"

Shit! I said her name at the end of the call . . . Right?

Jake tried to sound cool, "In my dreams, bro. The Lucy I spoke to is gonna get a whole lot of me on Friday night, if you know what I mean."

He grinned at the locker room banter, but the jovial man remained stoic.

Change the subject.

"So, what's the text about?"

"She wants me to review the cemetery bids."

Jake tried to hide his anger as Rudy added, "Stillwater trusts your judgment, you know that. She just thinks another set of eyes might help."

Doubt that, landscaper boy.

Jake lied affably, "It's cool since you're in the biz and all. Here, sit at my desk while I make some calls. And holler when you're ready to talk. If you think the job can be done for less money, I'm all ears."

The men soon debated the merits of each bid. Both preferred the solution which would rebuild the bluff with rebar, concrete and large rocks. When finished, the cemetery would appear as pristine as ever from the top. Grasses and vines would later soften the artificial cliff wall visible from the creek.

Jake said, "I think the price tag makes sense given the scope. You?"

"I didn't see an estimate for moving remains. Red tape like that can be costly."

"Think I'll ignore those regs. The freshest body over there is three years gone. Plenty of time for it to be all bones."

"Stillwater would go for that?"

"This ain't a time to ask for permission. She was frantic about getting the bids in, so it is what it is."

"Well, I'm on board with the selection. But she'll need to know that three hundred thousand dollars is the floor."

Whatever . . . Just keep quiet about Lucy. The boss ain't no fool like you.

"Thanks. I'm going to see her now. She'll be pissed about the cost, but I'll get the green light. You weren't at the cemetery the other day, but she's hell-bent on doing this."

Or was until that financial call.

WEDNESDAY AFTERNOON

DERAILMENT

PEDERSON LEFT THE AUDITORIUM STAGE to enthusiastic applause.

He'd just pitched RASC's mission statement—'Ethically discovering billions in treasure'—and the importance of culture. It seemed that the new employees, or kids as he affectionately called them, understood how vital both concepts were to the company's success.

He found his up-and-comer handler outside of the room. Since Q&A with the energized group had gone long, he was late for his next meeting—the third quarter financial review. As they walked along a well-lit corridor, he thought about when to hang up his CEO boots.

Announce the change in January?

Gomez—easily the best hire he'd ever made—was ready to take over. And the timing seemed ripe. RASC was riding high, logging one successful hunt after another. He'd of course stay on as Chairman of the Board and make sure the transition went smoothly. Full retirement would come later. Golf, golf and more golf.

His good humor evaporated when Doom and Gloom were in the packed conference room. The corporate attorneys bookended his general counsel, the one lawyer he appreciated. Near as Pederson could tell, the others came around only when there were problems. He greeted the key players in attendance, including Gomez and her operational leads. They sat across from the CFO and members of her team. Everyone seemed on edge, like prize fighters before the opening bell.

After Pederson settled in at the head of the table, the CFO slid over a hard copy of the charts and began the presentation. As the others followed along on a screen, he peeked ahead in the deck.

Well, fuck me.

The projected financials for the year now looked rough, quite a departure from the last such meeting in June. He'd always preached the importance of beating published targets. Consistently doing so had convinced investors that RASC was well led, which in turn contributed to a higher valuation and stock price. But such hard-earned goodwill could quickly vanish. He sat there flummoxed while waiting for the finance team to catch up.

"As you can see," the CFO said, "we'll miss our revenue, profit and cash flow targets for the third quarter by a wide margin. Q4 still looks okay, but it won't fill the hole."

Everyone was stoic. Pederson was no dummy, he knew that difficult corporate news travelled fast before it stalled near the very top. But he stayed cool and asked about the shortfalls. After a few minutes, he decided that crisp messaging to investors should overcome a one-time performance blip.

"Okay, I understand where we are. Is it time for the plan?"

The projected values for next year crushed his idea.

"I'm extremely concerned," the CFO said. "We've never been this far behind what Wall Street expects. And the issues are not isolated. Every operational leader here has sharply reduced their numbers."

Pederson chewed on that. His team changed treasure estimates all the time. After all, no one knew for sure whether a hunt would be successful, or if it was, how much loot would be found. But since he'd never seen across-the-board reductions, he quizzed his leaders about their suddenly anemic prospects. What he heard sounded like excuses. Since fortunes could not change so quickly, he decided that the third quarter misses had spooked them into artificially lowering (sandbagging) projections so they could easily be bested.

Not surprising. The bad quarter will tank this year's bonuses.

But he found it odd when no one backed down. Gomez just sat

there, presumably because she'd failed to produce an aggressive yet achievable plan. He'd explained when and how to club or encourage leaders during the process. Lessons which had obviously fallen on deaf ears.

The others were quiet. Likely wondering whether they'd get Mr. Congenial, soon headed off to pasture. Or the take-no-prisoners badass who'd built the company.

He opted for the latter. "Our stock will crash if we post a bad quarter, signal a lousy year and then tell investors that things won't get better in the near future. Everyone knows that our front-line folks low-ball initial estimates. Without good leadership, that conservatism becomes more pronounced as the numbers are aggregated. I think that's exactly what happened here. So, Eileen, I want you to help these fine folks fix their projections."

He then assailed the extra attorneys, "Why all the note taking?"

Doom spoke up, "We're documenting the situation."

Pederson stared him down. "There is no *situation*. It's an early hiccup in the process. You'd understand that if you came to these meetings more often."

The general counsel waved off Doom's attempted reply.

"John, we attorneys have a tendency to write things down rather than think. And you're correct of course, at least for now. We have a month to straighten this out before the next investor call."

That's good ammunition.

Pederson declared, "So, there you have it. One month to fix this mess. If we don't, consider what will happen to the stock price. And your jobs."

Taking the cue, his leaders gathered papers to leave. They were still stoic. After signaling for Gomez to stay, he wondered if their demeanor meant they'd accumulated 'fuck you' money or were simply concerned about the situation.

Hard to tell.

Pederson waited for the door to shut. "Eileen, what the hell was that?"

"Pardon me?"

"For starters, you broke my cardinal rule. Bad news never ages well."

"I just saw the roll up the other day—"

"Which means you didn't engage early enough."

"But—"

"What really pissed me off were the zeroes for 1589 and your precious *QAR*. When do I get briefed on those projects?"

"We have the 1589 session tomorrow and *QAR* on Friday. Your opus will be a challenge in the near term, but—"

"When I ask for meetings, make sure they happen. Right away."

She smoldered, then grudgingly said, "Yes, sir."

"Two gaping holes in the plan left me without a grasp of the big picture, so I had no choice but to blast everyone in the room. We're supposed to understand the operational details of key projects before things come together financially."

"I didn't realize—"

"That's why I asked for the updates weeks ago. What a fucking mess! Hell, you even have the attorneys riled up!"

Gomez nodded, but her look implied that she'd tired of the lecture.

"I'm not finished," he said angrily. "If you want to be CEO, you'd better act like this is your company. Which means you shouldn't be aloof while your people take the heat! If you do that shit, they won't have your back. And without them, you'll never be successful."

She stared back.

"Get out of here," he added roughly, unsure how to handle her. She'd always been passionate about RASC and her advancement. Now, out of the blue, she seemed disinterested.

Pederson looked at his watch. A few hours ago, he'd thought their culture was dialed in, that Gomez would be a good CEO and he was nearing easy street.

Now his legacy was on the ropes.

THURSDAY

LEAKS

SAL STEELED HIMSELF FOR THE phone call.

The doctoral student was responsible for the accuracy of old *QAR* files. Dead-end work performed in a small office far from his other colleagues in the facility. He often reminded Ben and the others that he'd been hired to analyze artifacts, but nothing changed. When his frustration boiled over, he thought about his first months on the team. When a permanent position seemed well within reach.

His fortunes changed after Ben—previously mild-mannered—implemented a host of process changes. They were designed to ensure that artifacts could safely and quickly be lent to the treasure hunters. If his team could not match their pace, Ben feared losing the new funds which had breathed life into a stale project. Sal repeatedly explained that state money associated with the RASC deal could not be withdrawn so easily, but his point fell on deaf ears. After missing a few deadlines which compromised the integrity of his work, he'd been shunted off to file management.

A man named Radcliff—English and low-key scary—introduced himself soon after the demotion. Sal enjoyed speaking with a real archaeologist about his problems. Seemingly sympathetic, Radcliff arranged a follow up dinner where he offered the young man five thousand dollars plus reward money to be a spy of sorts. All he had to do was call the Englishman if and when the RASC team found a clue to Blackbeard's treasure, something Sal thought would never happen. He'd accepted the following day, both to strike back at Ben and pocket much-needed dough.

Sal's only escape from Greenville all summer had been a trip to the dive site on *Shell Point*, planned before he was unfairly punished. Other than that, no one paid him much attention until earlier that morning.

He picked up the phone and dialed.

The name 'Toad' flashed on Radcliff's cell.

About fucking time.

"Hello."

"Uh, hi Mr. Radcliff. This is Sal from the *QAR* team."

"It's been a while since I've heard from you. Are you well?"

"I'm okay. Sorry I haven't called, but it's been business as usual, so to speak. At least until now."

"What's happened?"

"B-Before I start . . . I think . . . well . . . you said there'd be more money. Ben—the guy who runs the show here—just told me that my grant's not being renewed. S-so, I'd like to put some cash away in case another project isn't readily available. It's kind of weird. The leaders here continue to staff up. They even hired a second dive team! And my peers have all been renewed or promoted."

Shocking.

"Please sir, I'll give it my all through December. After that, there are still one or two people here who—"

"Sal?"

"Y-yes?"

"I hope there is a point to this conversation. If not, that would frustrate me."

"Yes sir . . . er . . . I mean, no sir . . . what I'm trying to say is that I have some intel! You see, there's been a development with the guy you told me to watch—"

"Lucas?"

"Yes, he—"

Radcliff made a snap decision. "Meet me tonight at your favorite pizza place. I'll spring for dinner and reward you as appropriate."

"That won't be necessary, Mr. Radcliff. I'll just tell you right—"

"Be there at nine."

"But—

Radcliff hung up. He'd been tempted to listen, but Sal was the type of kid you had to look in the eye to get the full story.

Later, the Englishman scouted the area from the upper deck of an adjacent parking garage. When Sal entered the brightly lit restaurant, he shimmied his chubby frame into a booth and read on his phone until it was nine. After the young man rose to order, Radcliff left his perch and a minute later slid into the vacated seat. He frequented high end establishments, not ones with checkered table coverings and gaudy prints of Italian villages. But with the other customers on the far side of the place and two workers busy behind the counter, it was a good venue for a clandestine meeting.

His stooge soon turned away from the counter with pizza slices on a tray. When Sal saw the Englishman, he almost tossed them into the air.

"Mr. Radcliff! You startled me!"

"Come here."

He was impatient as the young man sat, tugged at his shirt and then fidgeted with the tray. A most painful windup.

"I thought you might not make it," the student finally managed, his expression suggesting dashed hopes.

"Tell me what you've learned."

"Well, as I started to say on the phone, the RASC leader you told me about—"

"His name is Lucas! Surely you remember that?"

"Y-yes, of course. We were recently on a dive trip together, and

I thought the guy was going to kill me. I mean, when did tossing crackers to seagulls become a capital—"

"Is he aware of your extracurricular activities?"

"No, it's nothing like that. He's just a jerk like everyone else here. Which makes me appreciate you even more. Anyway, it's weird—I haven't seen him since that day."

What?

"Back up, Sal. What did you want to tell me?"

More nervous tics played out, this time on the man's face.

I want to tear out those blinking eyes.

"If what you have is good, you'll get the same amount as last time, the same way.

Apparently encouraged, Sal breathlessly described the silver telescope and inscription.

"Did you bring a picture?" The kid nodded and passed over his phone. Radcliff zoomed in on the artifact.

That's one hell of a find.

Oxford . . . England? Somewhere else? A lover there?

"Have your colleagues evaluated the inscription?"

"Sort of. They cooled on it a while back after Lucas and the lab head agreed that the telescope was captured loot."

"Sal! Just how long has it been?"

"Well, let's see. It all went down before the hurricane hit . . . but I can't remember the exact day."

Unbelievable.

"Sorry about not calling sooner. Lucas convinced everyone that it's not a big deal. Then the storm displaced us and—"

"Are you sure he's gone?"

Sal spoke rapidly, "Yes! It took me a while to notice, because I'm stuck in the back and he's not always on-site, but now I'm sure. Believe it or not, I think the inscription might be an important clue."

Radcliff almost slapped the kid. He'd become rich after vacating his archaeology doctorate years before. Which had largely insulated him from losers like Sal. Prior to taking that plunge, the Englishman had accurately convinced himself that his knowledge of artifacts and history would ensure success once connected with the right people.

"Sal, I'll send your reward later. But I would have doubled it had you called sooner. Enjoy the rest of your evening."

Summarily dismissed, the young man apologized again and hurriedly left without his food. As Radcliff considered the new information, he reached across for a slice.

A head start for a guy like Lucas is lethal.

After the man beat him on a number of searches, Radcliff changed his entire approach. Now, instead of hunting for valuables on his own, he let others do the work. Then swooped in to steal their prizes. The switch had proven wildly successful, but it remained untested against his nemesis. Lucas had left the shadows at about the same time to work for angelic RASC, where he initially targeted valuables outside of Radcliff's sweet spot.

But when the company announced that Lucas was after Blackbeard's treasure—jaw dropping news—the Englishman enthusiastically joined the chase. Money and fame were always top of mind, but mostly he just wanted to best the man. Radcliff's first move in that regard had been to find a manipulatable person in the Greenville facility. He'd targeted Sal after spotting the kid race toward food trucks before noon and the exits at quitting time.

Radcliff shook his head, dismayed about the late start.

It's worth a shot . . . but I need a break to get into the game.

Lucy was asleep when the phone rang.

"Hello," she said groggily.

"Lucy? This is Meghan Patterson. You probably don't remember me, but I've served you drinks over at the Cracked Claw."

"Meghan, of course!" Lucy said, faking it. "How are you?"

"I'm fine, thank you. Sorry to bother you so late."

"Not at all. What's up?"

"I'm calling about your big story."

She sensed opportunity. "Girl, I really enjoyed writing that. I just wish there was another angle to chase."

Come on, whatcha got?

"Girl power, right?" giggled Meghan. "Anyway, the article is the most exciting thing that's ever happened around here. Everyone keeps yapping about it! Now, I'm not a big reader, so I didn't get to it until this evening. But I'm glad I did. I've got something that might interest you!"

"Stop teasing! If you have the goods, I'll put your name up in lights!"

"That would be amazing. You see, there's this flag at the bar that MacGuire and Dillon, you know, the two guys mentioned in your article . . ."

When the call ended, the astonished Lucy compared what Meghan had sent over to the medallion picture, then furiously read up on Blackbeard. While it was too late to get the game changer in the morning paper, she'd try to publish the follow up piece online.

Yeah, right.

No matter how hard she'd tried, her dinosaur boss refused to move quickly in the electronic world. But to be fair, she'd never presented him with a story which could break nationally. And make her and the little paper famous.

1589

HURRICANE

THE CONQUISTADOR SCANNED THE SMALL cabin for aid.

His trusty armor over in the corner was useless. Its extra weight, once invaluable, would drown him should the galleon sink. The blade and harquebus he'd wielded with ferocity were secured on a wall but . . . stabbing or shooting at water would be absurd. He felt powerless and weak—territory as unfamiliar as the sea—then promptly threw up.

The first sign of trouble after leaving Havana had been dark clouds on the horizon. When the size of the storm became evident, the captain sounded a horn and turned his vessel toward clear skies. Other galleons in the immense fleet followed suit and spread out across the blue sea. The precisely executed maneuver indicated experience with dangerous weather.

When the winds reached them, the ship sailed westward at a breakneck pace. The closer the storm came, the more the vessel had shuddered and groaned. Yet the masts and sails remained majestic, awe-inspiring. The conquistador had laughed when the captain balled a fist and shouted, "Don't worry, men! We'll ride this puta as hard as the others!"

Not long after, the conquistador sensed fear amongst the crew. Similar to the scent that most savages expelled before death. The captain, however, stayed true to his rank. The louder and more hectic things became, the more he'd raced about the vessel encouraging his men. A true leader in battle.

As the galleon rode impossibly large waves, some had washed over the deck. When two men were swept overboard, the captain waved the lookouts below and sent the conquistador to his quarters. He'd complied as the brave man lashed himself to the large wheel.

Time had passed slowly in his dimly lit cabin. Eventually he'd stopped pacing to lay down. After one particularly harrowing roll, he retrieved the box of bottles from beneath his bed. He put one aside before wrapping the others in cloth. Once done, he'd returned the cushioned bottles to the box and wedged it into a small closet. Gear and blankets piled on top had completed the job. Whatever happened, the most valuable treasure aboard must survive.

When the conquistador closed his eyes after the bout of vomiting, all he could think about was the native woman. She'd warned him about the fountain, and the dangerous storm seemed poised to deliver on the curse. Unable to clear his head, the conquistador tucked the unprotected bottle under one arm and unsteadily made his way to the door. After wrenching it open, one of the crew shouted at him to hunker down. This time, he tied himself to the bed. Then watched a gold statue shake loose and roll around the floor for what seemed like hours.

Drink, Spaniard. More elixir could get you out of this mess.

He readied his knife to slice open the wax seal. When a violent lurch paused the stroke, he curled himself around the bottle. He clutched it even tighter when men screamed. Then, the conquistador felt weightless for a moment before his head slammed against wood. As darkness took him, he cursed the Godforsaken continent a final time.

THURSDAY

TRACTION

KEV STOOD UP, STRETCHED AND looked out at the river.

The heat and humidity had settled back in after yesterday's thunderstorm. But the ceiling fans on the porch kept him cool enough, especially since they spun chilled air coming from the cottage. Leaving the door ajar felt like cheating, but it helped with one of his goals: Spend every waking hour outside. While he still could.

Kev had not, however, expected to read journals, articles and pirate books overnight and into the following day. The manic effort, spurred on by his pending cancer treatments, left him weary and sore. But he shrugged off the discomfort and disappointment. Kev was determined to finish the materials then assess where things stood.

Because Tuesday's experimental drugs might bring me to my knees.

After making another coffee, he picked up the 1749 journal. Loose, yellowed pages inside made his adrenalin flow.

March 1750

My long journey is almost over, so it is time to chronicle events that should be remembered, perhaps celebrated. Our troubles might dampen the tale, but such is life. You see, my anger threatens to boil over—much like it did before I met Elizabeth. Writing down dark thoughts should help, but she must not see them, so I will store this letter in last year's journal.

Elizabeth's tumors are back and worse than before. She suffers from the affliction that killed her father long ago. And her pain gets worse each day. The bottle of elixir, which reduced the lumps the last time she was seriously ill, is nearly empty. I implore her to drink what remains. But she refuses to flaunt God's will again.

My love particularly regrets our taking the elixir to satisfy vanity. She is right of course, but we were younger then, stupid. And I was convinced that more bottles could be found. When that proved incorrect, we no longer drank the elixir for silly reasons, which left enough to cure Elizabeth a few years ago. And perhaps again if she agrees to use the immense power at our fingertips.

But if not, I pray for a swift end to her misery. When she is gone, the world will become a dark and insufferable place. Regardless of what she may think, I will never drink what remains, for every minute we are apart is too long. And I do not wish to meet my Maker stained by more sin.

But enough about our nightmare for now—it is time for a story about Blackbeard. While that perhaps is a peculiar reward for someone interested in our affairs, you might profit from it in some way. Most importantly, your life could forever change if you find the Flash Ken. This letter and my first fourteen journals point the way.

Kev put the papers down and felt his heart thump like a freight train. After collecting himself he reached for his phone.

"Get over here, big fella. I found something unbelievable." He hung up before Rudy replied.

Stillwater did not answer, so he sent her a text. "Come to the cottage ASAP."

He then paced around, thinking.

Drinking some kind of liquid stopped Elizabeth's cancer, at least for a while. And possibly made the couple look . . . younger? Better?

If only I could get my hands on some . . .

Hope for more time or a cure, however unlikely, grew within him. But after a long minute Kev squashed it. A potion or elixir like that could not exist, period, end of story.

He picked up the letter and read more.

Later, Rudy bounded up the porch steps as Stillwater came around the corner.

"What is it, Mac?" Kev waited for the angry looking estate owner to join them.

"This better be good!" she snapped. "The other commissioners were floored when I left the meeting. That's never happened before."

Kev replied, "Oh, it is! Drum roll please . . . Armistead did know the son of a bitch! When I opened the 1749 journal a little while ago, a goddamn letter fell out. Poof, just like that!"

Stillwater's eyes were cool; Rudy's danced with excitement.

She asked, "Who are you talking about?"

"Blackbeard of course! It's crazy but . . . well . . . you'll see."

She crossed her arms. "You're serious."

"I am! And—"

"Mac," Rudy interrupted, making a subtle gesture toward the estate owner. "Why don't you take it from the top? I bet everyone's had a long day."

He's right. Slow the fuck down or you'll freak her out again.

"Okay, let's tackle the letter in chunks like we did the journal notes. Just give me a sec." After copying all but the last sentence and returning the letter to its journal, he gave them the first page. Then anxiously awaited their reaction.

Rudy soon looked smug. "That anger and sin stuff is from his pirate days."

"Strike one," Kev intoned.

"Really?"

"Yep. People worry about shit like that near the end."

"How the hell would you know?"

"Because I'm an educated man."

"Damn. Guess my batting average ain't so good these days."

Stillwater now appeared resolute. "Mine stinks as well, and I'm a fool to boot. I'm so sorry about yesterday."

Kev moved her along, "Water under the bridge."

"Thanks for being kind."

Rudy observed, "Ma'am, how can you be so calm? Your life is about to change!"

"I refuse to get my hopes up. Plus, I feel sorry for that poor couple . . . what they went through sounds horrible."

Kev coached himself to stay patient. He did not care about the sorrows of dead people, but at least his friend and landlord seemed intrigued by what they read.

"Did Armistead off himself after she died?" Rudy asked.

She shrugged. "Perhaps he just gave up on life. History is full of such examples, but the really soul crushing ones involve the spouses of dead Civil War soldiers. Hope, or rather the lack of it, can be a powerful thing. Whatever happened, he passed away three months later."

Kev declared, "She should have taken the elixir."

Rudy looked at him strangely. "You bought that crap?"

"Not really. But Armistead sure did."

"Yeah, because of a placebo effect. The liquid must have been castor oil, a blend of herbs or some other homeopathic bullshit."

Stillwater said quietly, "Watching someone you love waste away is . . . well, I wouldn't wish it upon anyone."

Both men nodded.

She said, "But let's talk about something else."

Rudy smiled. "Okay. I said it before, and I'll say it again. The Flash Ken must be full of dough!"

"Or what's left of dried leaves," Stillwater replied. "Tobacco was the principal currency around here for years. Armistead probably thought his journals would be found before the crop rotted. But no one bothered with them until Kev came along."

Rudy re-read the relevant passage. "You may be right, 'could forever change' is not exactly a promise."

Kev said, "I bet he hedged his words in case someone unintended discovered the Flash Ken. But there's only one way to find out. Ms. Stillwater, can you take a shot at those fourteen journals? I obviously missed the breadcrumbs Armistead left behind."

She nodded. "Of course. But Rudy's right—even if I find a clue, it might be tricky to solve. The words on the first page are quite nebulous."

"Find something," Kev said as he doled out the rest, "then we'll figure it out."

The pirate's fame grew after soldiers from the Virginia colony murdered him in 1718. Yet details about his life remain elusive. Since I had the pleasure of his company, it falls upon me to explain how he became a most feared buccaneer.

We first traded together before he was a captain. Those transactions, struck in Oxford, were quite lucrative. After that, we conducted similar business here and there. We got on well, and he was quite the conversationalist. One day, he told me his real name—Edward Teach—and so much more.

His stepfather was a wealthy landowner with estates in and around Bristol, England—a port city full of privateers. They would gather and drink rum near the docks, which was where the young man examined their trophies and listened to tales of conquest. Once the allure of blue seas, sunny lands and plunder hooked him, he signed on with a successful captain. The decision angered the stepfather, who had specific designs for the young man.

Teach became a skilled sailor and dangerous fighter. But his run as a privateer ended years later in 1713 along with the War of Spanish Succession, also known as Queen Anne's War. Peace meant that men like him could no longer legally prey on French and Spanish vessels. Doubting a welcome home, Teach wandered to find work. Like many privateers, he landed in lawless New Providence. The golden age of piracy had begun.

"Wow," Stillwater said, shaking her head.

"Yeah," Rudy added, "that's some shit right there. I can't blame the guy for sailing away. But, just to make sure I've got it, what's a privateer?"

Kev replied, "Think of it as legalized piracy by privately-owned ships. The sponsors, England in Teach's case, were able to weaken their rivals *and* get some loot—a win-win."

"So, being a pirate was similar, but no one had their backs?"

"Exactly. And the rewards were greater without a third party involved."

Stillwater asked, "Does that passage refer to the Bahamas?"

"Yep. Nassau, also known as New Providence, was once a pirate haven. It was close to the shipping lanes which connected Europe, Africa and the colonies—you know, the triangle trade thing we learned about in school. Which meant there were merchant vessels sailing all over the place."

"I'm surprised the former privateers kept at it," Stillwater said. "Didn't they worry about being caught?"

Kev said, "Probably, but they had to eat. And there was a safety valve of sorts. Even after the war, the British regularly granted pardons. It was an effective way to reduce the number of pirates."

"Still, they must have led rough lives."

"It's all relative, I guess. Privateer captains often beat their men, even for minor transgressions. They also stiffed sailors on pay. On pirate ships, everyone aboard had equal say in most matters."

Rudy looked doubtful. "The inmates ran the asylum?"

"Not exactly. After choosing their captain, the men would follow his orders as long as they respected him."

Stillwater asked, "Is the original letter back in the journal?"

"Yes," he said, pointing to the volume. It stood next to a half-empty container of antacids.

"Good. We'll have it authenticated at some point. I wonder who does that sort of thing?"

Kev frowned, reticent to share the mystery with others.

"That the bottle you got the other day?" Rudy asked with an uncertain look.

Oops . . . Glad my other meds are tucked away.
"No," he lied. "I forgot there was one here. Keep reading!"

He joined a group of pirates led by Benjamin Hornigold and steadily rose through the ranks. By 1715, Teach had become quartermaster, a most important officer. That was the position he held when I first traded rum, food, weapons and munitions for captured sugar, furs, tobacco and indigo.

We met periodically in warmer weather, mostly on the Tred Avon. The pirates had a favored spot upriver where they removed barnacles, worms and debris—a process known as careening—that either damaged or slowed their ships. Evenings were reserved for drinking and feasting on blue crabs. Teach frequently indulged with the men but sometimes went to town with other officers. He enjoyed socializing with wealthy planters and merchants. Perhaps a reminder of his youth.

Stillwater shook her head. "And not a whisper about Blackbeard visiting the Oxford area. Unbelievable."

Kev said, "Keep in mind that he would have used an alias when interacting with others. And pirates were very secretive about careening locations. That's where they were the most vulnerable to attack."

The pirates, both dangerous and unpredictable, greatly respected Teach's charm, size and shooting prowess. And he had an uncanny ability to think a step or two ahead of others, including his adversaries. His gifts had many convinced that the pirate made a deal with the Devil. Teach enjoyed such stories since they enhanced his burgeoning reputation.

"His flag makes more sense now," Rudy observed. "Quite the actor, that one."

Stillwater snorted. "Armistead enjoyed using hyperbole. The pirates respected Teach because he got results."

After being nominated for command of a captured sloop, he easily won the vote. During the first half of 1717, the little fleet seized many vessels in the Caribbean without firing a shot. Yet Hornigold had, for the first time, allowed British shipping to sail by unscathed. During a meeting with the crew to address that concern, he was deposed—a common occurrence aboard pirate ships.

Teach became captain of the fleet. While the men admired their former leader, they wished to follow an aggressive man. One ready to unleash his brand of terror on the high seas.

Exhausted, Kev re-affirmed an earlier decision. He'd share the last sentence later that night or first thing in the morning.

Stillwater asked, "So where's the clue? We're in trouble if the fourteen journals are as vague as this letter."

"He can't leave us hanging like that!" Rudy said. "I mean, what's not to love about pirates, loot and power struggles?"

Kev offered, "At least we learned how the African got here."

"Perhaps," Stillwater replied. "But not how he died or came to own an Incan medallion."

"He might have been killed in battle," Rudy said. "I mean, some targets must have defended themselves."

"That's possible," Kev admitted, "but I doubt the pirates would have attacked a ship near a careening spot. Or toted a body around for days. Guess we'll never know unless Armistead tells us."

The others stared at him.

Did I give it away?

He added, "Speaking of which, the last page of the letter didn't print."

Rudy gave him a shitty look while Stillwater appeared relieved. Smiling, Kev retrieved the letter from the journal. He read aloud:

The next letter is near the Top.

"The top of what?" Rudy asked.

"No clue," Kev said. He yawned big while showing them the sentence.

"The word 'Top' is capitalized," Stillwater observed, "so it may have a specific meaning."

Rudy added, "Could be more slang."

"Folks," Kev said definitively, "I need a nap. Let's get after this in a few hours."

The big fella chuckled. "Mac, I suggest you go inside and fire up that fancy coffee maker. We're thinking this through first."

It had been worth a shot. "All right. But while I get some java, one of you figure out what 'Top' means."

"Hang on," Stillwater said, then went inside. She returned with a cup of coffee for Kev and a large dictionary.

"An older definition might be helpful . . . Here you go. It's either a high point, like a summit; the highest position or rank, like a king; the first half of an inning, like in baseball; the highest pitch, as in sound; the choicest part of something, like a cut of meat. The next one is a mouthful—a platform surrounding a lower mast that serves to spread the rigging and furnish a standing place for men aloft. The last two are a forward spin given to a ball by striking it near the top . . . and a fundamental quark which has an electric charge."

Kev asked, "What's a quark?"

Stillwater dog-eared the page, then flipped backward. "Quarks combine to form hadrons, which include protons and neutrons, components of—"

He interrupted, "It's hard to imagine our guy knowing that. Can you repeat the ones which refer to places?"

Stillwater marked off items with a pencil. "A high point . . . or a platform."

"Surrounding a mast," Kev added. "Armistead wrote about pirates, so that must be it. Let's see . . . without any old ships around . . ."

Rudy put his phone away. "It's not slang. Ms. Stillwater, both definitions instruct us to look up. What are the highest points on the estate?"

"Well, Rose Haven is pretty flat from the road to the house. There's a steady grade from there down to the river and, to a lesser extent, the creek. You've seen a good chunk of this place. The topography varies, but there's not much here except trees and fields."

Rudy snapped his fingers. "The graveyard bluff could be the summit!"

"That's up there," Kev allowed, "relative to the water at least."

Stillwater said, "We may be screwed if that's where Armistead hid the letter. The bluff has eroded a lot over the years."

"Roger that," Rudy replied, looking disappointed.

Kev drummed his fingers on a table. "Masts were once made from trees . . . Ma'am, how big do you figure the oak was back in the day?"

"I'm not sure. Should I look up their growth patterns?"

"Never mind," Kev said, shaking his head. "It wouldn't have been the landmark then that it is now . . . What about poplars? Those things get huge."

"The ones you see wouldn't be old enough. They grow quickly but eventually topple over due to shallow root systems."

Kev nodded. "How about other varieties?"

"None that get super big."

He said, "Damn! A tree just seems like the obvious choice. Okay, let's try a different angle . . . if it's not something natural, then it has to be—"

"Man-made," Rudy said. "Ms. Stillwater, what did the house look like in Armistead's time?"

"Come with me," she said, then led them outside and around the cottage.

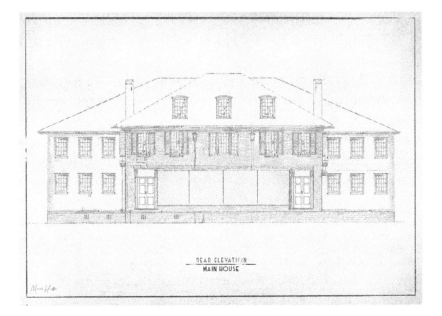

REAR ELEVATION
MAIN HOUSE

"Okay. Imagine it with a flatter roof, but without wings or a third level."

"Got it," Rudy said. "Those chimneys . . . hmmm."

Kev said, "You may be on to something, big fella. A flat roof with chimneys on either side would resemble a platform between two masts."

"You think?" Stillwater asked. "They were only a few feet higher than the roof. My money's on a tree, perhaps another oak."

"Armistead mentioned some," Kev said, "but we're cooked if the clue refers to a long-dead tree."

Rudy seemed concerned. "Ma'am, do you have fireplaces on the upper level?"

Stillwater nodded. "Yes, one in each bedroom."

He added, "I'm with Kev—I like the chimneys for this. But if Armistead did not anticipate a third story, the builders might have accidentally destroyed the hiding place."

They kicked around other possibilities when back on the porch. Afterward, the men were adamant about searching the chimneys.

Stillwater eventually said, "Okay, I yield. Let's find out if you're right!" She filled her arms with journals before leading the way.

Good. She's all in now.

"I need to grab some tools first," Rudy said. "Removing bricks is easy enough. We just have to make sure the chimneys don't collapse."

After stopping by his truck, they entered the house and went upstairs to the third floor. Their first stop, the north bedroom, was adorned with paintings, antique furniture and a four-poster bed. An odd ceiling—high in the middle, quite low on one side, made the place interesting. But the star of the show was the squat fireplace. Stacked wood and the usual tools stood nearby, a setup which appeared more ornamental than practical.

Stillwater announced: "Have at it, gents! I'll be in my room reading if you need me. And Kev . . . be gentle."

Gawd.

His friend offered a knowing look after she left. "See what I mean, hot stuff?"

Kev ignored the dig as he stooped to examine the fireplace.

Rudy said, "Mac, newer bricks rarely match the originals. But there aren't many here . . . and they all look the same."

"Is that good or bad?"

His friend shrugged. They each took a side and worked their way toward the middle, manipulating and probing bricks as they went.

"Zippy," Rudy said. "Let's check the other one." After the fireplace in the next bedroom—a twin of the first—was also a dud, Kev opened a window, removed the screen and peered outside. It was getting dark.

"The roof looks pretty steep."

Rudy replied, "Move over." He climbed out and disappeared. Once back he added, "Come out so we can game plan."

Kev crawled from the window and edged along the roof. After reaching a corner, he gingerly stepped onto the side elevation. The roof there sloped sharply down to the chimney. When their flashlights converged on it, Kev could discern newer bricks from the old.

Rudy said, "All of the originals are accessible, which is good. But if our man hid the letter to the outside, we'll need scaffolding to reach it."

Flying critters swirled around as they pulled and prodded bricks within reach. None gave an inch. When the north chimney yielded the same result, they collected bug spray, extension cords and construction lights from the truck. Once they were in place and powered up, Rudy removed a chisel from his toolbox. After chipping out mortar, he carefully pried a brick into Kev's waiting hands.

"Good," Rudy said, eyeing the bright red color in the gap. "We can safely remove the outer layer."

Kev asked, "Is it normal to have more than one?"

"Nowadays? No."

The pile of bricks grew rapidly as the men worked. When done, Rudy sized up the amount of scaffolding needed if the other chimney did not easily yield a prize.

Kev asked, "Could there be a third layer?"

"Hang on." Removing another brick revealed the flue.

Rudy said, "That's all she wrote for here."

Stillwater's voice rang out, "How's it going?" After working back to the window, they explained their progress and plan.

She smiled. "Sounds like you've made quite a mess! Do you think it's visible from the ground?"

Rudy replied, "Depends on the angle. But don't worry, I'll bring a crew over in the morning to re-install the bricks and clean up. By nightfall it'll look like we've never been here."

She teased, "Jake will pitch a fit."

Kev pounced, thinking her playful mood meant good news, "Any luck with the journals?"

"Not yet," she said, stifling a yawn. "I'll get back to them first thing. I'm dead tired, but I can't sleep with you two on the roof."

Kev happily agreed, "Tomorrow's another day!" Some rest would allow him to go hard in the morning.

Rudy checked his watch. "Mac, it's already here."

MANIPULATION

Pederson swept into the boardroom.

He greeted the execs who were seated in white, plush chairs around a long table. After joining them at the far end, he eyed a series of exquisite paintings that celebrated RASC's most significant discoveries. Circling the interior walls, they ended with a large 'X?' directly to his right.

Gotta fill that sucker. Pronto.

The Human Resources team was up first. As they discussed changes in the performance evaluation process, Pederson fretted about the upcoming investor call. His operational leaders had collared him shortly after the troubling financial review. Interestingly without Gomez. It took some time, but they'd finally convinced him that next year would be rough. The culprit was not plan sandbagging as he'd suspected, but rather an unusual alignment of treasure search life cycles.

Yesterday brought hope. The 1589 team ran a simulation that compared weather data which had been mined from a variety of sources—ship logs, port reports, personal letters, etc.—to the known movements of Spanish treasure fleets. They sailed twice each year in those days and the ships naturally encountered storms, even the occasional hurricane.

The latter probably happened in 1589. A large number of galleons and other craft left Havana that year shortly before a powerful storm hit the area. If his team was right about its direction and speed, the hurricane would have reached the fleet soon after it cleared the Florida straits. Standard operating procedure at the time was to ride out big storms, which in this case could have driven the ships straight into the coast of the sunshine state.

The simulation even produced a 'sweet spot' to search—a stretch of land south of where the 1715 galleons wrecked. From there, the team had eliminated places where human sprawl should have uncovered at least a few coins if a shipwreck was nearby. That narrowed the target areas to a handful of parks and nature reserves. A final algorithm estimated sand movements over the years. Heavy accumulations in the preserved areas could explain why no ships had ever been found.

The joy about his opus was tempered by reality. Only a thoughtful, methodical approach would confirm that there was treasure in one or more of these places and bring it home. The process could take three or four years; incredible really, but far too late for his current needs.

His CFO wanted to announce the news, believing it would offset their shitty numbers and projections. But Pederson was hesitant. Alerting competitors and the authorities would make an inherently tough job more difficult, or even worse put the valuables out of reach. After going to bed last night, he'd tossed and turned thinking about it, unusual for a man who habitually slept like the dead.

He perked up when Lucas and Yvonne arrived for the next module. Both wore snazzy gray suits. No tie and a blue shirt for him, while a colorful neck scarf suited her ebony skin. Once they were done, he'd figure out how to survive the investor call.

He grumbled, "Let's get started. As usual, our goal today is to fill the big X."

Gomez stirred next to him. "Sir, to that point, everyone here has signed a non-disclosure agreement."

She looked serious. NDAs were distributed when the company was close to a find.

Curious, he played along, "Well, we're due for some good news—it's been a grueling week. Lucas, take it away."

"Yes, sir. Most of you know our star researcher—Yvonne Shay—who'll kick things off today. Once you're caught up to where things stood last Sunday, I'll describe this week's exciting news and a few barriers to our success."

Pederson again turned to Gomez.

Is she right about the goddamn pirate?

She caught his eye and smiled sweetly. "I tried to tell you."

Yvonne addressed the telescope, research and tours in the Oxford area. Her projected charts were easy to understand, and she hit only the important stuff, attributes that signaled a bright future.

When Lucas had the floor he announced, "Sometimes it's better to be lucky than good. Here's what we learned from a police report and newspaper article."

The execs absorbed the latest from Maryland. When he clicked to a map of the estate stamped with a large X, most of them glanced at the empty frame on the wall.

"Folks," he said, concluding his first set of charts, "it's highly unlikely that Blackbeard had a treasure hoard. But if he did, it might be hidden on Rose Haven."

Pederson frowned at the apparent contradiction.

Gomez snapped, "Get through the details first. Then I'll help explain what they mean." Her face was beet red.

Lucas nodded, but his face was inscrutable.

Pederson tried to hide his anger.

How many cluster fucks must I endure this week?

His number two believed in the *QAR* deal, which was the sole reason he'd let it move forward. Now, right in front of her and every senior leader in the company, his best treasure hunter had just crapped all over its prospects.

The CEO eyed the man. "Don't take this the wrong way, but if your team shares that view, we'll never get anywhere. We've invested a lot of resources in this project."

Lucas nodded again. Gomez was still red. A standoff of sorts.

"Well," Pederson continued, "what I've learned today makes me cautiously optimistic. Let's try a different tack to move this along. Assuming the treasure is legit, what makes us so confident about the estate? I get the significance of the medallion, but the bones and gold might have come from the river. With tides and such, I bet they moved a fair distance over three hundred years."

Lucas seemed relieved by the question. "A few reasons, sir. You heard where Elizabeth Armistead lived and how she had the means to gift the silver telescope. Well, if the hurricane freed the African's remains from the muck at the bottom of that creek, Rose Haven and its only young lady rise to the top of the list."

"Muck?" Pederson asked, expecting humor to ease the tension. "There you go using technical terms again."

Lucas chuckled along with the others. "Quicksand may be a better word. I learned about it the hard way when my favorite sunglasses went overboard during a recon mission."

"Okay, I'll buy that. Next tell me why we believe the spyglass belonged to Blackbeard. Did I miss something in the inscription?"

Lucas smiled thinly. "You never miss a trick, sir. Any officer aboard his flagship could have owned the telescope. But it was more likely captured loot, destined to be sold or traded before *QAR* sank."

"How many were there?"

"In total? Ten or so . . . with no more than five on *QAR*."

Pederson declared, "So, there's a twenty percent chance Blackbeard owned that telescope."

"Well," Lucas allowed, "if it was an officer's prized possession, the odds are even better."

"Why?" Pederson demanded, sensing an opportunity. His normally on point project lead was all over the place.

"Only senior officers visited nearby towns like Oxford. That's how one of them might have met the girl."

The CEO boomed, "Lucas, why didn't you say that in the first place? That's an important revelation!"

The treasure hunter looked uncomfortable.

While Pederson seriously doubted there was a treasure hoard, the odds discussion had just blazed a trail to salvation. Now he had to convince his whip-smart CFO and general counsel that the valuables were likely within reach, and therefore reasonable to include in their projected numbers to Wall Street. They'd be hesitant, but passion and a bit of logic should appeal to their greed. After all, they too owned a bunch of RASC stock.

"Now," the CEO said, "tell us why you're so pessimistic about the project." He wanted every negative thought on the table before making his move.

"Sir," Lucas replied, "Blackbeard and his men mostly captured goods on the high seas, not valuables."

Pederson asked, "Are you positive?" A trick question of sorts. No one could be sure about much when hunting for treasure.

"Well . . . no. But we've examined hundreds of ship manifests and contemporaneous news reports. Owners would have insisted on cargo accuracy for insurance purposes. And reporters were all over the sailors who encountered pirates."

Gomez asked, "Lucas, are you referring to colonial reporters?"

"Yes."

"Well, isn't it true that Blackbeard and his crew spent half of each year on the Spanish Main? Where accounts of piracy were spotty at best? We know from experience how much treasure moved through that area. Frankly, the Incan medallion makes me wonder if the clever pirate captured a galleon."

Pederson jumped in, "Or maybe found one. From 1589."

Lucas shook his head decisively. "Pirates couldn't help but show off that kind of wealth. Which is why we should manage our expectations. Even if the telescope belonged to an officer, the sharing custom would have made it inherently difficult for one of them to collect a substantial amount of treasure. Regardless of who he was."

Pederson poked away, "Captain Kidd accumulated enough to bury. That's what inspired Robert Louis Stevenson to write *Treasure*

Island. There must have been others like him."

"Sir, that account has become blurred over the years. Kidd hid only a small amount of gold for a short time, and he did so long before Blackbeard came around."

Gomez purred, "I think the example is relevant regardless of the amount buried. Kidd hiding his treasure led to a popular song of the day, so it's feasible that inspired Blackbeard to do the same thing. And let's not forget that his famous contemporary—Charles Johnson—claimed the pirate did just that."

Lucas raised his hands in mock surrender. "I'm really not trying to argue with a pirate expert. Most of you know that I'm an analytical guy who values evidence over myths and rumors. Eileen here takes a different approach, and guess what? Her instincts about Blackbeard have been dead on so far."

The project leader had again minimized their prospects, albeit a bit more cleverly this time. Yet the CEO sensed something odd about his ace's demeanor, like the man was optimistic about something.

But if not the treasure, what?

He said, "I agree. Eileen's been all over this from the start. And when I take a step back and think about it, there's a lot to go on here. Lucas, did we already hammer out those challenges you mentioned?"

"All but an obvious one, sir. We don't own the property."

Pederson asked, "Does the Treasure Trove Doctrine apply in Maryland?" In order to be successful at the uber-compliant company, his people had to be well versed in the intricate web of state and federal laws that govern searches.

The general counsel replied, "It does."

Lucas said, "It's been drilled into our heads, but you can see on the chart that a treasure trove is money, coin, gold, silver, plate, bullion or similar items. For us to keep anything, the owner must be dead without heirs and—"

"Could that trip us up?" Pederson asked.

Gomez shrugged. "Someone always claims heritage after a big discovery."

The general counsel said, "Thankfully, those rarely work. Records, if they exist, are thin. And genetic evidence is hard to come by. I'm confident that we could knock back a claim unless there's a nasty surprise."

Lucas intervened, "Since no one knows Blackbeard's name, I'm more concerned with how to search the estate in a manner which protects our interests."

Pederson slapped the table. "That's critical if the world's foremost authority on Blackbeard is right about the treasure!" His passion clearly surprised the other execs.

The general counsel replied, "Well, the doctrine can be favorable to treasure hunters. Unless caught trespassing."

"Right!" the CEO declared. "So, Lucas, what's your plan?"

"We're still sorting through it, sir. I expect to have a recommendation by Sunday evening. Which means that's all we have for today."

Pederson grinned. "More than enough, I'd say. You and your folks have moved the ball to the goal line! Congratulate everyone for me but press forward. I want to score."

After others around the table offered similar accolades, he added, "Come back Monday to pitch your plan. Consult our playbook for these situations as you put it together. And keep an eye on that reporter. If she writes another article before then, get us together to talk it over. Outside interest could sink us."

He turned to Gomez, anticipating a winning volley. "Final thoughts?"

"Yes, thank you. In our business, the odds of success increase exponentially when multiple data points line up." She next counted on her fingers. "Like a telescope pointing to Oxford. The medallion figure and flag. Plus, Africans on Blackbeard's crew. And don't forget about a rich girl who lived by the creek. Taken together, they tell us to look for the treasure on Rose Haven. And I believe that's where we'll find it."

Attagirl!

As the others packed up, he thought ahead to next week. When, after describing hours of careful consideration, he'd pimp the hell out of her narrative. And later be just as convincing with analysts and shareholders. Doing so would violate every meaningful investor protection law. But when push came to shove, desperation had overwhelmed his preachy integrity.

FRIDAY MORNING

GALLEONS

Kate sipped hot tea on the front porch.

She enjoyed the crisp air which had settled in overnight. And hoped it meant the end of another grueling summer. Then, most days would unfold just like this one had, with low humidity and bright sunshine. Sandy barked happily at a pair of gray squirrels in the maples. In just a few weeks, their leaves would turn a breathtaking crimson.

Hydraulic brakes announced an arriving tour bus. When the big vehicle reached the circle, its driver slowed and waved Rudy's truck past. Once he and two men hopped out, both Jake and Kev appeared. The bus driver, having settled on a spot, opened the door for a chatty group of senior citizens.

Yes!

Stillwater loved her place when it was busy or quiet, but she'd awoken that morning ready to sell. That would no doubt remove a chunk of her soul, but at least she'd ditch the 'Ms. Stillwater' straitjacket once and for all. If something remarkable was found on the estate, Kate could always change her mind before a buyer emerged. Yet the more she thought about it, a fresh start might be good regardless of what transpired.

I could re-invent myself. Then explore things with Kev.

I like the sound of that.

When Jake losing his cool erased the daydream, she moved swiftly to where he stood toe-to-toe with Rudy.

The red-faced estate keeper said, "You're not touching the god-damn chimneys!"

Rudy objected, "Your boss—"

"I said no!"

She hollered, "JAKE TILGHMAN!" Both men froze while the tourists looked over in surprise. After counting to three, she calmly added, "We need to replace some bricks."

He looked up at the roof and scrunched his face in confusion. "That many need fixin?"

Kate was uncertain how to respond. She despised deception of any sort.

"Never mind, I'll go look for myself."

"Mind who you're talking to! Your behavior is ridiculous, and on a tour day no less! You're not to concern yourself with the chimneys. Rudy and his folks will be gone before you know it."

"But—"

"Enough already! The cemetery contractors will be here soon. That should be your focus today!" After a staring contest, the large man wheeled and stomped toward the storage building. The estate owner immediately regretted the interaction. She'd been taught never to yell at the staff regardless of circumstance.

Kev broke the silence, "Well, *that* was awkward." Jake's head twitched at the dig, but he went inside and slammed the door behind him.

Rudy said, "Appreciate the assist, ma'am. This face is too pretty to take a punch! Is it still cool to be here or—"

"Absolutely," she said, then lowered her voice conspiratorially. "You still have bricks to search! And in case you're wondering, I haven't had any luck with the journals. But I'll get back to them soon enough. Adios—text if there's news!"

She then approached the tour group. "Good morning! I'm Ms. Stillwater. As you probably heard, running a large estate can be stressful . . ."

The two friends removed older bricks from the south chimney.

Soon, one cracked in half as it fell into Kev's waiting hands. The pieces looked small and felt light, so he reached into the vacated space.

Jake cranked open his office window.

Since his boss had shooed him away—one of her stranger maneuvers over the years—he guessed that the rooftop search was related to the medallion. Same as their clandestine meetings in the cottage, sessions he'd tried to spy on without success.

He perked up when the men froze. MacGuire then held something up . . . cloth? . . . before unwrapping it.

The man said, "Let's go read it!" His voice carried surprisingly well.

Dillon asked, "Should we wait for Stillwater?"

"No, she'd want us to start right away. I'll text her to come over as soon as possible."

"Roger that. We brought extra bricks, so there should be a decent match for the one that broke. No one will notice the difference except Jake."

That's because I care about this place, asshole.

Wait, MacGuire said 'read' . . . Did they find a message of some kind?

If so, could it save my job?

"Leave it out for now, big fella. She might want it that way for posterity."

After making copies, Kev and Rudy read on the porch.

You found the letter. Well done.

Each day at Rose Haven gets worse. Elizabeth wears a shawl to cover her gruesome lumps and disfigured mouth. And she is terribly thin. When awake, my love prays a lot to distract herself from the pain. Sleep thankfully softens her features, perhaps a sign of peace.

She is clearly at death's door, yet my prayers for a swift end remain unanswered. I do not understand why He waits. If this is vengeful penance of some kind, He should reserve it for me. Elizabeth deserves relief, for she is kind and most pious.

Teach's story resumes after he became captain of the fleet. With British shipping again in their sights, the pirates sailed to colonial waters for the summer. Soon, they were back on the Tred Avon, this time for supplies. Subsequent weeks brought much success in the Virginia Capes and Delaware Bay, along with a warning of sorts. One surrendering captain labeled my colleague 'Blackbeard.' The moniker spread quickly in the press, which meant the authorities could easily distinguish the man from other pirates.

When they careened their vessels on the river in early September, I found Teach incredibly self-assured. And he loved the notoriety. As for my part, we traded like always, except the volume of plunder was larger and more varied than before. The men overindulged each evening, pleased with their new captain.

Once back in Delaware Bay, they looted arriving ships while blockading Philadelphia. Nearby governors took notice of the force which could threaten their existence. But before they could act, Teach sailed away. He sought rigging, spare masts, cable and other items needed for a winter refit. The pirates captured a large ship after reaching the Caribbean—a slaver with beautiful lines—then hunted for heavy cannon. Teach renamed the vessel Queen Anne's Revenge. After the captain made her his flagship, the men insisted that he take the largest cabin to himself.

"Damn!" Rudy said. "They closed an entire port with just a few ships."

"That shows how vulnerable most of our colonies were at the time. The Royal Navy had vessels stationed in New York, Baltimore and Virginia, but Teach knew to avoid them."

The British had recently assumed control over New Providence, so Teach and his men sailed for an anchorage in Florida. He had seen it twice before on journeys near the 1715 wrecked galleons. There, far away from any known settlements, he expected to winter unmolested.

Rudy said, "Tell me about those wrecks."

"Hang on," Kev replied, pulling out his phone. "Eleven Spanish galleons sank in a hurricane that year. They were full of coins and other valuables."

"Where?"

"Near Cape Canaveral."

"They pretty well picked over?"

"Yep. Some company found most of the treasure a few years ago."

"How much we talkin'?"

"Billions."

Rudy gave a low whistle.

When they arrived in late December, numerous trees had fallen down, and debris was everywhere. While area sandbars had shifted wildly, the main channel and berth were clear. He was grateful for that as well as their timing. Not only had they avoided dangerous weather, but his ships were in serious disrepair after months of unbridled aggression.

Half of the men would refit and clean the vessels. Most others were to convert QAR into a configuration suitable for piracy. Originally designed to be a privateer, she had undergone substantial revisions as a slaver. Prison bulkheads had to be replaced with gun ports, and the main mast returned to its original location. Once ready, she would be a force on the high seas.

"Interesting," Kev murmured, flipping through his notes. "Historians confirm that the pirates were off the grid by Christmas that year. But most believe that they hid in the Caribbean, not Florida."

Rudy's face lit up. "Mac, that's what you can do! Write the book that sets everything straight!"

I wish, big fella.

"Why not?' he answered lightly.

Teach wished to ensure the area was free from threats and navigational hazards; the latter in case they had to leave in a hurry. He selected three favored pirates—former slaves freed years before—to come with him on a trip south into unfamiliar waters. His quartermaster joined as well. Their skiff meandered through small coves dotted with jagged coral.

After entering an inlet which opened to a bay, they spotted the remnants of a ship in the distance. Half of the once-large vessel rested on its side, much of it buried in sand. As they approached, reflections from the sun flashed near the wreckage. Soon, it became clear that the timber—barnacled and rotted—had recently been underwater for a long time.

Once out of the boat, his men raced about collecting the gold coins responsible for the flashes. When their pockets and fists were full, they danced and screamed like wild men. Teach meanwhile studied the glittering pieces. Each had the Hapsburg coat-of-arms on one side, with a cross, lions and castle on the other. He could hardly believe their good fortune. They had found the remains of a Spanish treasure galleon.

Rudy shouted, "This is nuts!"

A wide-eyed Stillwater barged in. "What did I miss?"

Both men smiled.

"Sorry it took so long," she added. "I double-timed those folks through the house and then palmed them off on Jake!"

Rudy said, "They'll forever remember his grunts." He turned back to the letter.

Kev handed her a copy. "Your lottery ticket was under the seventh brick."

"What do you mean?"

He read aloud:

The coins looked new, but each one had been minted in 1589. Rumors of lost treasure galleons that year were legendary. Few however believed the tales, because neither the wrecks nor any valuables had been found. Teach took a deep breath and scanned the area. No other timber was evident in the calm waters or on land. Regardless, he wondered what other looting opportunities might be nearby.

Stillwater read feverishly afterward.

"The Spaniards sure had trouble keeping ships afloat," Rudy observed.

Kev searched on his phone. "This website claims that every vessel in the 1589 treasure fleets made it to Spain, but it does acknowledge rumors to the contrary."

"How many ships are we talking about?"

"The largest fleet that year had over a hundred; the other was somewhat smaller."

"Maybe losing a single galleon was acceptable, no big deal."

"If it carried goods that would spoil, perhaps. But the Spaniards would have searched high and low for lost gold."

"But how could that be kept secret? Imagine the number of distraught widows and family members, not to mention a big ass ship missing from port."

"Hence the rumors, I suppose."

Pirates shared loot, but only with those who helped capture it. Teach demanded secrecy, however, because their incredible discovery would undoubtedly shatter the custom. When the others happily agreed, he had the Africans expand a nearby cave— just out of sight from the wreck. They were well-armed in case there was trouble, however unlikely in that forlorn place. As they labored in the hot sun, he and the quartermaster returned to the ships.

After reaching the anchorage, the two men assembled the crew. Teach announced that there were men to the south, likely just Indians, and the Africans would sound a horn should a threat move against the ships. All were satisfied when the quartermaster—supposedly independent from the captain—corroborated the tale. He added that the two officers would later scour the area to ensure it was safe.

Many volunteered to come along. While Teach acknowledged the gestures, he reminded them that they needed to prepare the ships for the next round of assaults. Then, since the Africans were on watch, he encouraged everyone to celebrate that evening. When the others fell asleep after hours of revelry, Teach and the quartermaster loaded shovels and tools onto the skiff. A full moon lit the way back to the inlet.

It took hours of digging—first by torchlight—to reach the remnants of the hold. There, thousands of coins spilled forth from rotted chests, including some still chained to the timber. As the Africans ported gold and silver to the cave, Teach and the quartermaster dove to find the rest of the hull. Reef sharks cruised about in the warm, clear water above a spectacular display of fish and coral.

They were dismayed when the rest of the ship lay in water too deep for diving. But after circling the reef, they came upon another wreck, this one relatively intact. The men dove on it for hours while filling bags with coins. The following morning, they hauled heavy ingots and statues ashore with canvas and rope. When the sun was directly overhead, Teach spotted a clump of material wedged between large rocks. Bones, likely human, littered the area.

He dove down and freed a bottle from the rotted material. After reading 'Fuente de la Eterna Juventud' on the glass, he hid the prize in his belongings. If real, elixir from the legendary 'Fountain of Youth' would be priceless. A later dive revealed more bottles, but they were in a well out of reach box.

Kev looked up, awestruck.
Was that Armistead's bottle?
If so, how did he get it from Teach? Trading?
And that box . . . the plantation owner tried to get more elixir . . .
Damn. This shit gets crazier by the day.
He looked over at the others. Stillwater was focused, but Rudy winked. "Two wrecks and counting, Mac."

The digging and diving continued. Piles of coins in the cave grew so large that the men playfully laid on them. About half were Royal Eight Escudos—both rare and valuable. The pirates separated them from silver pieces of eight, blackish after exposure to water, as well as smaller gold coins. Dozens of statues and ingots, surrounded by sparkling gems, rested against the cave walls.

Teach had always dreamed of capturing a well-protected treasure galleon. So, he knew full well that they each carried two hundred thousand coins along with other valuables. Although the pirates had uncovered only a quarter of what should be around, it was a vast amount of wealth. After a final trip to the cave, he had the reluctant men conceal it with stones and brush. On the way back to the ships, it struck him that his pirating days would soon be over.

The next letter is in a place of quiet reflection.

Kev raised an eyebrow. The words were familiar.

But where did I see them? The journals? An article?

"He can't do us like that!" Rudy hollered, then looked thoughtful. "What's a Royal Eight Escudo go for these days?"

"Good question," Kev said, then searched on his phone. "They range in value from a few hundred dollars to seventy-five grand. The most expensive ones are in excellent condition and associated with a famous event."

Rudy thought for a second. "So, if they found fifty thousand royals, that's—"

"A cool billion . . . at twenty thousand a pop. That could be conservative given the circumstances, and when you factor in the other coins and valuables—"

"My God."

Stillwater's eyes danced as she caught up. "Kev . . . Rudy . . . the valuables might be in the Flash Ken!"

"That thought crossed our minds," Kev teased.

"You know," Rudy said, "what they found sounds a lot like 'La whatever' you mentioned the other day."

"Llanganatis. It's named after the mountain range where the Incans first hid the hoard. But big fella, galleons often carried gold, silver and gems."

"You forgot the statues. And who's to say a medallion wasn't in the mix? I bet one of those Africans claimed it as a prize."

Kev nodded. "Seems logical."

Stillwater asked, "Was the Fountain of Youth part of Incan lore?"

"No clue," Kev said, "but I'll find out."

She looked sad. "That part sounds like a fairytale."

He ignored her as his mind raced.

If that bottle is nearby, could any elixir be left? After so many years? And does it really have unique properties?

Rudy said, "Ms. Stillwater, you're gonna be rich! Can I be your pool boy, by the way? You'll have to put one in, though. But don't worry, I know the perfect spot."

Kev interrupted, "Simmer down, Cato. Armistead might lead us down that path since it sounds like he had the bottle. But he hasn't mentioned a thing about treasure." He'd said it calmly, but his stomach was twisted in knots.

Rudy stood. "Well, I'm a believer. In the coins and other valuables that is, not the Fountain bullshit. Ma'am, since you seem okay with the pool boy idea, how about adding free beer for life?"

"*If* we find a treasure hoard, you'll get a lot more than sunshine and suds."

"Who am I to argue with such wisdom? Hey, you guys are gonna kill me, but I have to run."

"Why?" Kev asked, incredulous.

"I have to check in on my jobs before the weekend hits."

Stillwater said, "And I should get back to the journals. My so-called lottery ticket will never hit without finding the clue."

"So-called?" Kev asked.

"Yes. I was stoked at first. But the Fountain stuff makes me wonder if Armistead or Teach fabricated the entire story. Even if it's true, I bet the pirates never returned to Florida. I mean, he was killed less than a year later. And if the others made it back to the cave, it would have been difficult to move treasure all the way to Maryland. Especially for black guys in a slave region."

Kev's hopes waned—she might be right. "That medallion though . . . and the elixir . . ."

"That piece could have come from anywhere. And been worn by anyone. As for the elixir, don't forget that Teach was conniving. Perhaps he carved words into the bottle and spun a tale about the treasure hoard to cement a trade. Armistead clearly bought in, so it must have cost him an arm and a leg."

"But that doesn't explain how one of the Africans died here."

"He wasn't necessarily one of Blackbeard's men. In fact, the odds are very much against it."

"The skeleton carving suggests otherwise."

She darkened then shrugged. "I've been wrong before . . . maybe the next letter will clear things up."

Kev said, "Do me a favor, when you need a break from reading, see if there's been a big discovery in Florida. If not and we strike out here, you guys can resume the search down south."

And maybe save my ass.

Rudy looked at him strangely.

Kev quickly added, "Even if we don't find anything of value, the letters themselves are pretty damn incredible. Ms. Stillwater, why don't you build a museum to showcase them and the real story of Blackbeard? Lots of folks would pay to see the journals, letters and such."

"Yes, if what they say is true. But a project like that would cost millions . . . which I don't have."

"Get the bank to help. Maybe the state or county as well. And you could always take up a collection in town. You've done an awful lot for those folks over the years, so they might return the favor. There has to be a way to monetize what we've learned."

"Spoken like a deal guy . . . but I'd rather have the damn treasure."

Kev smiled. "From your mouth to God's ear."

Once alone, he thought about the clue and dreamt of good health.

FRIDAY MORNING

OFFER

GOMEZ WAVED LUCAS INTO HER conference room.

He sat next to her at the table. After finishing up some paperwork, she eyed him like prey while shutting the door with a remote.

"Well, well, if it isn't our hero. Pederson's off the ledge and everyone got their weekend back." The sarcasm was palpable.

"Glad to hear it. He was pretty chipper toward the end."

"Yes, it's almost like the week from hell never happened. He even touted you as my successor."

Lucas raised an eyebrow, surprised. Thoughts of passing colleagues and those above him on the corporate ladder greatly improved his mood.

The COO's stare prompted him to say, "Thanks for the kind words."

Her face clouded. "They were his, not mine."

Here we go.

"You're unhappy with how things went?"

"The charts were fine, but you undercut me in there. A future exec would know better."

"The points that Yvonne and I made were spot on. But if we're here to debrief, why did you raise everyone's expectations? That's going to screw us both in the long term."

"You're unbelievable," she said, shaking her head. "Get your shit together before it's too late."

Something about her words rang a distant bell. But his focus wavered as he tried to place them.

Thought the COO job was out of reach for a few years . . . even for me.

"Am I clear, Lucas?"

"Yes, ma'am." If he had to spread more sugar her way, so be it.

Anything for that type of promotion. And the leverage it would give me in custody court.

"Good. I'd rather discuss next steps, not distractions."

"Fine by me."

"So, what do you intend to pitch on Monday? You must have something in mind."

He'd hoped to iron out some details over the weekend, but such is life. "I've come up with three options. Two are clean, the other not so much." He wouldn't phrase it that way next week, but she was just different than other execs.

"Go on."

"Buying Rose Haven is my favorite. If we do that, we'll hammer the grounds with our sensing technology. The entire process should take a month or so."

"Any downside?"

"Losing money when we offload the place. But the value could also go the other way."

"What's it worth?"

He slid over a sheet of key terms. "One hundred million dollars. Our real estate folks suggest adding a restriction which protects our interests. Once everything's in order, we'd make the offer through an intermediary. That should keep things on the down low."

She enthusiastically scanned the paper. "Buying is usually our last resort, but that would certainly speed things up. And I like the protective covenant . . . but why thirty days before close?"

"That's fairly aggressive for a large real estate deal."

"Perhaps, but if we frame it that way the little people will fill up the time. Have ownership cut over to us once the customary steps are completed, but no later than a month after acceptance."

Like that will make any difference.

"Sure. Would you like to hear the other options?"

She nodded.

"Okay. If we can't get the green light to buy the place or Stillwater turns us down, we could approach her only employee, a fella by the name of Jake Tilghman. He has a checkered past—assault and battery convictions, DUIs and the like—so his judgment appears questionable."

"What do you have in mind?"

"We'd offer him a cut of any valuables found in exchange for his sponsorship and silence. If he's amenable, our folks—disguised as contractors—would search the estate. But at a measured pace to maintain cover. He hires lots of outside help so the ploy should work."

"What kind of cut are we talking about?"

"Guy like that . . . ten percent, twenty max."

"That's tolerable. What's your sense of the risk?"

"Moderate. He could rat us out right away or string us along. Even if he kept his mouth shut, success might trigger him to do something foolish . . . but that can be managed."

"How?"

He chose his words carefully, "The cemetery bluff is very unstable." Being vague was the way to go until he felt her out.

She nodded. "What happens when he's not around to support us?"

"We take the treasure and run. And later show the authorities a written invitation to search the estate."

"I like it. What's the last option?"

"We lay our cards down with the estate owner. Ask for a piece of the action in return for doing the search and recovery work."

"She'd partner with us?"

"If it were me, I'd politely decline then go it alone. Presuming I could afford it."

"I can't imagine money being an issue here."

"Well, Stillwater's in debt big time—over $80 mil. But that may be irrelevant given the value of the estate."

"Interesting. If she bites, how much would we give up?"

"She'll be savvy about the circumstances, so the economics would be far worse than with Jake. We'd end up as a minority partner for sure."

"Ugh. Any dirt on her which could flip that script? Improprieties, scandal?"

"No, she's squeaky clean."

Gomez sat back. "Nice job, Lucas. Why didn't you bring these up earlier?"

"Figured you'd want to hear them first."

The bullshit made her smile. "The only option I don't like, at least for now, is engaging Stillwater. She'd blow us off for sure. But let's pursue the others. In fact, send the offer today with a Sunday deadline."

Say what?

"Oh . . . and figure out how to approach Jake. He's clearly a backup plan due to the risk and length of a clandestine search, but let's get a head start in case we need him."

"How about we get the boss on the horn? He'll freak out if we send an offer this large without approval."

"He trusts me to make those calls, but you raise a fair point. Have Stillwater decide by Tuesday. Then, if Pederson's hard over for some reason, we can retract the offer before the deadline. That way we move fast *and* give the boss a bite at the apple—a win-win."

He frowned at her not getting the point. "Let's at least get the functional approvals before the offer goes out. I'll get the ball rolling right now."

She darkened. "They don't matter on something like this. And purchasing property is in our bag of tricks the boss referenced. Trust me, he'll love the idea."

Then why not get air cover?

Lucas changed tack, "Even a Tuesday deadline could force a bad answer."

"I doubt it. Her debt might be a real problem. And she's lived alone in a mansion since the hubby died. Think about how lonely that must be. Our offer could be the nudge she needs to move on."

"Seems more like a shove. Why assume that she's ready to sell?"

"Call it . . . women's intuition. And why not? We make educated guesses all the time."

This could get her into serious trouble with Pederson and the Board. Wait, that's perfect. I'd be a step closer to her job, possibly even the options.

"Okay. But I'll need an email directing me to make the offer."

"You got it. One last thing—could Stillwater and company have linked the figure to the flag? If so, she'll never sell."

"Well, she has a history degree . . . but I doubt it. Only the torsos match up."

Gomez looked thoughtful. "We should monitor Rose Haven with a drone. And get equipment to tap her phone lines and jam cell coverage. I want to make damn sure these novices haven't tumbled to the answer."

He chewed on that.

Both measures seem like overkill right now.

And if I task employees to help, they'd burn up the ethics hotline.

"Is there a problem?"

"No, I was just thinking . . . there are some guys in Baltimore who are good and fast. Hiring them would be pricy, but if they're available we could be up and running in a few hours."

"Do it."

DEADLINE

KEV LEFT FOR THE CEMETERY.

Armistead had put the benches there for 'quiet reflection.' Excited by the revelation, he blew by Jake and a group of men near a treaded digging machine, two skid loaders and a dump truck. Each one canary yellow.

Better beat those guys to the punch.

Kev sped up while daydreaming about the Fountain of Youth. But that proved costly when he turned an ankle near the big oak. Kev sat for a bit and glared at the uneven ground.

Only city boys need sidewalks.

He continued on after the pain subsided. Once in the cemetery, Kev examined the first couch-like bench near the creek, which he guessed weighed several hundred pounds. With no apparent hiding place on its exterior, he dropped to the ground and reached under the bench. In the narrow space, Kev felt spider webs, along with what might be old leaves and grass clippings. But there was nothing of interest there or beneath the other two benches. For grins, he put his shoulder to the one near the river and heaved. It didn't budge.

Damn.

Just then a drone flashed into view, moving left to right along the water. Once the gadget disappeared, he dismissed it as a neighbor's new toy. Kev sighed. Feeling defeated, he left to make his meeting with Stillwater's pastor friend. Optimism soon flooded back.

We ain't dead yet.
Rudy can help with the benches.

Kate put the journal on her desk.
I haven't found a thing.
The phone rang—a surprise call from her financial advisor.
"Ms. Stillwater—glad I caught you. I have two urgent matters to discuss."
That upset her. "What are they?"
"I just got a call from a buddy who works at the bank. He's heard from the higher ups that there's a big project underway at Rose Haven."
Jesus Christ.
"Yes, as of today. How did they find out?"
"The company you hired called them. Part of pre-project diligence I guess."
"Is that legal?"
"If your contract gave them permission, sure."
"Well, the owner's here with his team and machines, so I'm not sure I appreciate the concern."
"That's because the vice-president told the guy you've made every scheduled payment, which is all he can say at this point."
"I would hope so. But I'm confused . . . did your friend call for a particular reason?"
"Yes. The bank is spooked about your finances. First it was the higher tax bill, then when the VP heard about the project . . . Let's just say he's done his homework."
"I don't care what he thinks, I'm fixing the cemetery."
"That's your prerogative. But you'll run out of money this fall."
I know.

He continued, "Ma'am, it's time to make a decision. Waiting to miss payments will create that fire sale I warned you about."

She sank deeper into the chair.

"Ms. Stillwater?"

"Tell your friend that the bank will be paid in full. Your briefing the other day left me with no choice but to sell."

"Will do," he said, sounding relieved. "For what it's worth, I think that's the best decision under the circumstances. And a perfect segue to the second matter . . . did you get a package today?"

"Yes, but I haven't opened it."

"I got one as well. Take a look."

Stillwater could hardly believe it when she read the offer. But her thrill faded when she realized a key restriction impaired their search plans.

Stress made her lash out, "Why are you so involved in my affairs?"

"My buddy called to be helpful. As for being copied on the letter, maybe the law firm—an impressive one by the way—found my name in a tax filing."

She chilled since her situation was not his fault. "Well, what do you think?"

"It's fair, right in line with our market assessment."

"Agreed. But accepting as is kills my cemetery project."

"Make the bluff someone else's problem. Even if the new owners don't fix it, your husband's plot is far enough inland that it will be safe for ages. Tell you what—I'll take the liberty to draft a response which includes visitation and burial rights. And Ms. Stillwater? When things slow down, I'd love to hear more about the bones and medallion."

Yeah, you and everyone else.

After the call ended, she was startled by a sharp knock on the sliding glass door. It was Kev.

She barked, "Did you find the letter?"

"Not yet," he said, clearly surprised by her intensity. "But it might be under a cemetery bench. Rudy's coming by later to help look."

She felt dumb as Kev explained the relevant journal passage.

If I missed something like that, how on earth will I find the Flash Ken clue?

He added, "I'm leaving to meet with your pastor friend. You mentioned some sort of letter?" Kate handed over the old-fashioned introduction. Prepared just like her mom had taught her.

Kev paused on his way out. "Is something wrong?"

She wanted to cry. "Kev, I'm selling Rose Haven."

"Why?" His stunned look made her feel worse.

"I'm almost out of money. And I just received an unsolicited offer for the place that's valid through Tuesday."

He shook his head. "Do you plan to accept?"

"I have to."

"But ma'am—"

"The kicker is I can't alter the grounds or buildings in any meaningful way before close."

"A buyer can restrict you like that?"

"Apparently."

"Don't do this! That clause will stop us in our tracks."

He doesn't get it.

"Kev, the letters are no good without the journal clue. Which we can't find. And I'm staring foreclosure in the face."

"How about countering—"

"That would only delay the process. You must understand that my family's reputation is more important than a treasure hunt."

He looked exasperated. "Please don't do *anything* before I get back. Say, why don't you come along? The fresh air might do you some good."

"No, thanks. I want to finish the journals. To be sure."

Kev jogged to the garage.

After his silver sports car started—a pleasant surprise since it had been parked for some time—he carefully backed out. Once on the road, he drove angry and fast. After missing the ferry, he went around the river. He stewed over their predicament on the way, even more so when a combine harvester blocked the road for few miles. Eventually, he passed the large vehicle and made it to St. Paul's.

The small, red-bricked church had an outsized façade, above which stood a white cross. Fearful of interrupting a service, he climbed the front steps to listen at the double doors. Hearing nothing, he opened one and peered inside. His eyes slowly adjusted to the dim light. White walls and wood pews stood out at first, then a gold cross on the altar. Just above it, a large stained-glass window featured a colorful figure of Jesus Christ near a sailing ship.

"Mr. MacGuire?" He'd jumped at the rich, velvety voice. The person it belonged to emerged from the shadows wearing trousers and a button-down.

"Yes. You must be Pastor Matthew. Sorry I'm late." After shaking hands, Kev decided the guy looked more like an accountant than a member of the clergy.

"Do you like our big window? Some parishioners say it's a poor match for this simple church."

"I think it's cool. But I feel like that ship is unusual."

"I've never seen another like it. Perhaps it's a nod to our nautical past, with which I'm sure you're familiar."

Like you wouldn't believe, pal.

"You're not positive, sir?"

"No. Some of our records are missing."

Shit.

Kev produced the estate owner's letter to move things along.

"Thanks for meeting with me."

The pastor gave it a cursory glance. "Anything for Ms. Stillwater. And you're in luck—the files from the 1700s are still here. Follow me."

Kev brightened as they ducked through a right-side door onto a mossy path. A squat and similarly red-bricked building stood directly behind the church. After the pastor led him through small rooms decorated for children, they entered a larger one. Books and files packed its shelves.

"You couldn't walk in here a few years ago. We've cataloged hundreds of items since and sent them to a storage facility. But I left the really old records here. They just look the part."

Kev nodded, impatient to begin.

"You have an hour or so before the children arrive for religious education. Everything's chronological, and the 1700s are in the far-right corner. If you find something interesting, please bring it to the church. I'm always on the hunt for new information about this place or its parishioners."

Once alone, Kev located several dusty items from the 1750s. They documented regular services, baptisms, weddings, funerals and donations. A thin file tucked in between revealed familiar handwriting on yellowed paper:

> *Being of sound mind and body, we bequeath all of our belongings, including Rose Haven, to the White Marsh Church. We ask only that its pastor consider building the next house of worship on the plantation. It is a wonderful place for prayer and reflection.*

None of the listed assets struck him as unusual, but he perked up when the next set of papers addressed the 1752 sale. After using his phone to convert the old currency, he wondered if the meager price would someday make church leaders weep.

The last page in the file read:

This letter recognizes the generosity of two recently passed parishioners. As a young pastor, I performed the marriage rites for Edward and Elizabeth Armistead. Then, over 30 years later, I put them to rest. Elizabeth—a Devon—was a deeply religious woman. Edward, less pious when I first met him, also became a staunch believer over the years. Both were quick to donate money to the needy or lend their plantation for important events. They also left Rose Haven to this church, for which I am both humbled and thankful.

Sadly, their gift has again emboldened some to speculate why Edward settled his obligations with pieces of eight instead of tobacco. The same people also wondered how the couple—particularly him—looked youthful until the very end.

In a sermon designed to counter the silliness, I explained that the man earned his coins honestly, not through some sort of illicit endeavor. And I thundered that some folks age more gracefully than others. I closed with a reminder—to no small effect—that the couple had helped many people during difficult times, including the gossipers themselves.

Regardless, after much thought and prayer, I plan to sell Rose Haven once we find the right family. While the Armisteads wished for us to build the next church there, the location is far from a central meeting point. The tobacco operation also requires skill which none of us possess.

Rest Ye With God.

Kev felt lightheaded.

Youthful . . . the evidence keeps piling up.
Did those silver coins come from the hoard?
Or did Armistead really earn them by trading?

After taking pictures of the papers and letter, he found the pleasant pastor at the altar. The man marked his place in a large bible before saying, "You found something!"

Kev handed over the files. "Ms. Stillwater will be pleased. The pastor back then must have thought very highly of her family."

"I'm not surprised. Any other revelations?"

"Yes. The Armisteads wanted this church to be built on Rose Haven." He'd purposefully excluded the coins and youth chatter. The pastor could learn about that on his own.

"How interesting! The estate would have been an extraordinary setting, even if a bit out of the way. I'll read these later and update the parish history on our website. Please give my best to your landlord."

When back in his car, Kev captioned the photos 'PIECES OF EIGHT!' and sent them to the others.

FANTASIES

JAKE LED THE CONTRACTORS AND their machines down the creek side of the peninsula.

He'd kept them off the main path to protect its twisting, wild sections. The company owner—wearing overalls, grimy cap and muddy boots—droned on about material deliveries and how the project had filled a worrisome schedule gap. When he finally piped down, Jake wondered why the job was still a go.

She can't have sold the place already. Or found farmers to work it. Something's changed . . . even before that rooftop celebration.

Once at the tip of the peninsula, he directed the men where to park. Later, he escorted them to the front gate where they piled into pickup trucks and drove away. Another workweek gone by. That always gave him a lift, but it felt different this time, more intense.

Are things finally going my way?
Let's find out with Lucy.

Back on his porch, Kev read about the Fountain of Youth.

It turned out that people have long sought to improve their health or looks. Alexander the Great searched for a healing river some two thousand years ago. Centuries later, a prominent crusader was rumored to have curative waters on his estate. Over the next several hundred years tales from newly discovered lands teased the masses. Modern times delivered hope, if that was the right word, in the form of stem cell research, side effect laden pharmaceuticals and plastic surgery. But most of the material was about Ponce de Leon, the explorer Kev remembered being key to the legend.

Spanish royalty directed the man to explore the Caribbean island of Bimini. He'd received the standard charter for conquistadors—steal valuables and subjugate the natives. While unclear if de Leon made it there, historians agree that he landed in 1513 near what is now St. Augustine, Florida. Both places celebrate him to this day. Island tourist attractions include a mysterious pool of healthy minerals. And the city promotes a spring which perhaps once had special properties.

Disappointed by the lack of clarity, Kev put his phone down and gazed at the river.

Ponce never mentioned the Fountain in his writings. He was later connected to it by others, perhaps to demean the man killed by an Indian arrow.

But if we're to believe Armistead's letters, a Spanish galleon with bottles of elixir sank seventy years after the explorer's death. Does that mean someone else discovered the whereabouts of the Fountain after de Leon died?

Either way, lots of folks may have sampled the elixir. But there are no reports of unusually long-lived royals or explorers.

And what to make of the bottle? Since its markings were apparently clear, was it hidden from the crew?

Blackbeard was intrigued by what he found, perhaps no surprise given the legend. And the Armisteads clearly believed in its properties.

It can't be real . . . but what else could have sent Elizabeth's cancer into remission for a few years? Surely not some sort of placebo as Rudy suggested.

And why would a Fountain prophecy—'Its waters save only the worthy - others beware'—exist if it has no basis in truth?

Perhaps most who drank the elixir failed to meet that standard.
Wonder how I'd fare if given the same opportunity . . .

Rudy bounded up the steps. "Why do you look so weird?"

"It's nothing. Let's roll."

As they rode in the truck along the tortured new path, Kev briefed him on the prospective sale of Rose Haven, his search of the benches and the church gossip. Rudy had been too busy at work to read texts.

"No way your landlord sells now, Mac!"

"Why do you say that?"

"Are you serious? Those pieces of eight came from the treasure galleons!"

"We'll have to convince her of that. I'm surprised—she seems bound and determined to move on. Almost like she's anxious for a change."

"How the hell does an estate owner run out of money? They're all filthy rich."

"She is if you think about it. But her wealth is illiquid."

"Come again?"

"It's tied up in Rose Haven. Stillwater is selling to pay her debts, which means they must be monumental."

"A loaded Flash Ken might take care of the problem."

"No doubt. But I wouldn't be surprised if she agrees with the old pastor. Pieces of eight were just one of many currencies back then, and Edward was a trader."

"Even after some parishioners questioned their appearance? I still don't buy the Fountain stuff, but the chatter has to intrigue Stillwater. We need more than three days to puzzle through this!"

"You and I are in violent agreement, but—"

"Mac, could selling the necklace help?"

"I checked—it's not worth as much as you think. There are a number of Incan medallions floating around. Many pristine, unlike that one."

"Bummer. Well, I'd bet the ranch those coins came from the

hoard. We just have to get her to the same place."

"Funny you put it that way. If Stillwater rolls the dice, she literally risks losing Rose Haven."

"But—"

"Let's just find the letter. And hope it helps with the journal clue."

After arriving in the cemetery, Rudy led the way to the middle bench. He frowned while examining it.

Kev asked, "What do you think?"

Rudy said, "My hydraulic jack could help, but it's back in the office."

"Just push it over with the truck. The stone can take it."

"She's too tall, Mac. The bench will tear out the splash shield, maybe more."

"There must be a way to do it now."

Rudy looked at him strangely then went over to a skid loader. He smiled while dangling a set of keys. After it started, he drove over, lowered its bucket to the back of the bench and goosed the throttle. Once the relic thumped onto the turf, Kev moved in and cleared debris away.

Nothing.

Rudy next drove toward the creek. After the bench there tipped over, Kev's cleaning efforts uncovered something wedged into a corner. Further inspection revealed it was a narrow cylinder.

"Booyah!" Rudy said while peering through the cage.

Excited, Kev dug crumbly material from one end and then removed a piece of cloth. Rudy pumped his fist when it contained another letter.

An idea made Kev re-wrap the papers.

Rudy asked, "What are you doing?"

"Let's get Stillwater fired up, too."

The men raced to the truck and drove along the new path. Soon, Kev pointed to the veranda. The estate owner had just removed a plant with colorful flowers from a terra cotta pot. When she stood and looked over, her hands were filthy with dark soil.

"We found it!" Kev called as he hopped out.

She looked intrigued. "And?"

"We haven't read it yet."

"What are you waiting for?"

"You! Clean up and come over. We'll go through it together."

She looked at her hands. "I'll be right there."

Back at the cottage, Kev made copies and brought them to the porch. Stillwater arrived a few minutes later carrying the journals. Rudy helped place them on a table.

She said, "Sorry guys, but for the life of me I can't figure out the clue."

"You read all fourteen?" Kev asked.

"Carefully. I'm not sure what else to do."

Disappointed, he handed out the letter. "This might help."

Rudy asked, "Ma'am, are you excited about those pieces of eight or what? Or how the couple looked?"

"Not really. The silver is likely all gone. And I'm sure the pastor had the right bead on aimless gossip."

Shit.

Kev said, "I took it to mean there's gold left in the Flash Ken."

Rudy said, "Hell yeah!"

Stillwater shrugged. "Did Kev tell you what I'm up against?"

"Yeah. Sorry to hear about your troubles."

She nodded her thanks then read.

You found the next letter. Well done.

The doctor believes that Elizabeth will pass any day now. She still refuses help for the pain, which sometimes makes her say the most awful things. When she sleeps, I consider what must be done before I, too, leave this world. But there is no task more important than finishing the letters.

The revamped pirate fleet was a sight to behold. It was led by the now ready-for-battle QAR. She absolutely bristled with heavy

*cannon and smaller weapons. And the fast, nimble sloops com-
plemented her well. With hundreds of seasoned men aboard four
vessels, Teach now led the most capable pirate force in the world.
But instead of being drunk with power, he was consumed by how
to move the treasure.*

*The crew was anxious to test their prowess, so he set sail
for Spanish dominated seas near the West Indies and Central
America. There, they captured a fair amount of cargo, including
a shipment of wine carried by an ideally configured sloop. After
the pirates removed the bottles from its large trunks and storage
racks, Teach announced that she would join the fleet.*

*Their journey soured after a large party went ashore to gather
supplies. When dozens of those men became feverish, achy and
nauseous, Teach sequestered them aboard the new vessel and
towed it behind the flagship. He then waited for the familiar pattern to play out, one that he and others had successfully endured.
True to form, each infected pirate appeared to recover. But a day
later, twenty of them turned yellow and spewed black bile.*

Stillwater looked up. "Yellow fever I presume?"
Kev nodded.
"How did they get it?" Rudy asked.
"From mosquitos."

*Teach struggled to maintain calm, but the fear from those
yet untouched by the fever proved inspirational. After a furtive
conversation with his favorite Africans, he dispatched them and
other immune sailors to the new sloop. Those back in good health
returned to QAR.*

*The smaller vessel soon made way. Days later, when the fleet
reached Florida, the sloop split off from the others headed back
to their winter berth. The Africans anchored just outside of the
inlet where a spit of land shielded the wrecked galleon from
view. Once the vessel was secure, they volunteered to care for the*

stricken men. The other helpers accepted the offer and hurriedly left by skiff. The Africans then placed bedrolls on deck and flattened the sails to provide comfort and shade. The sick would rest there between bouts of vomiting.

"See," Stillwater said, "Teach was no angel. Using the men like that was heartless."

Kev smiled disarmingly. "You mean clever."

As darkness fell, one African stayed with the men. The others took the empty trunks by skiff through the inlet, then over to the cave. After removing debris from its entrance, they gazed at the treasure which glittered in the torchlight. It was intact and just as mesmerizing as before. Once the trunks were full—no small feat—they closed the cave and returned to the sloop.

The Africans spent the next day tending to the men. Most looked better; some even shuffled about every few hours. When nightfall came, the three men hauled heavy trunks from the cave to the water, then rowed them one at a time to the sloop. The jack—a Godsend—lifted each trunk to an open cannon port, where they swung it inside. Wrestling the treasure from there into the hold was most difficult and noisy, yet the sick men rarely called for help. Once finished, the Africans surveyed the six double stacked trunks running lengthwise across the back. They would be easy to shield from prying eyes.

Five men died the following afternoon—about the expected number—and their bodies were dumped far from the ship. That night, the Africans wedged the trunks into place with chunks of wood and then walled off the area with spare planks. Teach arrived in the morning after checking the cave. The sloop sat lower in the water and its hold was shorter, but he felt certain that only his co-conspirators would notice. Since those still alive seemed destined to survive, he and the Africans sailed the sloop to the anchorage. Once there, Teach assembled the crew. He announced that they would attack colonial shipping earlier in the year than normal. By disrupting a well-known pattern, he expected to capture better prizes.

Teach smiled inwardly when the quartermaster voiced his concern about the British. Additional ships and men were reportedly coming to eliminate the pirate threat once and for all. Like Teach and his crew, most buccaneers had wintered far away from New Providence. With the pirate ships now dispersed, the quartermaster expected the British attacks to occur along the colonies as the weather improved.

Citing likely capture and death, he pressed Teach to seek a pardon from the pirate-friendly governor of North Carolina. Others had successfully done so; more would follow suit. Some of the men supported the idea, while others were unsure or downright hostile. The apparent split was not workable.

Teach, though, had planted a seed with some influential men who suffered from syphilis. Before participating in a formal vote, they wanted medicine which could not be found in a backwater colony. Others, fearing that the fever could still spread, joined the chorus. Teach proposed that they loot medical supplies from Charles Town before deciding their future. He celebrated their agreement by later sipping from the bottle. Perhaps the perfect time to satisfy his curiosity.

They sailed for South Carolina the next day. Teach would of course be aggressive there, but this time for a reason held close. He felt that if the pirates stirred up enough trouble, most of the men would agree to seek a pardon. Only then could he execute the rest of his plan.

The next letter is in the Flash Ken.

Stillwater looked rattled. "We're screwed."

Kev said, "Maybe not. Let's think about what we've learned. They sailed to Charleston . . . after which they presumably followed his plan. Whatever that was."

"When did they reach the port?" Rudy asked.

"End of May. The pirates blockaded the harbor and demanded help for the fever and syphilis. They captured arriving ships until the governor gave them a chest full of supplies."

"I would have filled it with hemlock. What about North Carolina?"

"They got there in June. After wrecking his flagship and a sloop in shallow water, Blackbeard and his men were pardoned. But there weren't many pirates with him."

Rudy asked, "Most of the crew went against him after Charleston?"

Kev shrugged. "Whatever happened to them, the governor and Teach became friendly. The pirate split time between Bath Town, the capital, and a sloop anchored not far away at Ocracoke. Which, as you know, is where he was killed that November."

Rudy nodded. "That allows for what, six months or so to move treasure to Maryland?"

"Teach apparently never left. But he *must* have connected with Armistead during that time period and told him the news. Since it's in the letter and all."

Stillwater said, "They could have met in Carolina to keep things quiet. Or somewhere nearby."

Rudy looked thoughtful. "I've changed my mind. The treasure is in Florida or North Carolina! That old pastor was right. Armistead earned his pieces of eight the old-fashioned way . . . which means there are two piles of money hidden somewhere!"

Kev smiled. "That's the spirit!"

"Or Armistead was an aspiring fiction writer," Stillwater said dourly.

Kev shook his head. "Then why hide the letters?"

"I have no idea. It just seems like a growing possibility. I mean, if the Fountain water was legit, why didn't Teach use it to heal the men?"

Kev felt the cancer gnaw at his gut.

First time in days.

"Ma'am, please request more time from the buyer."

She shook her head. "We can't find the Flash Ken clue, much less solve it."

Rudy stood and swept up the stack of journals. "You know, I've never read on a weekend night unless I was sick or incarcerated. It will take me a while to get through these bad boys, so I bid you *adieu!*"

They watched him march off.

"This is a lost cause," Stillwater said, "but at least we gave it our best shot."

FRIDAY AFTERNOON

INTEL

Lucas pushed Theresa on a creaky swing set.

She flew back and forth near a gnarled orange tree. A rusty chain-link fence separated the weedy, compact backyard from way too close neighbors. After sending his little girl higher to a squeal of delight—that sound of pure joy only small children can produce—he resumed a normal pace.

"Again, Daddy!"

They'd been at it since she led him through her mother's concrete block house. Playing with her was exactly what he needed after the rough meeting with Pederson and Gomez. A break enabled by having the boys from Baltimore up to speed and in position.

He tensed up when one of them called. Lucas answered with his right hand while pushing Theresa with the other.

"What's up?"

"Something's happening here. There are big machines in the cemetery."

Lucas frowned. "Tell me more."

"The largest one has treads and a scoop. There's also a dump truck and two front-end loaders. Looks like quite the operation."

"Are they digging?"

"They're parked for now. Some workers drove them in then left the estate. Maybe for the weekend since it's Friday."

Stillwater might be fixing the bluff.

"Well, keep watching—"

"Wait, there's more. Before they arrived, another dude took a hard look at the benches there. Then spotted the drone."

Benches? I don't know enough about Rose Haven.

"Okay. Keep flying but take it higher during daylight hours. I don't want to risk another sighting. And hang tight—I'll be there later." After making the decision, he arranged the logistics which included a ride on the smallest RASC jet.

The swing set fun continued until the girl's seething mother arrived.

"Jesus Christ, Lucas! I haven't chilled with the ladies in forever!"

"I know, but something's come up."

"Is Theresa not as important as your job?"

He sighed. "She's number one on my list."

"Talk is cheap. You just promised me—us—that you'd stay the weekend."

His daughter began to cry. Her anguish made him angry, but he checked himself. Arguing would only make things worse.

"I know. But I'm running a project that could change our lives."

"Poor Lucas," she jeered, "always after easy street. RASC is taking advantage of you just like the Colombians did."

"No, it's different—"

"Bullshit! It's always one thing after another."

Like any good job.

She continued the rant, "You'll regret days like this when she's older!"

"Please calm—"

"Lucas, here's the deal. If you go, I'll make sure the custody court hears about it. This is yet another example of why she belongs with me and not you."

He almost lost it. Without him paying the bills, the woman would have nothing, not even a shitty house. But he always stayed cool in front of Theresa. He'd sworn to never act like his parents.

"I'll make it up to her, babe." The mother's face reddened further.

"I'm not your wife anymore, Lucas. Hell, I never really was. You know what? Just get the fuck out of here. And try not to screw up the light of our lives."

"That'll never happen."

"If you say so."

Relieved to escape the tears and anger in an Uber, he clicked on a video sent by the surveillance team. He advanced it until the man—likely MacGuire—examined the benches. The hulking machines arrived soon after he left.

What's he looking for?

If its treasure, wouldn't Stillwater have done some low-key digging before bringing in machines? Or maybe we just missed it.

I should have put a drone up right away.

Gomez makes surprisingly good calls—she has better instincts than I thought.

An idea formed on the way to the airport.

I'll have Jake followed.

Then try to connect with him while the others watch the estate.

Radcliff and his four men were hard at work in Atlanta.

Seated at long tables in his narrow ops center, they'd just spent hours searching for Lucas in Miami and Greenville. After coming up empty, he'd divvied out the many Oxfords in the U.S., each tagged on a big screen at the far end. Radcliff now typed away on a laptop while investigating the one in North Carolina. The others worked quietly on their assignments, each mimicking their leader's intensity.

The Englishman had also entered the tail numbers of the RASC jets into a flight tracking application. It allowed him to view real-time departure, in-flight and arrival information sent by companies and the wealthy to the Federal Aviation Administration. While

Lucas might not rate high-end corporate travel, Radcliff figured it was worth a shot.

His screen soon revealed a new flight. A RASC jet would depart Miami International airport within the hour. He rolled his chair over to a desktop computer and entered the destination into the mapping program. The big screen zoomed in on the mid-Atlantic, then to Easton, Maryland. The airport was close to that state's only Oxford.

He barked, "A company jet is flying to Maryland! Mickey, Garrett, canvass the Oxford there online. And be aggressive—we've got nothing to lose. Ryan and Tyler, grab your go bags. We roll out in five minutes."

His admin booked them on a flight to Baltimore-Washington International. After landing there, they would pick up a few essentials and head to town.

Radcliff smiled—the game was afoot.

Jake was about to suggest a nightcap at Lucy's place.

Dinner had gone well. After some opening jitters, the conversation flowed—no easy feat for him—and there'd been lots of laughter. Her visiting the restroom afterward gave him a chance to hone his pitch.

You've got this.

Every eye in the place watched her glide back to the table. The men obvious, the women not so much. Jake understood. Her red curls were luxurious, the petite floral dress form fitting.

He grinned as his confidence grew. He'd slicked back his hair and put on wrinkled khakis and red flannel for the big night out. A more chill look than the stiffs wearing dinner jackets and trousers.

Lucy sat down and smoothed out her dress. "So, have things

calmed down for you at Rose Haven?"

"Yeah. Wednesday and Thursday were nuts with the phone calls and TV folks, but they didn't show today. Reckon they've moved on to something else in the twenty-four-hour news cycle."

"They'll be back if they learn about the digging."

What in the hell?

"Why? It's no big deal."

"Are you sure?"

"You're still playin' reporter!" he groaned. "Who told you?"

"A source of course."

"Well, we're fixin' the cemetery. Like I said, no big deal."

"Stillwater may be using that as an excuse to search for more valuables."

He flushed after considering the odd activities on the estate.

Could they relate to the cemetery project?

Nah.

He was brusque, "I told you what's going on."

"Jake, I have a strange question for you. Has anyone at Rose Haven ever mentioned pirates?"

"No, at least not in front of me. Why?"

"I've come across some choice information. Believe it or not, that medallion may have something to do with a famous buccaneer. And apparently MacGuire and Dillon know it. So, if your boss directed you to get those machines . . . Jake, are you picking up what I'm putting down?"

Buccaneers . . .

He chuckled. "Who, Captain Hook?"

"Trust me, the name will shock you." She looked at him expectantly, her smile radiant.

"Can't help you."

Lucy set her jaw. "The boss wants confirmation that Stillwater and company are interested in pirates before we run a second article. He's worried about looking foolish. Which means I need you again."

"I don't know nothin' about buccaneers or pirates."

She glared at him.

"I'm serious!"

Lucy snapped her fingers. "I know! Let me onto the estate tomorrow! There's more to those machines than what you say, I just know it!"

"Staring at them won't help. And I don't work weekends."

"How about making an exception for little ol' me? I just want to poke around some. And Stillwater will be none the wiser. She's supposed to be in town with the other commissioners. When I go to print, you'll be an unnamed source like before."

"It felt dirty last time."

"Jake, I can't trespass. My boss is terrified of Stillwater, so everything has to be on the up and up."

"I'll think it over."

"Come on, I'll be your best friend!"

Can't get laid without giving her something . . .

He feigned thoughtfulness. "You know, she hangs out with the men in the cottage an awful lot."

"Now we're talking. Any idea why?"

"It might relate to something they found in a chimney," he replied, then explained what had transpired that morning.

"You held out on me!"

Close the deal.

"Look, whatever they're up to has nothing to do with the machines. Go on, shake your head, but it's true. I did the hiring. Let's talk more over a nightcap—"

"Jake, I never took you for the naïve type."

"I'm not. Material deliveries start next week."

"When?"

"Thursday or Friday."

"Which gives Stillwater and the men plenty of time to dig."

"With what, shovels? The contractors aren't scheduled to return until the material arrives."

She looked flummoxed for a few seconds then said, "Wait,

Rudy's a landscaper."

"So?"

"I bet he knows how to use those machines."

"Maybe. Come on, let's go—"

Her phone rang. Lucy apologized before answering, then stood after a quick conversation.

"I have to run."

No!

"Is it about Rose Haven?"

"Not this time," she said abruptly. A hug good-bye got him hard. He made sure she noticed.

Lucy eyed him seductively after breaking away. "Don't forget about tomorrow, handsome. Then we can have that nightcap you mentioned."

He croaked a whisper, "Okay."

She left cash on the table then walked out.

Valuables and pirates . . . what did Lucy learn?

Could the boss and those bastards be looking for buried treasure?

The RASC jet landed in Easton.

After it came to a stop near a long line of similar aircraft, Lucas took another call from the surveillance guy.

"Jake's at dinner with a lady friend, real pretty. I sent you the address and more drone footage. That cemetery is a busy place."

While tempted to ask about the video, he instead found his rental car and drove over to the modern looking Italian restaurant. After relieving his guy in the parking lot, he played the new file on his laptop and watched two men make a discovery.

MacGuire and Dillon?

Looks like papers of some sort. Not good.

A stunning redhead soon left the restaurant. She matched the description he'd received but . . .

No way Jake's pulling that.

The big man emerged afterward and climbed into a pickup. Curious about the woman, Lucas went inside and asked for his old pal Jake.

The maître-d' said, "I'm sorry, but you just missed him."

"Bummer. He with that girl again?"

"Lucy? Wait. Are they dating?"

"One can only hope. He's been chasing Ms. Johnson for a long time."

The man looked confused. "It was Lucy Simmons."

The goddamn reporter!

Lucas raced out, hopped in his car and then sped toward Oxford. After catching the truck near a stoplight, he mixed in with traffic. Fewer cars on a back road soon allowed for a safer distance. His target eventually turned into the parking lot of a lively bar outside of town. Jake was quick to the door. Lucas entered a few minutes later and took an empty stool next to the man. The greasy fireplug of a bartender came over while drying a glass.

Lucas ordered a vodka soda then inconspicuously studied Jake. The man stared straight ahead as he drank beer, and soon received another.

The treasure hunter held out his hand. "Name's Lucas. You look familiar, so we must have met before." The big man reluctantly shook it.

"Yeah, you toured Rose Haven the other day."

"That explains it! What an amazing piece of real estate."

"Yeah, it is."

"You look after the place, right? What a challenge! But you're obviously up to the task."

"I try."

Big talker.

"Come to think of it, I drove by earlier and saw construction machines pulling in. At least I think so. I get the estates around here mixed up."

Jake looked at him strangely. "Did you hear about the cemetery?"

"Yes, I read the article. Must have been a crazy week for you folks."

"Yeah. Well, I hired a company to fix the bluff. Those are their machines."

So, I was right . . . or he's a good liar.

"Do you think they can stop the erosion?"

"Mister, I've already said too much. My boss is kinda private about estate business." As if to emphasize the point, Jake drained the last of his suds.

Lucas said, "Bartender, his next round is on me. Sorry Jake, I can be nosey sometimes."

The big man accepted the fresh beer with a nod. After a deep pull he looked guilty.

"The boss introduced you as a writer."

"Yes! I'm working on a novel. It's set around here, which is why I toured the estate."

"Makes sense," Jake grunted, a conversation killer.

Lucas did not push it further. He'd secured potentially valuable intel and made a solid connection, but Jake's relationship with the reporter was a problem. He seemed like the type who'd leak news about a treasure hunt to score some high-end tail.

Lucas sipped his drink as he watched the Baltimore Orioles finish off a big inning.

What did the men find?

A map? A message?

How the hell can I find out?

OVERNIGHT

INSOMNIA

KEV STARED AT THE MOONLIT ceiling in his room.

Before Stillwater left for the evening, he'd again pressed her to delay the sale or reject the restrictive clause. But both logic and passion fell on deaf ears.

She'll accept the very day I'm due back at Hopkins.
Where the treatments will be debilitating and useless.
Ain't life grand?

He rolled out of bed and opened the liquor cabinet. After finding the right bottle of scotch and a glass, he went to the porch.

Give up, bro. It's over.

Stillwater lay awake in bed.

Her financial guy had shot down the idea of a counteroffer before she hit the rack. Always calm, the man patiently explained that wealthy buyers often target multiple properties at the same time, so pushing back on terms important to them might queer the deal. Which she could never let happen.

So, three days it is.
But finding the Flash Ken is a fool's errand.

With sleep not in the cards, she put on joggers and went for a walk.

Lucas paced around the inn.

Anxious about what the men had found, he soon left and drove into the countryside. Once near base camp, he killed his lights. The moonlight made it easy to follow wheel ruts through the trees. They opened to a small field near the creek, where he parked next to a tent. Two of his men were fast asleep while the other guy operated the drone from a conversation van.

Lucas watched footage with him for a while. Wildlife heat signatures ruled the screen until someone—presumably Stillwater—left the house and entered the cottage. When she did not re-emerge, he stepped out to call Gomez.

Her voice was faint, "Lucas?" He brought her up to speed.

She said, "Papers under a bench . . . damn."

"Yeah, they're on to something. The question is what."

"I have the same question as before—could they have linked the medallion to Blackbeard's flag?"

"We have to assume so now."

"Agreed. Any sense why Stillwater wasn't with them?"

"No. But she's with Kev in the cottage."

"At this hour? Are they sleeping together?"

"It's a strange time for a social call."

"Then she must be in the know. Which means they're about to dig for treasure with those machines."

"Jake says they're on-site to fix the bluff."

"And you bought that?"

"He seemed truthful."

"Tell me about him."

"He's gruff and unfriendly, a man of few words."

"Was he suspicious?"

"Didn't seem to be. He even asked about my writing, but only because I bought him a beer."

"Interesting."

"Yeah. If it wasn't for that reporter, I'd be inclined to bring him under the covers."

"Did your surveillance folks secure taps and a jammer?"

"Yes, everything's ready."

"Great. Get started."

"Will do, but they might not yield much. That trio is together a lot."

"You told me that Rudy works most days. And Stillwater's often in town."

"Fair enough. But what if she bitches to her wireless carrier?"

"Easy. Stop jamming until she waives off the service call."

"Okay. I'll call you again tomorrow night. Earlier if need be."

"Don't worry about it, I'm coming your way."

What the fuck?

Radcliff drove his men through the countryside.

He eventually pulled into a closed service station near Oxford. After parking the large SUV between two other vehicles, the Englishman took stock of a fluid situation. His folks back in the ops center had found the newspaper article. Not long after, they identified the skeleton figure. He'd of course recognized the Incan symbol straight away.

As the rush of discovery faded, Radcliff called around to area lodging establishments. When he spoke with a friendly clerk at the Robert Morris Inn, she casually revealed that 'Mr. Lucas' was asleep in his room. And usually came down for breakfast at seven AM.

The Englishman then drove to town. He'd drop Ryan off near the inn where the man would wait for Lucas to emerge. The plan was to follow him and react as appropriate.

Hope we're not too late.

Kev spotted Stillwater strolling by.

"Hey there!"

"Hey yourself," she replied, then came up and sat on a chaise. "Why are you up so late?"

"Couldn't sleep. Failure drives me nuts."

"Same here. My mind's racing like crazy."

"Care to fog it up with booze?"

"Why not? I've already had some wine. A glass or two more should get me to bed."

He went inside while wondering about the likely innocent wish. On the way back, he flipped a switch which bathed the porch in soft light.

No bra . . .

Aroused, he handed Stillwater a full glass before looking away. He wanted her badly.

Don't complicate things.

"Ah, thank you," she said, then savored the red blend. "This hits the spot."

They sipped their libations in silence for a bit.

"Kev, don't beat yourself up over my problems."

"I just wish we had more time to figure things out."

"Me, too." With a wink she added, "Should I triple the price and tell the buyer about Blackbeard?"

"That would go over well."

"No kidding. But like you said earlier, the information itself *must* have value. Perhaps the new owners can figure out how to uncork it."

"And profit from our leg work. That would be par for the course."

"How so?"

"The sale is just the latest punch in the nuts this year. Work problems, personal issues, it's been a real mess."

"Things are never as bad as they appear. You'll turn it around."

Not this time.

"Well, at least I met you and made peace with Rudy."

"There you go!"

"Everything else fucking sucks though." He immediately regretted the language and tone. "Uh, sorry about that, ma'am."

"Please—call me Kate. And I'm not offended in the slightest. You and Rudy are choir boys compared to my father. His mouth was in the major fucking leagues."

He smiled wanly. "Kate . . . using your first name feels strange."

"Why?"

"You know how it is. Estate owners are like royalty."

She laughed softly. "When my reign ends in a month, I'll be good ol' Kate again. Think I'll enjoy that."

"But you belong here."

"Don't feel sorry for me. I'll clear millions and travel like a starlet. I just need someone along for the ride."

"You'll miss this place like crazy."

"Trying to cheer me up?"

"Sorry Ms—Kate. I'm lousy company tonight."

"Would you prefer to be alone?"

"No."

"Okay."

More silence.

"Kev, is something else bothering you?"

Time to reveal the cancer?

Nah, the big fella comes first.

"I'm fine, just bummed out like I said." He forced a smile. "I'll try to lighten up since I'm in the presence of a queen."

She raised her arms, and the suddenly taut fabric of her top outlined both breasts. "Do I look like royalty to you?"

Kev was stunned when she stood and undressed. He tried not to gawk, but her fine figure made that impossible.

She said, "Stop staring," then pulled him to his feet. As they kissed deeply, she slipped a hand into his shorts and stroked him. He responded in kind, and they stayed like that for a while. Kev broke away before he lost control. He sat on the chaise, breathing heavily.

He muttered, "Maybe we shouldn't . . ."

Without responding she tugged at his shorts. Once they were free, Kate pressed him backward—then mounted him with a gasp. At first their lovemaking was slow. But, with her eyes closed and mouth slightly ajar, she rode him faster and faster. He tried to hold out, but this time the wave of release proved unstoppable. When he exploded, she collapsed on his chest with a cute whimper.

Kate rose up after her own convulsions faded. With him still inside of her, she moved in tight circles for what seemed like forever. When Kev got hard, he turned her over and they did it again, more patiently this time.

After they were finally spent, she said, "Give me your shirt. We've made quite a mess."

He handed it over. "That was—"

"Wonderful, I know. We should both sleep great now, but don't be surprised if I want more of that in the middle of the night. It's been far too long."

She led him to the bedroom and quickly passed out, half covered by a sheet.

Shouldn't have started something I can't finish.

But damn that felt good.

SATURDAY MORNING

DIRECTION

KEV AWOKE WHEN RUDY BARRELED into the room.

The big man froze after seeing Kate in bed. Panicked, she pulled the sheet to her chin while Kev made sure his junk was covered. Rudy, after opening his mouth a few times, finally muttered, "Sorry to interrupt."

Kev smiled. "Doesn't anybody fucking knock anymore?" He glanced over at Kate. She still looked sexy, even with tousled hair.

What a wild and unexpected night.

His friend spluttered, "I did! You two sleep like the dead."

Since the estate owner still looked stricken, Kev offered, "It's not like he's your dad."

She laughed and threw a leg over him, obviously ready for round three. "You're right! Make him go."

Rudy cleared his throat. "Folks, I'm still here. And Mac, I couldn't reach your cell."

Kev looked around. "I don't know where it is."

"Can't imagine why."

"All right, big fella. Tell me where the fire is before my naked ass gets out of bed."

"Put some clothes on and you'll see."

After joining his friend in the living area, Kev spotted the journals. Stacked on the kitchen counter near coffee and bagels.

Did he actually find something?

When Kate emerged, Kev eyed her taut legs poking out from

an old work shirt. But desire had taken a back seat to whatever was about to unfold.

"Ms. Stillwater," Rudy said, "I'm disappointed. I thought you had standards."

She smiled demurely. "I'm going by Kate now. So, what's the big news?"

He patted himself on the back. "Just yesterday, I was like Watson to Sherlock Holmes or the Boy Wonder to Batman. Now, we'll see whether Mac handles his demotion with class." He poured steaming coffee into paper cups.

Kate said, "Typical male, forgetting who's in charge. But come on, tell us what you found!"

Rudy handed the drinks out. "There's cream and sugar over there. And Ms. Still—er . . . Kate, don't worry. I'll reveal everything in good time."

Kev waited patiently. His pal could rarely be rushed.

After tearing into a bagel, Rudy said, "Okay, here's the deal. I read some of the journals in order. Which was a complete waste of time. It took until the wee hours of the morning before I remembered an important lesson."

"Okay, Sherlock," Kev said, avoiding a Robin compare. "I'll bite. What was it?"

"Do you remember our sixth-grade teacher?"

"Ol' Mother Hubbard. How could I forget?"

"Right! Well, one day—while you were on a field trip with the so-called talented and gifted kids—she gave us mere mortals an interesting test. The last question asked, 'What day of the week is it?' And get this, if you answered just that one correctly, you got an A!"

Kate declared, "You found a clue in the fourteenth journal!"

"Sort of! Now, whatever her intent, Hubbard's lesson taught me to look for shortcuts whenever possible. So, I spread the journals out to see if anything caught my eye. Remember the fancy drop case letters?"

Kev nodded eagerly.

"Here," Rudy said, producing papers from his pocket. "I made it easy for you amateurs."

For the sake of posterity, I will chronicle our lives on this beautiful . . . Leap into 1724 with me, it will be an exciting . . . A bald eagle rang in the new year on a cold . . . Great adventures are ahead as . . . The river is frozen as we begin another . . . Outstanding party last night to celebrate . . . Farmwife she is not! Yet Elizabeth runs much of our tobacco operation . . . Looking forward to a growing season with expanded fields . . . Another rewarding year behind us. If only we could have . . . Silence looms over Rose Haven, almost like the animals . . . Her countenance is beyond beautiful, I am so lucky . . . Killed a large buck with a bow, fresh meat for the table . . . Elizabeth looked stunning at the ball in Oxford . . . Nature on Rose Haven always amazes, there were turkey everywhere . . .

Kev, having raised an eyebrow after making out 'flag,' finished the code using the first letter of each line.

FLAG TO FLASH KEN.

"You did it, big fella!" Rudy pantomimed hitting a home run then slowly circled furniture as if rounding bases.

"I want to play," Kate said. "But I'm not sure what it means."

Rudy held up at the chair which served as second base, looking uncertain. "You guys want me to figure out everything."

Kev sipped his coffee then asked, "May I step in for the great Batman?" The thought of being Robin now seemed okay.

"By all means, young ward."

"You know how we caught the medallion then later spotted Blackbeard's flag? Well, since the jewelry could not have been part of his plan, Armistead expected us to follow a different sequence. We just upended things with those two discoveries."

"But how do we know that's the right flag?" she asked. "He hasn't written anything about it, at least not yet."

"In the first letter, he teed up the pirate stuff as a reward. Well, that was a red herring of sorts. Blackbeard was part of the clue."

She said, "So, he expected someone to figure out the message first, then identify the flag."

"Exactly."

Rudy asked, "But what on it points to the end of the rainbow?"

"I'm not sure," Kev said, then spread papers out on the counter. "Let's take another look at the flag and estate sketch."

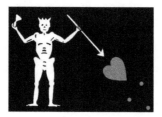

"Once again," he added, "the skeleton has raised arms. One hand holds an hourglass, while the other thrusts a spear downward toward a red heart. Below that are three drops of blood."

They stared at the papers until he had a thought. "The cemetery benches might fit the blood pattern."

"I'm not digging up graves," Rudy declared.

"I said benches, goofball."

Rudy nodded, obviously relieved. "Well, let's get after it. The contractors are gonna tear the place up anyway."

Kate said, "Not true. I have to call them off by Tuesday."

Perhaps sensing Kev's surprise, she added, "Don't get me wrong, I want to dig . . . but I'd feel better about the cemetery if one of the other flag symbols matched something on the estate. Otherwise, we're jumping at what popped into your head. I mean, there were also three docks then, and maybe similar groupings on land."

Rudy observed, "The spear could be important. It points to the spots."

"I can't think of anything that looks like that," she replied.

Kev suddenly felt unsure. "You're right, I'm just guessing. And now that I think about it, Armistead may not have built the Flash Ken where he intended to hide a letter." Kev looked down at the floor before adding, "We need more time to figure this out."

She set her jaw. "I'm sorry, but I'll need something concrete before I counter. There's just too much at stake."

After a long minute, Kev snapped his fingers.

"Rudy, does Tremaine still run a helicopter service out of St. Michaels?"

"Sure does. You want to go up?"

"Yep. Something might pop out from the air."

Radcliff called the inn after Lucas did not show for breakfast.

The same lady he'd spoken to earlier had not seen the man, but she mentioned that his room was being cleaned. After thinking things over, Radcliff had Ryan stay put. He dropped his other man off a few streets away to stroll around in case Lucas was out and about. Then, since the bones and gold were found in a creek adjacent to Rose Haven, he drove in that direction and eventually found a quiet field away from the road. The others would make their way over if Lucas did not show in a few hours.

Time for the drone.

Pederson struck the golf ball.

It arced high over a pond and landed two feet from the flag. He laughed at the reactions from his companions, "My boy! . . . Lucky shot! . . . Such bullshit!" He'd been relaxed ever since the meeting with Lucas and Yvonne.

He led the golfers across a small bridge then replaced his ball with a marker. After the others finished the hole, Pederson squared up over the putt for the win and a thousand bucks. When the ball rolled in, he gave a Tiger-like fist pump.

They shook hands and settled up, then headed to the nineteenth hole. On the way, he admired the club's crisp acres of Bermuda grass set amidst palms, pine and water. Once the men had cool drinks, they toasted another glorious weekend in south Florida.

Gomez felt tense as hell on the way to the airport.

This is it.

She'd showered, dressed and packed while waiting for the big jet to land in Miami. The long range one, in case she and Lucas secured Blackbeard's treasure. Once in Easton the flight crew would bunk there and await her call. If all went well, she would somehow transport valuables to the plane then direct the captain to fly to Central America. He'd push back, the stewardess as well, until the COO produced her gun. Then, after feigning a return to Miami, the plane would fly into international airspace and dip below radar before the authorities realized what happened.

But what if we don't find anything?

Or have to make multiple trips to the airport?

Whatever . . . my plan is shitty, but it is what it is.

I'll react as things unfold.

After being whisked through the executive air lounge without so much as an identification check, Gomez strode to the parked jet and dropped a bag near the stairs. The captain gave her a warm welcome. Once inside the lavish cabin the woman sat in her favorite chair. Plush leather of course, and up front where she belonged.

The stewardess approached with a smile. "The usual, ma'am?"

"Yes, please." She glided to the aft galley as Gomez buckled in. The captain briefly went over the flight plan through the open cockpit door. Once she had her tea, the plane taxied to the runway.

Her mind raced as they shot into the sky.

I've got to save Padrino.

PERSPECTIVE

KEV TRIED TO DECIPHER RUDY's phone call.

"Tree, it's Dillon . . . No, from a landline, the nearby tower is on the fritz . . . Hey, I realize this is totally last minute, but can you take me and Kev up this morning? . . . He's better now, I swear . . . Come on dude, you owe me a solid."

Rudy hung up. "We might get his morning slot if two newlyweds play ball. He thinks they'll jump at a discount on a later flight. If so, we're on the hook for what he loses plus fuel for our trip."

Kev nodded. "When will we know for sure?"

"He'll call me on the way if it doesn't work out. Worst case is we go this afternoon."

The men raced to the truck—without Kate who had schedule conflicts. Thirty minutes later they reached the small heliport on the outskirts of St. Michaels. There, the men signed their lives away at the front desk before a sturdy woman led them through the building. When they reached the tarmac, the chop was overwhelming. Tremaine had the sleek, black helicopter ready to go.

He grinned and waved them over. After instinctively ducking under the spinning blades, the men climbed into the passenger cabin. Kev slid across to the far window; Rudy stayed by the door. Once it shut, the interior was fairly quiet. They looked around appreciatively at the cream leather couches and mahogany trim.

Rudy asked, "You travel like this on your deals?"

Kev chuckled. "Only when slumming, big fella."

The intercom crackled, "Welcome aboard, gentlemen. Fasten your seatbelts."

Take off was smooth, and the bird rose effortlessly into the clear sky. After Tremaine leveled off, Kev nodded. The altitude offered the right balance of perspective and ground detail.

"Thanks for making this happen," Rudy said loudly. "We really appreciate it."

"No problem. What's so urgent?"

"You heard what happened on Stillwater's estate?"

"Hasn't everyone? I moved heaven and earth to get some scoop!"

"Sorry to disappoint you, Tree, but that article had it all . . . unless you want to hear about our crabbing exploits. But seriously, Stillwater asked us to look for other problem areas."

"Too lazy to walk around?"

"She's got an insurance adjuster coming this afternoon, so there wasn't enough time. And getting a bird's-eye view of the place makes sense if you think about it. I just wish she'd given us a head's up, so we didn't have to screw up your day."

"She worried about the rest of the shoreline?"

"Primarily, but it's best to start at the buildings and then work our way out. That'll give her the peace of mind to file a claim or whatever."

Kev was impressed by the smoothly delivered bullshit. It was as good as what he once fed the government.

"Got it," said Tremaine. "Since we're up, I'll swing over town and give you the usual spiel. Who knows, you may learn a thing or two. And don't forget to enjoy yourselves. It's a gorgeous day to tour God's country by air!"

He banked sharply over the restaurants and shops that lined the streets. Many people strolled about. Yachts of all sizes were in the harbor, some anchored to buoys, and a water taxi buzzed around. The scene was markedly different than Oxford's busiest day.

Tremaine said, "St. Michaels became famous when British warships tried to shell it one night during the War of 1812. But they missed! The clever townspeople hung lanterns in the surrounding woods to draw off the fire. When the Brits saw everything intact the following morning, they got spooked and sailed on to Baltimore. That's where Francis Scott Key wrote the 'Star Spangled Banner' during an attack on Fort McHenry. I'd like to think our soldiers manning its defenses were inspired by what the folks here pulled off."

Rudy smiled big. "Suck it, England!"

"Right on! But these mics are pretty sensitive, so there's no need to shout. Anyway, a few years ago, part of the movie *Wedding Crashers* was filmed here. That brought even more tourists as well as the rich and famous. From up here, it's easy to see why."

They left the harbor area and flew along the water. Visibility was excellent. He could make out every detail of the long bridge which crossed the middle of the bay. Seeing where his parents died triggered a deep sense of loss.

Tremaine said, "As we come east, check out all the nooks and coves. Boaters love to overnight in them and sometimes get one all to themselves."

Soon, acres of fields, trees and waterways played out to the horizon, beyond which lay the frothing Atlantic.

"Our shore is as flat as a pancake and one big socioeconomic melting pot. As we cross over, you'll see mansions next to modest homes, posh towns near trailer parks and crab shacks that compete with highly rated restaurants. Add rivers, creeks and farms of all shapes and sizes, and we have most everything in our neck of the woods. If big cities and sports teams are your thing, Baltimore and D.C. are only ninety minutes away."

On the approach to Rose Haven, Kev became anxious and broke out his trusty sketches.

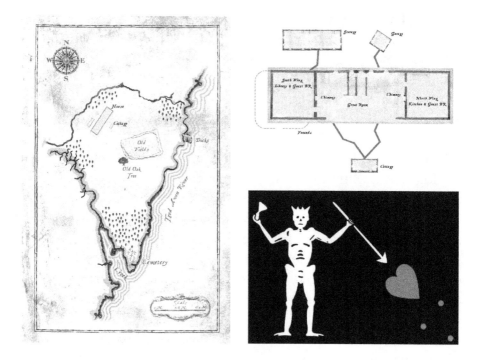

Once the helicopter was over the house, Kate waved from the veranda. Jake was also there. They were re-potting more plants.

He never works on Saturdays.

After dismissing the thought, Kev looked for anything that resembled a symbol on Blackbeard's flag.

He muted the intercom. "Big fella, why would the Armisteads build a guest house there? It kind of hoses up the view from the ground floor of the house."

"Would you rather the cottage be in Kate's front yard? What drives me nuts are those crooked paths. You don't notice them much on the ground because of some clever landscaping, but the layout from up here looks awful. I'm kind of surprised goat-jigging Eddie didn't go for soft curves like we do today. Get it? *Soft* curves!"

Kev ignored the foolishness and snapped pictures of the buildings, which he compared to the sketches and flag. He grew irritated when nothing stood out.

Come on . . .

He reactivated the intercom. "Tree, can you take us to the river and back?" After that approach proved unhelpful, they flew in concentric circles over the rest of the estate. The big oak impressed even from altitude. Once they reached the cemetery, Kev's hopes dimmed.

"That's about it," Tremaine said, then banked sharply to the left. He quickly leveled off. "Sorry fellas, I did that to avoid a drone! I swear one of those things will kill me someday."

After watching it do a lazy turn, Kev muted the intercom again and told Rudy about the cemetery sighting. "What do you think? Is someone spying on the place because of the necklace and bones?"

"Nah, Mac, it's just some kid having fun. Or a nerd flying a new toy."

Makes sense—Tree obviously sees them a lot.

Once the drone disappeared across the creek, they flew back to town. Upon landing, Kev thanked the man with a wad of cash. When back at the truck, he placed the sketches on its bed and spun through photos from the flight.

"This can't be that hard, big fella. We've got buildings, benches, docks and a few headstones to consider."

Rudy replied, "Don't forget the other two hundred acres. Maybe we're trying to match an apple to a banana. Hell, we've seen part of a bluff collapse this summer. Think about what else could have happened over three hundred years."

He's right.

Kev cycled through the pictures again. One inspired him to turn the buildings sketch counterclockwise.

Whoa! Could it be that simple?

He showed the sketch and flag picture to Rudy. "Take a look."

After studying them closely he said, "I don't get it."

"Focus on those paths you bashed. And how the cottage and garage sit relative to the house."

Rudy looked bewildered.

"They look like the skeleton! Hang on, I'll show you." Kev grabbed a pen and crossed a few things off.

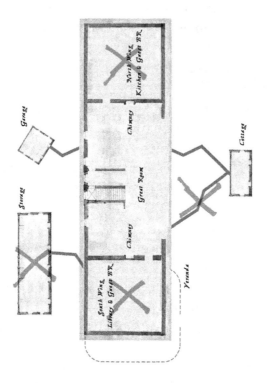

"Ignore the additions this time."

"So, you think the garage may be the hourglass, and the cottage is—"

"The heart! Which makes the long part of that path a spear! Armistead designed the damn buildings to match symbols on Blackbeard's flag!"

"But the cottage is a rectangle."

Instead of responding, Kev rooted through a toolbox and found a straight edge. He used it to color in the paths and extend the 'spear' on the estate sketch through the cottage and beyond.

I was right!

Three benches. Three drops of blood below the heart.

Rudy now looked excited. "Holy shit!"

Kev called Kate. "Great, you haven't left yet! Blow off the art festival so we can search the cemetery!"

"What did you see?"

"We made a connection that at least puts a museum in play. We'll be there in an hour."

"Why so long?"

"We're starving. Want anything?"

SATURDAY MORNING

INVASION

Lucas ripped off his headphones.

The prospect of getting whipped by amateurs made him boil. He rarely lost a treasure hunt. When it happened, at least there were professionals involved, competitors he respected.

This project is FUBAR—fucked up beyond all recognition.

Gomez was with him in the van, looking ridiculous in a fancy pantsuit. Her unwelcome presence on his field op made the apparent setback feel even worse.

She finally noticed his anguish. "What's the problem?"

"We may be toast. Kev's fired up about the cemetery."

"The treasure's there?"

"Didn't say, but he was pretty animated. Even jabbered something about a museum. They'll be back in an hour."

She muttered, "A museum?"

Gomez was concerned.

For what? The treasure?

Stillwater loves history . . . And if that's her plan, she'll tell the world about a discovery.

Which would bury Padrino.

Or was MacGuire joking?

She turned back to Lucas. "If he was serious about a museum, Stillwater might go public or involve the authorities when they find something. Either kills our chances."

"Slow down. We have time, and he could be wrong. Let's monitor their progress with the drone."

"The video from that altitude sucks."

"I'll risk flying lower again."

"Fine. But I need intel, and that's not coming from the air."

Lucas asked, "Does it really matter? This hunt appears to be going against us. If we lose out, we're supposed to accept it and learn from our mistakes, remember? Pederson will hang our asses from a flagpole if we don't follow the credo."

She snapped, "How about ideas instead of roadblocks?"

"Fair enough. In my old job, we'd occasionally use parabolic devices to listen in on conversations. You know, those things sideline reporters operate during ball games. But getting close enough to hear the trio talk would run us afoul of the Treasure Trove Doctrine. Not to mention our boss."

"How long would it take to get one?"

"A few hours? If we can't find a device nearby, I'm sure the boys from Baltimore could hook us up."

"This search might be over by then," she said, drumming her fingers on a cupholder. "How can we quickly learn more without getting into trouble?"

He shook his head. "I'm not sure."

So uncreative.

Gomez said, "Let's pay Stillwater a visit before the men return. I'll introduce myself as the person who made the offer."

"But she'll recognize me from the tour. And Jake's there today. If he sees me, our backup plan is history."

"Don't worry—I'll just tell her that you're my guy on the ground. And as far as your new friend goes, that ship sailed after his dinner date with the reporter."

"Okay. But I bet Stillwater tells you to pound sand."

"I'll win her over by acting eccentric. That'll give us a chance to gauge whether she'd shirk wealth for a museum of all things. Unless you've already formed an opinion."

He paused. "Can't say for sure . . . Wait, why are you so dressed up?"

Gomez smiled enigmatically. "Meeting her was always a possibility."

"I don't know about this . . . tipping our hand has little upside. At best we learn whether Stillwater planned to sell before the men spotted something on the flight. And I doubt she tells us that much."

"Nothing ventured, nothing gained."

"Play that out for me. What happens if we think there'd be some sort of announcement?"

Gomez hid her anger at the many questions. She needed his help, at least for now.

"We retreat and call Pederson. I suspect he'd increase the offer or try to partner with her. Before it's too late."

"That's it?"

"Yes, except get the parabolic thingy—just in case."

"You think the boss would go for that?"

"Enough already! He'll drop the lily-white façade for a shot at Blackbeard's treasure. He needs *something* to keep Wall Street off his back."

"Let's just call him now. This is getting serious."

"Grow a pair, Lucas. You've got a lot riding on this."

"The stock options?"

"Yes. And becoming COO."

She'd broach their other connection later—if necessary.

Lucas reluctantly trailed Gomez to the big house.

She rang the bell and a dog barked. When Stillwater opened the door, the excited animal raced out and darted around. The estate owner smiled when Lucas crouched and scratched its ears.

She said, "I know you—"

Gomez interrupted, "Apologies for the intrusion, Ms. Stillwater. I rarely meddle with a deal, but I just *had* to see Rose Haven for myself."

The estate owner examined her with interest. "You made the offer?"

"I did!"

"Which means Lucas here is no author."

She remembered my name.

"Subterfuge," Gomez said while looking around appreciatively. "Unfortunate but necessary. And he did a *terrific* job describing the buildings and grounds. Simply gorgeous, almost surreal actually. But there I go being rude again, not even introducing myself. My name is Eileen . . . dear, this is a bit awkward on the porch. May we come in?"

"I'm sorry, but I'm leaving soon for an engagement in town."

Lucas relaxed. Stillwater had clearly bought the act.

"Well, what do you think of the offer?"

"It took me by surprise, so it could be Monday evening before I make a decision. Hopefully that makes sense given the circumstances."

"Surely you have an inkling one way or the other?"

"Well, I'm not sure the price is fair. And I could use more time to think it over. Even if I accept, it will take weeks to finish an important project that just started. And packing up—whew! I've lived here my entire life. Anyway, I'll have a better sense of things tomorrow evening when my advisors brief me on the offer."

"Perfectly reasonable. When I get excited and do silly things like this, it drives *my* people insane. But it does allow me to clarify a few things. As you've undoubtedly ascertained, Rose Haven is my top choice in the area. So, if money turns out to be a sticking point, I'm sure we can work something out. But the offer and close deadlines are non-negotiable. I'm hell-bent on starting my new venture as soon as possible."

"Understood," Stillwater said flatly. "May I ask what you do for a living?"

"Of course. I own a vacation company that peddles unique combinations of lodging, fine dining and historical experiences. Speaking of which, I intend to turn one of the buildings here into a boutique museum that showcases Maryland history. Do you think something like that would interest folks?" Lucas smiled at the Oscar-worthy performance.

Stillwater glanced at her watch. "I'm not sure."

Gomez brightened. "I have an idea! Advise me as I put this together! I'll certainly make it worth your while. Let's chat about the possibilities over a cup of tea."

"This has been an unexpected pleasure, but I really must go. If I accept the offer, we can discuss anything you'd like."

Gomez said flatly, "That won't work for me."

Stillwater frowned; Lucas was concerned. He knew that tone.

His boss rooted through a fancy tote. "I must have a card in here somewhere."

Gomez assessed her options.

Should I back off? My career is lucrative, a sure thing. And I'll be CEO.

No . . . save Padrino . . . just like he once saved me.

If I can't, at least I'll be the next boss. As long as I score Blackbeard's treasure.

Worst case—I'm a regular gal for a spell. Before I rise again.

Gomez produced the pistol and waved it at Stillwater. "Take us inside."

The estate owner flinched then grew pale; Lucas was very still.

She finally managed, "Get off my porch or I'll call the police."

The COO looked her over with disdain. "Our cell service is terrible, darling. How about yours?"

Stillwater pocketed her useless phone then entered the foyer.

Lucas locked the door behind them.

What the fuck is Gomez doing?

She must have planned this all along. A gun, the nice clothes and a bullshit promise to call Pederson . . .

I just bought in.

Clever or crazy, she's way out over her skis.

Which may be a good thing.

She had Stillwater sit at the kitchen table, where the woman stared dejectedly at the landline across the room. Sandy plopped down nearby and rested her head on the floor.

No threat coming from that sweetheart.

Stillwater broke the silence. "Did Lucas scout the place for a robbery? I have money and jewelry. We can make this easy and I won't tell a soul."

Gomez smiled. "We're after the treasure, silly."

The estate owner looked guarded. "What do you mean?"

"We know everything. When MacGuire and Dillon arrive, we'll hide in the pantry and listen. But we'll have that little chat first."

"I don't know what you're talking about."

"Yes, you do. Tell me, was it the medallion that first piqued your interest? Something else?"

Stillwater set her jaw and said nothing.

Intervene before this gets worse.

He said quietly, "Just come clean, ma'am. You can't win this."

She shook her head. "Who *are* you people?"

Gomez narrowed her eyes. "We work for a treasure hunting outfit that's based in Central America. Lucas is right, you have zero leverage. And I'm losing patience."

Well, fuck me.

That explains why my old bosses let me go, that 'chance' meeting with Gomez and my subsequent hiring.

I'm so freaking gullible . . .

Stillwater said, "Lucas, you asked about Elizabeth on tour. Was she—"

Gomez firing (CRACK!) made him flinch, and the bullet tore into the wall above the estate owner. Her resolve broken, she shakily gave a hasty account of the journals, flag, letters and Flash Ken clue. It was hard to follow, but once he heard about the coins, curiosity overwhelmed his shock about the gunfire and Figuras Ocultas.

Damn—these folks are after the legendary 1589 treasure. And Blackbeard of all people may have brought it here. Incredible.

But what on his flag points to a nearby place? Guess we'll find out soon enough.

Wait . . . Has Gomez already told Figuras Ocultas about this?

Surprised by the locked door, Kev entered the code and led Rudy inside.

The house was quiet, so he called, "Kate? You here?"

As Sandy tore their way, he heard a faint voice, "I'm in the kitchen."

Kev launched when he spotted the seated estate owner, "The spear is a path off the house! It points directly to the cemetery!"

Her silence surprised him. Rudy asked, "What's wrong?"

"Tell us more," said a lavishly dressed woman emerging from the pantry.

Rudy pounced, but before he reached her a stout, bald guy leaped out and decked him. His friend dropped to a knee—nose gushing blood. Baldie then stood over him, fists at the ready. As Kev registered the gun, the woman stepped aside for a better field of fire. He shook his head, overwhelmed by the sudden turn of events.

What the hell is happening?

"Get over to the table!" she hissed at Rudy. "You'll get worse if you try that again." He sat then gingerly dabbed at the blood with his T-shirt. Sandy sniffed spatter on his shorts.

The woman gestured toward Kev. "You, too! Lucas, that was well done—the fat one's faster than he looks." It dawned on Kev that he'd met the 'writer' on a recent tour.

Is this a robbery?

She said, "You must be MacGuire."

"Yeah," he replied grimly.

"Excellent. My name is Gomez. Lucas and I are treasure hunters, much like you apparently. Except we do it for a living."

Ugh. I'm—we're screwed.

"I don't understand."

"Tell us more about the spear and cemetery."

He shook his head, confused. "What brought you here?"

The woman puffed up with pride. "A message on Blackbeard's telescope got us close, then the medallion pointed to Rose Haven. That's why we offered to buy the place and tapped the phone lines."

Shit.

Gomez continued, "Now tell us about the helicopter ride."

"But I don't get it. Your goon was here right after we found the jewelry."

She looked serious. "Show some respect, Lucas is the best treasure hunter I know. But if you must know that timing was coincidental. We scheduled estate tours in this area after our first Oxford search didn't pan out."

Damn, they move fast.

Better buy some time—Jake might still be around.

Kev said, "Things will only make sense if I start from the beginning." After Gomez nodded her approval, he methodically described the events of the past week—except for the Fountain of Youth. To his chagrin, the intruders were excellent listeners.

Gomez had them stand once he finished. "Remarkable progress. Particularly considering—"

"What was the message?" he interrupted, not interested in her compliments.

"Guide my love to Oxford."

My love? . . . The treasure and bottle must be here!

Gomez said, "Let's get moving. Rudy, you'll dig while we watch."

"With what?"

"The machines."

"I can't operate those things."

"Don't be silly—we watched you work in the cemetery with our drone. If you folks cooperate, you'll soon be rid of us. But if not . . ."

Kev kicked himself.

These people have been all over us. And we had no idea.

The trio shuffled out of the house under gunpoint. Gomez had them follow the new path to the cemetery.

Lucas considered his predicament on the way.

If Figuras Ocultas knew where things stood, they'd be here by now.

Which means if we find something, Gomez will call them in or fly the treasure to Colombia.

Where Theresa and her mother will join me.

My cut from the sales of coins and such could dwarf what RASC pays, even as COO.

But my wild-card boss might put a bullet in my back first. Those conference room pictures prove that she's not the sharing type.

I should be okay though, if she stays loyal to Figuras Ocultas.

Which happens if she's really Padrino's long-lost daughter.

He'd just tumbled to the idea. When Lucas worked for the organization, there'd been whispers that their leader had at some point planted his adopted girl in a legitimate company. And her age seemed to fit. The more he thought about it, the more logical it seemed.

Wait, what if they someday make Theresa do the same thing?

The thought sickened him. He needed a better outcome, one which kept her out of the fray.

Find the treasure, take Gomez out, don't piss off Figuras Ocultas, keep my little girl safe and stay out of jail.

He shook his head.

That's a lot of moving parts.

Kev spotted Jake moving furtively near the main path.

The man disappeared into the trees before the others noticed. He might have called the police before tracking them, but his actions suggested otherwise.

Yeah . . . I doubt he could see the gun from that distance.

Keeping him in the dark was a bad idea . . .

Since changing the status quo was up to them, Kev decided to go for the weapon if and when the estate keeper surprised the intruders. Rudy was far too wobbly, and Kev could not see Kate taking them on. Since Gomez's assurances about their safety seemed dubious at best, he silently apologized for his transgressions against the red-haired giant.

Need you, pal.

SATURDAY AFTERNOON

DECISIONS

ONCE IN THE CEMETERY, GOMEZ backed against a tall tombstone.

With the plots either beside or behind her, she could see the creek, two of the benches and about half of the grassy area which led to the woods. It was a good spot, so the COO had MacGuire and Stillwater sit down and cross their legs. Lucas was over on the river side of the peninsula. They were ready for Jake, whom the drone had recently spotted near the house.

Gomez signaled. Rudy, with dried blood masking much of his face, drove over in a front loader. Using the same technique as the evening before, he rolled the creek side bench further away from its original spot. When there was plenty of room, he dug. After a while, she inspected the hole and waived him on. His work eventually produced three heaping piles of clay.

Damn it.

Kev shrugged. He'd suggested the digging spots.

Is he fucking with me?

Rudy looked over for guidance as she considered what to do next. Lucas seemed to pick up on her indecision and edged closer while keeping an eye out for trouble.

"Boss, let's take a step—"

"Get back there!" she snapped. He gave her a strange look before returning to his post.

Future COO my ass.

More like a child who needs babysitting.

Kev asked, "You want Rudy to dig deeper? Or try somewhere else?"

Hmmm . . . of course! Search away from the graves.

She called out, "Try the grassy area, but this time use the excavator."

Rudy started it up. Gray smoke enveloped him at first but dissipated as he drove over to the designated spot. Once there, he lowered side stabilizers to the turf and dropped the bucket down. Its jagged edge tore into grass and clay, which he dumped near the woods. Back and forth he went.

Jake edged along the riverside bluff.

He'd slowed to a snail's pace once Lucas came into view. When the surrounding foliage thinned, Jake melted into the ground to assess the situation. He quickly realized that Lucas had a pattern. The man would glance toward Jake's hiding place every fifteen seconds or so, but mostly he watched the excavator dig. At just the right time, the estate keeper raised his head to see what was happening near the creek, but grave markers shielded the others from view. Without any further insight, he dropped back down and glacially thought about his next move.

Lucas is obviously on the lookout. For me, I guess.

But he acted like a stranger on tour. Then played dumb in the bar . . . I'm so confused.

Lucy might get it . . . but I lost track of her.

Whatever's going on, it makes me think she's right about pirates.

Buried treasure could save my job. Hell, I might even get my hands on a piece or two.

If that's what the boss is after, then these two people are what? Experts of some kind?

Jake had always been an outsider in town, but that was never the case on Rose Haven until MacGuire and Dillon came around. Now, adding insult to injury, Stillwater had embraced two other newcomers while purposefully keeping him in the dark. The perceived inequity uncorked his rage.

After an idea formed, he timed his launch and covered the distance to Lucas like a blitzing linebacker. He then drove through the unaware man, planted him on the ground and landed two solid punches.

He froze at the gunfire (CRACK!). Aware that a bullet had whipped by his head, he rolled off and stood, hands in the air. The woman who'd fired then backed MacGuire down. It looked like he'd made a move after Jake drilled Lucas. Stillwater was over there as well, sitting on the ground.

Jake had been ready to explain why he attacked Lucas. But his boss really being in trouble—just like the story he'd contrived—shook him up. As he stared at the stranger, common sense drowned conspiracy.

I misread this. Badly.

She called, "Lucas, what part of pay attention did you not understand?"

The bald guy looked pissed, but the woman shrugged that off. "Whatever. Jake, come over here and sit down. We've been waiting for you."

"Yeah? I've met this fucker, but who the hell are you?"

A man's voice erupted from Lucas' walkie-talkie, "A woman just left the other side of the woods. She's headed for the house."

He took off shouting, "We've got a runner!"

That's gotta be Lucy . . . Go, girl!

Gomez shook her head after baldie disappeared into the trees. "Jake, put your phone in the pile. And folks, the next person who does something stupid gets shot."

He looked her way after complying. "Lady, you didn't answer my question."

"Your friends can fill you in."

Aching from the tackle and punches, Lucas dodged trees and crashed through shrubs.

After leaping over a tall log, he wondered how the drone had spotted a woman but missed Jake's approach.

Doesn't matter. Catch her and live to fight another day.

Once in the open fields, Lucas poured it on. The redhead was slow, so he quickly closed the gap. She looked back when near the big oak, then stumbled and fell. He slowed to a jog after realizing his quarry was the reporter. And watched her chest heave from exertion as she looked for an escape.

He called, "Don't even think about it."

Her shoulders slumped. It was over.

Good. Her getting loose would have been a disaster.

"Get up, we're going back to the cemetery."

"Who are you?"

"Now!"

"But that woman shot at you and Jake!"

"Last chance, or we do it the hard way."

It was awfully loud in the excavator cage.

Dizzy from the pain and blood loss, Rudy dug for what seemed like forever. After he gauged that the hole might soon broach the water table, Lucas ran by and crashed into the woods.

What the hell?

Rudy craned his head around to see who'd escaped. But his friends were still there. With Jake.

We're really fucked now. But who's that asshole chasing?

He sighed, locked the bucket in place and killed the engine. Chipper songbirds taunted him.

Gomez called, "I didn't tell you to stop."

"I reckon we're close to hitting water. If something was here, I would have found it by now."

After looking uncertain, she snapped, "Okay, join the others."

He did so, then asked, "Jake, when did—"

The woman shrieked, "Shut up!"

She's losing her shit.

Lucas returning with his quarry—Lucy!—threw Rudy for a loop. The asshole held her arm tight and looked awfully pleased with himself.

Hope someone knows she's here.

Gomez lit up when she saw the pair.

"Well done, Lucas! Who's that?"

"Meet Lucy, the reporter who broke the medallion story."

The COO darkened. "What are you doing here?"

"I could ask you the same thing!"

"Never mind, I got it—you're a backwoods investigative journalist. Who'll be next, the mayor?"

Lucy said, "There is no—"

"It was a joke, genius. Now shut up and sit with the others. Lucas, have the guys stop jamming. I want comms up in case we have to call for help." He passed along the instructions by walkie-talkie.

Gomez's other thoughts were jumbled, panicked. When whispers distracted her, she demanded quiet.

One of these folks will be missed soon enough.

How can I spur things along?

She motioned Lucas over. "I'm changing things up."

He shook his head. "Have Dillon dig until he hits water. Then do the same where the benches were. We might as well be sure."

No, something's not right.

Gomez smiled and tried to sound calm, "I need your help. You see, my father's dying, and a bottle of liquid in the hoard might help him. Please . . . tell me where to search."

Everyone stared at her.

"Seriously, I'm just here for the bottle. You'll get the rest no matter what."

Silence.

I bared my soul for nothing.

Gomez waved Kev to his feet. "Tell me, MacGuire. It's now or never."

He stood and dabbed at sweat trickling down his face.

She's after the bottle, so it must be legit.

But how the hell do I—we—get out of this mess?

Gomez said evenly, "I'm not joking."

"You know everything I do!"

"Let's dig more," Lucas said reasonably. "If it's not here, we can—"

"Enough! MacGuire, spill the beans before I hurt you . . . or someone else."

The goon's expression made Kev hope for a split in their ranks. But the man did nothing.

Better change tack.

"I'm sorry about your dad. Is the bottle you mentioned related to the Fountain of Youth?"

She looked triumphant. "So, it does exist! Why didn't you tell me that before?"

"Armistead wrote about a bottle and the Fountain in his letters, but we figured it was a fairy tale."

"Well, you were wrong!"

"I guess . . . either way, I don't know where else to look. And even if there's a bottle around, it must be empty by now."

"Guys like you *always* have a backup plan . . . Lucy! Come here."

The terrified looking reporter did as she was told and stopped a few yards away.

Gomez said, "Last chance."

The worried Kev snapped, "I promise—"

When she fired (CRACK!), Lucy bucked and grabbed her left shoulder. He caught her on the way down yelling, "You fucking—"

(CRACK!)

The shot had gone over his head, so he gently lowered the pale woman to the ground. She whimpered softly and curled into a fetal position.

"Your landlord is next, then Dillon. Get over here, woman!"

Kate ignored her.

"Now!"

Kev hissed, "None of us knows where it is!"

Lucas sidled up to his boss and whispered in her ear. She listened for a second before waiving him off.

As Gomez aimed the pistol at Stillwater's back, Lucas pivoted and dropped his boss with a blow to the neck.

He picked up the gun in a flash then covered the others. Punching her carotid artery had done the trick—she was out cold. Everyone else looked shocked by the move, even the cool MacGuire.

Lucas announced, "Help Lucy but don't try anything."

He'd almost taken Gomez out when she mentioned a healing

potion, then again after the woman shot Lucy. He'd finally acted because a dead estate owner would limit his options.

Now, how to get out of this mess?

Figuras Ocultas is a phone call away.

They'll lock these people up and search the place with real tech. MacGuire and the others will be killed when they are no longer useful.

Then, treasure or no, Theresa and her mother would wind up with me in Colombia.

But there has to be a better answer . . .

"One of you call 911," he said, gesturing toward the stack of phones.

Lucas felt that he could avoid prosecution, at least for anything serious, while Gomez took the fall and went to jail for a long time. RASC would undoubtedly get hammered by the authorities and press for the day's events, but he was confident that Pederson would pull the company through and mount a stirring comeback. Perhaps with Lucas serving as the ethical hero, maybe even COO.

The rest depended on Figuras Ocultas. Padrino dying might very well distract the Colombians. Or the organization could implode without strong leadership. If they did come for him, he'd volunteer to be their new mole and hope like hell they still valued business prospects over revenge.

As MacGuire dialed, Lucas placed the gun on the ground and stepped away.

Kev retrieved it.

After completing the emergency call, he looked around. The goon had not moved, and Gomez was still unconscious. Rudy and Kate were crouched beside Lucy. They had pressure on her wound, but the woman's pallor had worsened. And those two looked shaky as well, especially Rudy who was caked in blood. Jake stood off to the side. He seemed forlorn, lost.

Kev tried to appear calm, but he was over the damn moon.

I still have a chance at the elixir!

But where could it be?

He said to Lucy, "There's an ambulance on the way." Then, without really knowing added, "You're gonna be fine."

Her answering smile was ghastly.

Lucas said, "Careful with that gun, MacGuire. I have a daughter to look after, and you sure as hell don't need it for my boss." Kev eyed the man, surprised at his aggression.

Rudy hissed, "Shut up or Jake will knock you into next week!" When the big man came over to enforce the threat, Lucas shrugged and stared at the woods. Everyone was quiet for a spell, even when Gomez propped herself up and looked around. She collapsed again after seeing Kev had the weapon.

He broke the silence, "Jake, you did us a solid back there. If it wasn't for the gun, you'd have kicked the shit out of that goon."

The big man nodded but still looked out of sorts.

Kate added, "Yes, you put your life on the line for us. Thanks for being so loyal."

As the man blushed, she asked, "Was that woman serious about her father?" Kev looked over at Gomez again and saw tears.

He asked, "Well, were you? And how did you learn about the bottle?"

Silence.

"Her interest in the Fountain makes it seem legit," Rudy observed.

Hope so.

Sirens blared in the distance. Soon, two police cruisers skidded into the cemetery, trailed by an ambulance. Chief Roberts, Daniel and a third officer burst out of the cars and drew their pistols.

The chief yelled, "Drop the gun!"

"What a joke," Stillwater said.

Daniel lowered his weapon. "The good guys have the upper

hand, Chief." After she did the same, he waived three EMTs out of the ambulance.

Kev engaged the safety and placed the gun at his feet. "Thanks Daniel, but I don't need it anymore."

He nodded on the way to get it. "What on earth happened here?"

Kate took charge. "Those two invaded my home and held us hostage. Then she shot Lucy. I was next before the bald guy knocked her out."

"Why would he do that?"

"No clue."

Rudy said, "Let's not make the prick out to be a hero. He's also responsible for this." The big fella pointed to his nose.

One EMT bandaged Lucy's shoulder while another prepared an IV. The third fetched a stretcher. Several feet away, Daniel hauled Gomez to her feet and cuffed her, then did the same to Lucas.

Roberts eyed the sullen pair. "Any idea who they are?"

Lucas perked up. "We're treasure hunters who work for Rare Antiquities Salvage Corporation. This is my boss, Eileen Gomez, and I'm Lucas Chilton. Just to be clear, if it wasn't for me, she would have shot Rudy in the kitchen."

He flushed. "That's fucking bullshit!"

Lucas continued, "It's not BS; you saw what she did to Lucy."

Kev considered the goon's role that day.

He aided and abetted several crimes but also saved our asses.

Taking that bitch out could really help him.

"Treasure hunters," Roberts repeated thoughtfully. She watched Lucy get loaded into the ambulance. After it sped off, the deputies read Lucas and Gomez their rights before shoving them into the back of a cruiser. Daniel came over once the other cop drove away.

The deputy said, "You folks have obviously been through the ringer." He grimaced as the remaining EMT reset Rudy's nose. The big fella handled it without a whimper, but the pain made his eyes water.

Daniel continued, "But we need to understand what happened here. Did those two see the article?"

Kev nodded. "That's what they said."

"Were they after more jewelry?"

"It's hard to fathom, but the Gomez woman thinks the medallion has something to do with pirate treasure. They watched the estate with a drone . . . which reminds me, the operator is somewhere around here, probably across the creek. You should send someone after him before it's too late."

Daniel gave the order by radio.

Kev continued, "Anyway, the digging machines triggered her, so they broke into Kate's house and took us hostage. The equipment belongs to the contractors Jake hired to fix the bluff, but Gomez refused to believe it."

Roberts narrowed her eyes. "No one in their right mind would bury treasure in a cemetery."

The simple logic made his mind race.

Stillwater eventually filled the awkward silence, "You know what, Roberts? I can't wait to lead an inquiry into this mess. Focused on the timing of your police report."

Disparate memories jolted him.

Yes, that must be it!

Radcliff chuckled when the cops cuffed the prisoners.

Down goes Lucas.

Sucks, though. I thought for sure he was on to something.

The Englishman watched the drone below his peel off and head for the creek. He kept flying just in case.

After the cops finally left, Kev brought his largest T-shirt out to the cottage porch.

"Put this on, big fella. I'm tired of seeing the blood Lucas knocked out of you."

Kate's laughter made Rudy fume, "At least I tried to do something—unlike some people I know!"

Kev clapped him on the shoulder. "Appreciate you. It was better than my weak ass attempt in the cemetery."

"Folks," Rudy said after he changed, "we're lucky to be alive."

"Gomez looked certifiable, didn't she?" Kev observed. "I guess we should be thankful the goon loves his daughter."

Kate said, "If eliminating us was his best option, something tells me we'd be dead by now."

Rudy added, "It'll drive me nuts if that asshole gets off lightly."

Kev smiled. "He's quite the actor that one, kind of like Teach. Speaking of which, what's our next move?"

Rudy looked crestfallen. "I guess Eddie was full of shit after all. He's probably somewhere laughing at us."

Kate said, "If so, it's because we dug in the wrong place."

"You serious?"

"I'm not giving up now. We have a map of sorts and just escaped from a sociopath who knew about the treasure. Not to mention the Fountain of Youth."

"Carpe Diem!" Rudy replied. "But where do we search next?"

"Let's take another look at the sketch."

Rudy noticed Kev smiling big. "Why the shit-eating grin?"

"Remember how Armisteads expanded the tobacco fields out to some oaks? If he meant three, we might be in business."

RESOLUTION

KEV AND KATE WALKED ALONG the main path.

He carried two shovels, her a bag of stakes. She was chatty while he felt nauseous.

What did Gomez say?

It's now or never.

Heavy stuff.

He thought about those he'd mistreated over the years. Rudy and his father, other friends from town, work colleagues, unwitting consumers, the many convenient women . . . All were serious marks against his character.

If the Fountain saves only the worthy and punishes everyone else . . .

He doubted that he'd fare well on any judgment day. Either now or when the cancer got him.

"Earth to Kev! Again—what made you think of the oak trees?"

"Sorry. Believe it or not, Roberts clued me in."

"No!"

"Seriously. She's the one who questioned why valuables would be hidden in a cemetery. Which is exactly right—Armistead would not have done that."

"Because a burial might have uncovered the Flash Ken?"

"Exactly. Once it had to be somewhere else, I thought about that line I drew on the estate sketch. But it was hard to focus because my ankle was killing me."

Kate looked confused. "Old injury?"

"No, I twisted it in a hole yesterday. Then tweaked it while going after Gomez."

She smiled sweetly. "I asked for the time and you're building me a watch."

"Hear me out, my mind works in mysterious ways. The pain triggered a memory of a similar depression in the yard we had when I was a kid."

"And how did that come about?"

"An enormous tree toppled over one summer during a storm. Took me and my dad days to cut it up. The ground sank later as the buried root ball rotted away."

Kate looked thrilled. "You think there's another hole!"

"Hope is more like it."

Think I'm right, though. Both the oak and depression are close to the line.

But will the bottle be in the Flash Ken? And could any liquid be left?

If so and it really works, that prophecy will screw me.

Chill, dude . . .

One step at a time.

Once near the big oak, Kev found where he'd hurt himself. After marking it with a stake, he canvassed the area and located a similar depression.

Three trees, baby!

After staking it as well, he compared the area to the estate sketch. The line ran right straight through what must have been a triangle of oaks. His anxiety was through the roof as he showed Kate.

"This has to be it," she muttered.

"As long as these holes were made by dead trees."

Kev gauged where to start. Without a better idea, he strode to the mid-point of the triangle as Rudy drove up in the front loader.

"Big fella!" Kev called, then slashed the ground twice with a shovel. "X marks the spot!"

"No shit?"

"No shit!" he said, unable to play it cool with his friend. "Looks like there were three trees after all."

"How should we play this, Mac?"

"Have at it with the blade—but be careful. If the Flash Ken's here, it won't be buried deep. Remember, Armistead paid his bills with silver coins."

"You let me dig to China in the cemetery!"

"Time was our only ally for a while."

After nodding, Rudy gently stripped away debris, grass and reddish soil. When Kev heard a scraping noise, he stopped his friend and moved in with the shovel. Scooping dirt revealed wood.

Holy fucking shit.

Rudy said, "We found it!" He hopped down and grabbed the other shovel. Kate stood by quietly as the men cleared a patch of wood, about ten-by-twenty-feet. A rusted padlock secured a corner hatch.

Kev pressed down on a few boards with his foot. "Feels pretty solid."

Rudy replied, "The clay protected the wood." After fumbling with the rusted lock, he added, "This thing's hopeless. Guess we'll have to smash through."

Kev raised his shovel.

"Wait!" Kate said. "Can't you just break the rings holding the lock?"

Thus redirected, he stabbed at them until they splintered. The hinges then groaned in protest as he raised the hatch. A musty smell emerged.

Whew . . . just like Nana's basement.

He dropped to his knees and switched on a flashlight. A ladder descended to a wooden floor eight feet below. The clay walls, bone dry except for a few seepage marks, looked sturdy. After taking a deep breath, he lit up the middle of the room. Six trunks were there along with posts that supported the roof.

Unbelievable.

Rudy and Kate peered in.

"Wow," she whispered.

Rudy said, "Those trunks sure came a long way."

The moment of truth.

"Should we try the ladder, big fella?"

"Nah, I'll get one from the loader. Some extra flashlights, too."

After it was set, they climbed down and looked around. Three beams of light soon converged on the nearest trunk.

Kev looked at Kate. "Go for it."

She reached for an ornate handle then paused. "What if they're empty?"

"Only one way to find out."

Everyone gasped when it was full of gold coins.

Kev moved in and scooped out a handful. After examining them he said, "All minted in 1589. How about that?"

Kate said, "This is crazy."

Now for the bottle.

The next four trunks held more coins, mostly gold, as well as ingots, statues and sparkling gems.

Rudy observed, "Everything we read about is here!"

Not yet.

The big fella continued, "And some of these statues remind me of the medallion."

Kev opened the last trunk—empty but for some papers and a sealed bottle. He reached in to get it, trembling. He studied its impenetrable glass before a shiver freaked him out.

Someone just walked over my grave.

He gave the bottle a little shake and heard liquid.

Oh, man.

Kev blanched when he caught the others staring, then read the etched letters aloud, "Fuente de la Eterna Juventud."

"The Fountain of Youth," Kate said, obviously awe struck. "Even that's real . . ."

"Too bad the bottle's empty."

Weird. Why did I lie?

Rudy spread his arms like a preacher. "It doesn't matter, Rose Haven is saved!" Kate smiled weakly then fell into Kev's arms. The estate owner sobbed breathlessly, like a small child.

After composing herself, she murmured, "Thank you both. For everything."

Rudy surveyed the open trunks. He selected a gold ingot from one, then plucked an intricately carved statue from another. After examining the leering man, he said, "I like this little dude. When I climb out this bitch, I'm bringing these along. To remind myself that the hoard is real and not a figment of my imagination."

Kev held the bottle like a football while retrieving the papers. Kate followed their lead and filled her pockets with coins and gems. He was the last one out.

Am I worthy?

Radcliff and his men approached the cottage.

After the drone captured the trio's discovery, he and his men armed themselves then stalked through the woods and fields. Loud conversation eventually drew them to a brightly lit porch.

The two guys. Celebrating.

He sent the others around to the far side then crawled closer. Gold artifacts on a chaise caught his eye—glittering, shiny, amazing.

But where's the woman?

Better hold off until we find out.

Kev refilled Rudy's glass with single malt scotch.

Kate soon arrived carrying a small bag. She was all smiles after months of worry and days of debilitating events. Kev fought his emotions—he wanted time alone with the bottle *and* drinks with his friends.

Rudy said, "Well, if it isn't the wealthiest woman in Bedford Falls!"

She played along with the movie quote, "No woman is a failure who has friends. And I can't imagine better ones than the two of you. Sorry I lost it back there, this is all pretty overwhelming."

Kev said, "We're just happy things worked out. Like I said before, Rose Haven is where you belong." He reached for the scotch. "Here—have a touch of the good stuff."

"Actually, I'd hoped to share something special with you guys." After removing a bottle of wine from her bag along with three stemless glasses, she filled them with ruby-colored liquid.

"Joe and I saved this Bordeaux for his recovery, which unfortunately . . . well, you know."

They clinked glasses and sipped the wine.

Kate said, "This is lovely. But he should be here to see this! If only I'd found that damn bottle years ago . . . But you know what? Since it's sealed, there may be some residue to study! How awesome would it be to eradicate disease! And save both victims and loved ones from experiencing so much pain!"

She's right. Drinking what's left would be selfish.

Rudy said, "After today, I'm willing to bet that shit sent Elizabeth's cancer into remission."

Kev almost spit out the wine.

"Then consider it settled," she said. "But I don't want to sound looney, so one of you can figure out how research like that gets done. Anyway, are you guys ready to read those papers or what?"

Kev said, "We should figure out how to secure the Flash Ken first. Maybe get a new lock, and rig—"

"Great minds think alike," she replied sunnily. "I just spoke with the chief of the state police barracks over in Easton. Several officers are on the way to guard the place."

Radcliff whispered into his microphone then slipped away.

The cancer bit had piqued his curiosity before the mention of cops ruined a grand opportunity. He reached the SUV before his men. After stowing his gun inside, he slammed the door in frustration.

So. Fucking. Close.

Kev said, "Great. That'll make Roberts lose her shit."

The flip comment belied his inner turmoil—he'd lost control of the situation.

But I'm keeping that bottle come hell or high water.

"No doubt," Kate agreed. "And I can't wait to tell our chief about it." She'd put 'chief' in air quotes. "But enough about Roberts, let's read before things get busy again."

"Okay—but keep the Fountain stuff between us for now. Like you said, we don't want to sound crazy."

"Agreed."

You found the Flash Ken. Congratulations.
Last night, I visited Elizabeth in the cemetery. While I feel

empty inside, at least she is no longer in pain. I am incredibly thankful for our time together, yet the fond memories only hasten my plans to join her, God willing.

I hope you enjoy the treasure as much as we did. Please help others in need and only use the elixir, if any remains, for serious illness at a young age. But enough preaching. Our story resumes when Teach and the pirates sailed from the anchorage to Charles Town. There, they looted arriving ships for days until the governor produced the requested medicine. Blackbeard's crew was both pleased with the result and terrified by his suddenly youthful appearance. The Devil rumors swirled anew amidst troubling news.

Captured sailors had confirmed the British plan to end piracy. An armada of warships would soon gather near the mouth of the Chesapeake Bay. From there, they would intercept and destroy the pirate ships which came north for the season. The grim situation stunned the crew and most now clamored for a pardon before it was too late. Teach kept an eye on a specific pirate—Cooper—during the proceedings. After he agreed, the remaining holdouts fell into line.

The man captained one of the sloops. He was quite capable and enjoyed the confidence of the men. Most importantly for me, his hair color, beard and size could pass for Blackbeard. Later, I approached him and suggested we exchange identities. Cooper found the idea appealing. He suspected that only a renowned pirate would escape the gallows, perhaps with a small cadre of men.

He was an able negotiator, but I would have parted with far more to escape the life. My confidence grew as our plan came together. Cooper, who now looked older than me, would pay a group of loyal pirates handsomely for their silence, companionship and protection. If I could scatter the other men before then, most would never have the opportunity for mischief.

Rudy smirked. "Anyone else catch the pronoun change?"

"I'll never hear the end of this," Kev groaned. "But a younger looking Blackbeard is the real revelation here."

Kate said, "Props to you for figuring things out first, Rudy. Let's be honest though—once we found the treasure, Armistead and Teach had to be the same guy."

Kev nodded. "I can't wait to hear how he ended up with the entire hoard."

Rudy rolled his eyes. "Don't tarnish my genius! I mean, where would you poor people be without me?"

Kate asked, "Kev, when did you know for sure?"

"The telescope message was what sealed it for me. If they were different dudes, Elizabeth would have professed her love to a pirate, eventually secured his treasure and later ditched the man. All to live happily ever after with Armistead. Throw in how religious she was and . . . I don't know, any other scenario seemed farfetched."

Rudy said, "Says the guy with a bottle from the Fountain of Youth."

They laughed at the absurdity of it all.

For the sake of brevity, I hid a final letter in the guest house. It explains how I peaceably reduced the size of my crew, purposely wrecked QAR *and completed the formalities with Cooper and his men. One final search if you wish to learn more.*

Eager to trade fame for obscurity, I cut my hair and beard and we set off. My conspirators and I maneuvered our sloop through inland waterways and shallow ocean waters, then the lower part of the Chesapeake. We mostly sailed in the morning to avoid attention and dangerous thunderstorms. Good fortune smiled on us, and we made our way without incident to the Choptank River, then to the lovely Tred Avon.

We anchored near the Devon property on a warm afternoon. Trees shielded us from view as we scouted the shoreline. A patch of heavy bramble looked to be a good, albeit temporary hiding spot for the treasure. The quartermaster's share, however, would remain aboard the sloop. He intended to hire a few men then sail onward to a secret destination.

After some debate, the Africans had decided to stay in Maryland. While they desperately wished to return home and find loved ones, safe passage there would be nearly impossible. To help ease their minds about living in a slave colony, I offered protection and land tucked away from prying eyes. As for me, I would again become Edward Armistead, my alias used in the Oxford area.

We hauled the trunks into position and lowered three onto separate skiffs. Afterward, I had the Africans row them ashore several minutes apart to avoid raising suspicion on the busy waterway. Once there, the men used a pulley to haul the trunks into the bramble.

Since the Devons might have learned of a ship anchored near the plantation, I went to the main house. There, Elizabeth hugged and kissed me before remarking on my youthful look. She seemed uncomfortable when I attributed it to a deep tan and clean shave. Thankfully, her parents were none the wiser since their eyesight was poor.

The quartermaster must have directed the Africans to finish the transfers at dusk. When I returned after dinner, the officer emerged from the bramble with one of the men. About to hail them, my jaw dropped when the quartermaster crushed the African's head with a hammer. He immediately dropped, a mess of brains and blood. Once over the shock, I sprang upon the officer and snapped his neck. It was the last violent act of my life, but a necessary one, for I would have been his final mark.

He'd hidden the other two bodies nearby. After shedding tears and saying a prayer, I lashed the lifeless creatures to the largest skiff. Several rocks finished the load. The boat rowed sluggishly, but I eventually made it to the far side of an oyster shelf. Once there, I pulled the plug and swam to shore, confident that the blue crabs would make quick work of the flesh. I sank another skiff to align with the story I was about to tell.

I had a terrible nightmare that evening. The men's ghosts, led *by the quartermaster, took great pleasure in exposing my identity to the world. After waking up in a cold sweat, I was comforted by the fact that dead men tell no tales.*

I told Elizabeth about the elixir and treasure. She believed my story that the others had left by skiff to pursue their dreams. Fortunate, because the devilish acts would have troubled her deeply. I frequently prayed for the souls of three outstanding men. As for my own, I found solace by helping others in need. Acts of kindness intended to offset years of gruesome deeds.

Elizabeth and I later married by the river. The happy event occurred a few years after the statuesque brunette caught my eye in town. I later visited her whenever our ships were on the river. While such trips were infrequent, we soon fell in love. The unusual courtship was embraced by her family. My upbringing and apparent wealth helped, as did the fact that Elizabeth had already spurned several suitors.

Once our bond seemed unbreakable, I told her about my life, first as a privateer then a pirate. I remember being both surprised and pleased when Elizabeth found my roguish activities endearing, but she insisted they end before we became man and wife. While a bit anxious about that, I promised to someday return a changed man. The treasure enabled me to do that sooner rather than later.

When Elizabeth and I parted ways before my final pirate voyages, we exchanged gifts as was our custom. She presented me with a silver spy glass of unusual quality. I thought about her whenever I used it, and privately wept after it went overboard in North Carolina waters.

"I'm glad those RASC fuckers found the telescope," Kev said, smiling. "Even though it almost killed us."

Kate nodded. "It should be buried with Elizabeth. *If* we can find her remains."

He winked. "Or featured in your museum."

Before my wedding, Cooper and his men received pardons from Governor Eden. They were free as long as they stayed in the colony. 'Blackbeard' married the daughter of a plantation owner and enjoyed some quiet time there.

Yet Cooper and his men—for whatever reason—returned to sea. After seizing a vessel, he convinced Eden that the prize had been abandoned by the French. The governor's acceptance of the tale made some believe he was privy to the scheme.

That attracted the attention of Virginia's Governor Spotswood, a man who was hell bent on ending piracy or finding pirate treasure. Perhaps both. However inspired, he sent an armed force to attack Cooper and his men in the neighboring colony.

The soldiers caught up to them in the Outer Banks. A fierce battle ensued, killing my twin and most of the others. By all accounts, the man fought bravely before succumbing to many wounds, forever enhancing the legend of Blackbeard. The few pirates still alive were taken to Virginia.

I would not be surprised if some of them revealed the true story of Blackbeard in a bid for clemency. If so, their pleas would have been ignored, for the captors had not yet received the bounties earned by killing 'me' and the others in battle. I was sad when the men were hung. But at least the well-publicized events further shielded my identity.

It felt strange to be pronounced dead when I was healthy, wealthy and married to Elizabeth. I often worried that our money or youthful appearance would raise suspicion. But those concerns were never realized, and I became an integral part of the community. Has there ever been a more perfect ruse?

Good-bye reader. The end of my life is bitter. But, if given another chance to re-live it, I would not change a thing. I pray He sees it the same way.

Kev whispered, "Hope so, pal," then heard sirens.

EPILOGUE

SPRING

KEV AND RUDY DEPLOYED THE baited line into the creek.

Once done, they motored off. While waiting for the crabs to feed, Kev took in his surroundings. Everything was bathed in early morning sunshine, including the imposing wall along the bluff. Elizabeth's remains were back where they belonged, and she and her husband both had new headstones. His read, 'Edward Teach—Notorious Pirate, Beloved Husband & Generous Philanthropist.' A most appropriate epitaph.

The discovery of Blackbeard's treasure had thrilled folks around the world. After the initial reporting, subsequent pieces examined Teach's transformation, RASC's assault on Rose Haven and the role conquistadors played in South America. Tabloid newspapers ate up the Fountain of Youth, but it was widely ignored by mainstream outlets. Once the media attention slowed, the academics took over. Reconsidering a chunk of history and assessing whether the statues and gems were from the Llanganatis hoard had them all aflutter.

After the trio announced the find at a September press conference, they celebrated its success on the cottage porch—the site of so many revelations. When Kate peeled off to get some sleep, Kev finally came clean about the stomach cancer. The stunned Rudy had wrapped him in a bear hug and promised to be there every step of the way. Once Kev divulged his other secret, the big fella pressured him to drink from the bottle. But he had refused in case the elixir could serve the greater good.

More booze, however, led Kev to remove the wax seal and peer inside the dark glass. Concerned that the meager amount might evaporate that very night, he downed it and licked the rim. When nothing miraculous occurred, the men crashed for the evening. Then drove to Johns Hopkins the next day for Kev's first cancer treatments.

Kate pressed him later that week about his long absences and apparent exhaustion. Too weary to maintain the charade, the cancer news poured out. At first, she'd cried and said all of the right things. But after spotting the uncapped bottle the woman stalked off without saying a word. A few days later, Kate told him they were through. Mostly since he'd robbed the world of an enormous opportunity, partly because of his deception and dishonesty. Their only pleasant interaction since was when she rewarded him and Rudy for the discovery. Money which, when added to the severance payment from G&R, would ironically last him several lifetimes.

As Kev suffered through his treatments, she'd been busy, first holding an exclusive auction for private collectors. They paid dearly for pieces of the hoard which had been valued at several billion dollars. After Kate satisfied her loan with a small part of the proceeds, she purchased a gorgeous home for Jake in Oxford's historic district. At about the same time, Rudy made it his mission to find the man a girlfriend, and in doing so uncovered his relationship with Lucy. While that seemed to finger Jake as the leak, Kev kept the information from Kate. He found her attacks against Lucy (for not revealing sources), Chief Roberts and him unfair. Even rats did not deserve that type of vitriol.

Her anger dissipated while planning for the museum, which would include videos of the treasure hoard and sample coins, ingots, statues and gems. Interactive displays about the pirate's life and race to find the Flash Ken would also be there, along with the telescope, letters, journals and trunks. Visitors would exit the museum from the underground chamber near the big oak, apropos in his view.

When Kev felt somewhat human, he and Rudy searched the cottage for the final letter. While that proved unsuccessful, they discovered an even better prize—a map hidden behind a dry-wall-covered brick. The single sheet of paper featured a prominent X along an unfamiliar coastline. After the men deciphered a note referencing a failed search for more bottles, they poured over satellite images of eastern Florida. Once they found a possible match, Kev brought the discovery to Kate just like old times. But she'd remained unmoved, more focused than ever on her big project.

Unsure about next steps given his health, Kev continued with his treatments. Toward the end of the experimental program, the cancer markers in his blood declined sharply, then disappeared altogether. His doctors were stunned, even more so when a second lab confirmed the results. After Kev learned that the program had not cured other participants, he became a believer in the Fountain. Then blamed the drugs for his ill health over the fall and winter. Mostly though, he was just thrilled to have been judged worthy.

By someone or something, perhaps even God. Whomever or whatever it was, he was humbled by the gift. It intrigued him that the Fountain water either healed deserving people or made them look younger. Kev surmised that he'd been spared to find the galleons, and with them more bottles and treasure. Such a discovery would assuage the guilt he felt from healing himself over others and keep the cancer away. If Elizabeth was a good gauge, he had a few years before it returned.

After celebrating his good health, he and Rudy booked a trip to Florida. Once there, the map led them to a nature reserve near a heavily populated area. The unspoiled landscape was promising, but the logistics of a search seemed overwhelming. They'd retreated home to consider next steps. Involving RASC, of course, would never happen.

Kev had monitored the company ever since its CEO fired Gomez. She'd pled guilty to an array of offenses in exchange for a long stay in country club jail. Most reporters who bashed RASC for the events in Maryland later trumpeted Lucas becoming COO. Its largest investors, however, ignored the chaff and dumped the stock due to weak financial projections. But when Lucas announced that the other 1589 ships were well within reach, the stock price rebounded and then roared to an all-time high. Kev had a hard time believing the tale. A company that elevated people like Gomez and Lucas into positions of power could not be trusted.

Kev snapped back to the present. It was time to crab.

"Let's roll, big fella."

"You got it, Mac. Hey, you know how I sold the business? Well, I've been thinking. If treasure hunting becomes boring, we should . . ."

Kev tuned him out as they approached an orange buoy. He snagged the attached line, placed it onto a U-shaped bar and readied the net. A series of thoughts hit him.

Why did the elixir work for a guy like Blackbeard? At face value, a nefarious pirate would not seem like a worthy candidate.

Could the Fountain or whatever have anticipated his later philanthropy?

Or maybe he served as a historical bridge between Spanish conquistadors and me. Part of some master plan to have the elixir re-emerge when modern medicine could cure disease once and for all.

If so, I hosed that up. But not for long.

Kev smiled at his new-found passion. They'd learned so much, yet the Fountain in many ways remained an enigma. He kind of liked it that way.

His pulse quickened when he saw the first crab, a big one. After scooping the creature out of the water and dumping it into a basket, his mind wandered to Kate. The two of them had developed a special bond over the summer, and their one night together was sublime.

More bottles might give us a second chance.

But is she worthy?

Kev laughed as he caught another crab. Much like Blackbeard long ago, he had a new lease on life.

ACKNOWLEDGEMENTS

First and foremost, I thank the love of my life, Keri Gregoire, and worldly mother, Nancy Jablinske, for their welcome criticism, encouragement and creativity.

Other big helpers included Kate D'Abadie, Scott Howell, John Matsko, John Mollard, Greg & Shirley Nelson, K.B. Owen, Jon Rambeau and Dave Weston.

Lastly, the publishing team at Canoe Tree was nothing short of superb.

It's been a long road since I first thought of an opening scene for a novel. And I have no idea whether folks will enjoy the finished product.

But I had a blast writing it.

ABOUT THE AUTHOR

CHRIS GREGOIRE LIVES IN CHESAPEAKE Bay country. When not writing or having fun with family and friends, he is obsessed with catching and eating blue crabs. The proud Virginia Tech alum hung up his corporate boots a few years ago to try his hand at writing. *Creek of Bones* is the result of that effort, his labor of love.